Titles by David Best

AMNESIA
THE JUDAS VIRUS

AMNESIA

DAVID BEST

BERKLEY BOOKS, NEW YORK

THE BERKLEY PUBLISHING GROUP
Published by the Penguin Group
Penguin Group (USA) Inc.
375 Hudson Street, New York, New York 10014, USA
Penguin Group (Canada), 10 Alcorn Avenue, Toronto, Ontario M4V 3B2, Canada
(a division of Pearson Penguin Canada Inc.)
Penguin Books Ltd., 80 Strand, London WC2R 0RL, England
Penguin Group Ireland, 25 St. Stephen's Green, Dublin 2, Ireland (a division of Penguin Books Ltd.)
Penguin Group (Australia), 250 Camberwell Road, Camberwell, Victoria 3124, Australia
(a division of Pearson Australia Group Pty. Ltd.)
Penguin Books India Pvt. Ltd., 11 Community Centre, Panchsheel Park, New Delhi—110 017, India
Penguin Group (NZ), Cnr. Airborne and Rosedale Roads, Albany, Auckland 1310, New Zealand
(a division of Pearson New Zealand Ltd.)
Penguin Books (South Africa) (Pty.) Ltd., 24 Sturdee Avenue, Rosebank, Johannesburg 2196, South Africa

Penguin Books Ltd., Registered Offices: 80 Strand, London WC2R 0RL, England

This is a work of fiction. Names, characters, places, and incidents either are the product of the author's imagination or are used fictitiously, and any resemblance to actual persons, living or dead, business establishments, events, or locales is entirely coincidental.

AMNESIA

A Berkley Book / published by arrangement with the author

PRINTING HISTORY
Berkley edition / December 2004

ISBN: 0-425-19934-7

Email the author at DBest22@aol.com.

BERKLEY®
Berkley Books are published by The Berkley Publishing Group,
a division of Penguin Group (USA) Inc.,
375 Hudson Street, New York, New York 10014.
BERKLEY is a registered trademark of Penguin Group (USA) Inc.
The "B" design is a trademark belonging to Penguin Group (USA) Inc.

PRINTED IN THE UNITED STATES OF AMERICA

10 9 8 7 6 5 4 3 2 1

ACKNOWLEDGMENTS

I couldn't have written this book without the generous help of Dr. Anice Modesto, who spent many hours with me discussing the operation of mental hospitals. Her constant good cheer and willingness to help whenever I had a question made me feel less like the pest I know I became at times. My understanding of the daily routines of a state mental hospital was also aided by discussions with Dr. Jim Mahan.

It seems that whenever I talk to Dr. Dianna Johnson about a book I'm working on, she tells me something useful for the story. This time, she gave me the idea for Blue Sky Farm. Unless you actually see it in operation, it's difficult to get a full appreciation for the sights and sounds of functional magnetic resonance imaging (fMRI), so the several hours I spent with Dr. Robert Ogg and his imaging colleagues at St. Jude Hospital were a great help.

There wouldn't have been a Clay Hulett in the story were it not for the demonstration of steer roping and discussion of the sport provided by Brown and York Gill. I'm grateful to Dr. Mark LeDoux for advice on neurological conditions that could lead to transient memory loss, and to Dr. Christie Brooks for insights into psychiatry residency training. Finally, thanks to Drs. Joseph Callaway and Randy Nelson for their perspectives on EEG recording and the theoretical considerations involved in making memory movies.

PROLOGUE

THE TWO ARMED sheriff's deputies standing guard in the hospital hallway were bored. You could see it on their faces and in their posture. Probably it was because the crimes committed by the man they were assigned to watch had occurred many years ago and in a different state, making it all an abstraction to them. They hadn't lived through the seventeen months of horror themselves, so it was old and yellowed news.

In the control room, the first color photo that was about to be shown to the patient in the MRI machine flashed up on the laptop controlling the display program.

"Jesus, I never saw anything like that before," the MRI tech said. "I may lose my breakfast."

On the screen was a dreadful array of bone and blood, sinew and skin. Through the gore, a displaced eye could be seen dangling like a spent flower.

"*He* did that?" the tech said, jerking his head toward the window that allowed them to see the lower third of the patient waiting for his brain to be scanned. The rest of his body was inside the putty-colored machine.

"With a hammer," the gaunt man supervising the test said. "He likes hammers. As nearly as they can figure it, she was his second victim."

"How many were there?"

"Fifteen, they think. Could we get started? I've got other things to do."

"Sure," the tech replied, working the MRI keyboard.

"How long does a run take with this model?"

"Ninety seconds. I'll get ten baseline images, then I'll show him your photo series as we acquire ten more images. We'll finish the run with a final ten taken as his brain returns to baseline after he's seen the final picture."

"I'm particularly interested in his prefrontal cortex and the amygdala."

"No problem. We'll be doing sixteen different planes of section simultaneously, so you'll get a good sampling of the area you want." He flipped a switch that turned on the mike communicating with the scan room.

"Mr. Odessa, we're going to start now. We'll need you to hold your head perfectly still for about a minute and a half." The tech flipped off the mike and looked at the man with him. "Why is he cooperating so well?"

"We have an understanding."

The tech began the run. In a few seconds, ghostly slices of Vernon Odessa's brain began to appear on the imaging screen.

The gaunt man's question about the length of the run had caused the tech to wrongly believe he didn't know much about this type of analysis. "Those are purely structural images," the tech explained. "After we get the functional series, a computer will calculate the difference in blood flow stimulated by the photos you've brought. The integrated images will appear on that monitor behind me."

The gaunt man's eyes flicked upward to the patient beyond the window as the run commenced. He was excited, but it wasn't obvious because he was a master at hiding his feelings. Observe and learn, but never let others learn about you. His patient, Vernon Odessa, was a prize, a psychopath of his very own, like a pet he could control and study whenever he felt like it.

The seconds struggled by.

"Moving into functional mode," the tech said finally. He flipped the mike switch. "Mr. Odessa, you should now be seeing the first photo in the mirror directly above you."

To control his anticipation, the gaunt man tried to imagine what was going on in Odessa's brain.

The photos flicked by on the laptop at six-second intervals until the tech said, "Tasking finished and returning to baseline." He looked up at the man beside him. "We should see the integrated results in about forty seconds."

His hands perspiring, the gaunt man turned to the monitor behind him.

Time in the control room now began to pass like a frozen river.

Waiting . . . waiting . . .

Then there they were, morphing onto the screen in succession from the front of Odessa's brain to the back.

Incredible . . . the deep-brain EEGs he'd done earlier were correct, for the frontal cortex and the amygdala on the functional MRI images were both glowing red with activity, like a normal brain . . . not dead like the brain of other psychopaths.

What then made this man kill?

It was puzzling, but so exciting.

The logical next step in his research slowly unfolded in his mind like the birth of something hideously deformed. And he found it appalling. But even as he stood there, marshaling all the reasons it couldn't . . . *shouldn't* be done, he knew that it was only a matter of time before he gave in.

THREE MONTHS LATER

The car slowed and pulled onto the shoulder halfway between the sparse light poles that illuminated the dark highway. Leaving the car's headlights on and the engine running, the driver got out, went quickly around to the passenger side, and opened the door. Inside, the young woman sitting with her hands folded in her lap looked at him with the most vacant expression he'd ever seen, which, considering what he did for a living, was saying a great deal.

He reached in and took her by the arm. He could have told her what he wanted, but it wouldn't have done any good. Eventually responding to the persistent pressure he was exerting on her, she hesitantly moved toward him. When he had her out of the car, he released her. Without a word he hurried back to the driver's side, slid behind the wheel, and sped away without even looking in the mirror.

Her name was Molly, not that it mattered anymore. She stood for a moment, watching the taillights of the departing car fade into the thin fog that had begun to move onto the highway from the river bottoms. She had no words to describe the image, but somewhere deep in the parts of her brain that had once served her love of poetry and Impressionist art and the color of leaves in the fall, neurons nudged each other in appreciation.

Though she was now totally alone and in a very unsettling place, she wasn't afraid, for she didn't know what that meant. She began to walk, moving toward one of the light poles along the highway, attracted to its brightness as an occupant of pond water might seek the sun. Feeling a sharp sensation on her bare arm, she looked down. There was a tiny something on her skin. She reached over with her other hand and nudged the object. But it was attached to her, so that without intending to, she flattened it and smeared her skin with a formless material much the same color as the objects that had gone away into the fog.

Already, Molly was learning. Though she didn't yet know the words *mosquito* and *blood,* it *was* a start.

HALF A MILE away, in the cab of his eighteen-wheeler, Jesse Ragland checked the time: three A.M.

Shit.

Jesse was hauling a load of potted palms up to a Missouri distribution center from Miami. The contract called for him to be in Kansas City by nine that morning. Five hundred miles to go and only six hours to get there. No way he was gonna make it. And with a 250-dollar-an-hour penalty for every hour he was late . . .

Damn . . . he should not have stopped to see Cheryl in Corinth. He'd never paid for a piece of tail in his life, but this one was sure gonna cost him. Despite the gathering fog and the curve ahead, Jesse nudged his speed up well beyond the limit for the chicken-shit road he'd had to take to get back to the interstate.

AS MOLLY WALKED along the shoulder, she nearly stepped on something, but it hopped out of her way just in time. Then it hopped again.

With nowhere to go and nothing better to do, Molly followed the curious object.

When she was close enough, she bent to pick the thing up, but it hopped again, coaxing her a little farther onto the highway. By now, Molly and the toad she was following were standing in the middle of the westbound lane.

Suddenly, the area was flooded by light.

Molly turned and looked in that direction. Coming toward her were two bright spots followed by a huge, dim shape. Molly cocked her head and watched the thing like a curious cocker spaniel. Then it emitted a horrible, loud noise that hurt Molly's ears. Reacting with only the elemental circuits available to her, Molly shut her eyes and put her hands over her face.

When Jesse rounded the curve and saw Molly standing directly in his path, he wet himself and leaned on the air horn at exactly the same instant.

What the hell was wrong with that woman? She wasn't gonna move. At the speed he was going and with the shoulder on each side of the road so narrow, if he tried to swerve around her, he was going right into the swamp. He slammed on the air brakes, knowing he'd never be able to stop in time.

The tractor trailer jackknifed and skewed sideways on the highway, sending five tons of screeching metal and rubber sliding to where Molly stood. And when it was over, she was standing there no longer.

CHAPTER 1

MARTI SEGERSON HURRIED along the flowered carpet, her heart pounding.

She should *never* have checked her bag. If she'd kept it with her, it wouldn't have been lost and she'd already be in there listening to Oren Quinn's talk.

Reaching the Magnolia Room, she grabbed the brass door handle and charged inside.

Oh great . . . the entrance was in the front of the room and at least a dozen heads turned to look at her. Feeling as though she'd audibly broken wind in an elevator, she moved quickly to the rear, where she looked in vain for a seat on the end of a row. But there weren't any.

Resigned to standing, she shifted her attention to the podium and was surprised at what she saw. Oren Quinn was a genius—a Ph.D./M.D., board certified in neurology and psychiatry, the holder of a half dozen lucrative electronic patents, a world authority on memory, and the author of three *New York Times* best-sellers on the many curious neurologic syndromes he'd encountered in his practice.

But the man on stage didn't look like the photo on the flyleaf of his books. This guy was gaunt and old, with silver hair and dark circles under his eyes.

Marti turned to the man standing nearby. "Is that Oren Quinn?"

"In the flesh."

Of course, Ann Landers hadn't looked like her picture either. Still, Marti felt a twinge of irritation that Quinn was intentionally misleading his readers about his appearance.

And you'd *never* misrepresent yourself, her inner voice said sarcastically. Needing to stop thinking about that, she turned her attention to what Quinn was saying.

". . . While it's true we know very little about where memories are filed in the brain, it is possible to electrically stimulate recall of a specific memory if the current is accidentally delivered to an appropriate point in the neural circuit where the memory is stored. This was shown years ago in the classic work on the temporal lobe of epileptics."

Though Quinn looked ancient, Marti noted he still had a strong speaking voice.

He continued, "I think it's highly likely that, as this stimulated recall occurs, it spreads over the visual cortex and re-creates the same pattern of arousal that occurred when the patient first experienced the event being remembered.

"It therefore follows that if we could record all the electrical signals produced by the visual cortex during the recall of a memory and send those signals into a computer equipped with the proper programming, it should be possible to turn those memories into movies that re-create everything the patient saw when the event in question initially occurred."

This generated a buzz in the room.

At the middle aisle a small, dark man with a full head of wavy hair stood up and approached one of the mikes they'd spotted through the audience for questions.

"Dr. Quinn . . . aren't you forgetting something?"

The moderator, who'd been sitting off to Quinn's left, leaned into his own mike and said, "Identify yourself, please."

"Dr. William Lane, from the Nelms Institute for Neuroscience."

"Thank you. What was your question?"

"Everyone knows that memories are not accurate reproductions of past events, but are a quilt work made from pieces of several actual events stitched together with some parts that *never* occurred. They merely *seem* accurate to the one having them. So how could your extremely fanciful scenario of memory movies ever come to pass?"

Good point, Marti thought. *It* was *a goofy idea.*

Instead of answering the question, Quinn looked away from the guy at the mike and focused his gaze at the back of the room.

"Dr. Segerson, perhaps you could respond to that."

The sound of people turning in their seats so they could see who Quinn had thrown the question to was actually not very loud, but in Marti's ears it sounded like an avalanche.

Me? *He wants* me *to respond?*

She felt her face flush. She had never even met Quinn, had never had any communication with him or anyone else about this topic. Why the hell was he bringing her into it? She looked at Quinn and then at the many faces turned toward her. This was bizarre. She was just there in Washington to interview for a job at the Gibson State Mental Hospital in Tennessee.

A part of Marti wanted to run for it . . . just get out of there, but the door was too far away for an easy exit.

What was the question? She couldn't remember . . . something about . . . memories and the visual cortex.

"Do you plan to speak sometime in this century, Dr. Segerson?" Quinn said.

And that made her mad. "First, let me say that Dr. Quinn and I have never met, nor have I ever heard his speculation before on memory movies, so I'm certainly not his shill, nor do I necessarily believe such a thing is remotely possible. But as for the objection that's been raised to the idea, I think it's possible that the errors present in any recalled event are laid on as the memory reaches consciousness. At more basic levels, such as any activated circuitry in the visual cortex, it could well be that there the activity is a far more faithful re-creation of the initial event."

Everyone then turned to look at Quinn.

Now that she was out of the spotlight, Marti wondered why on earth she'd said she didn't believe Quinn's idea was possible . . . no . . . she'd said it wasn't *remotely* possible. *Way to go kid . . . insult the one man who could get you in close. Stupid.*

"Thank you, Dr. Segerson," Quinn said. He looked at the man who'd asked the question. "You see, even someone who isn't my shill understands how it could work."

There were a few more questions for Quinn from others in the audience, but Marti was so unnerved by her sudden forced participation in the event, she barely heard them. Then, with a generous round of applause, it was over.

In his letter responding to her application, Quinn had suggested she come to Washington and interview for the job right after his talk. So, while he exchanged a few last words with a couple of men who caught him as he stepped off the dais, Marti waited for him by the door.

The group spoke for several minutes until Quinn excused himself and headed for the hallway.

"Good morning, Dr. Segerson," he said, as he swept by. "I see you arrived late."

Hurrying after him, Marti said, "The airline lost my bag."

"Have you always had trouble arranging your priorities?" he replied, not looking back at her.

"You're construing far too much from an isolated event."

Quinn suddenly turned to face her. "So you've never been late for anything before?"

"*Never* is a strong word."

"So is *isolated*." He gestured to two upholstered chairs facing each other across a small table. "We can talk here."

"In the hallway?"

"Do you need a more private place?"

"I don't *need* it. I just thought . . . Sure, this is fine."

A moment later, with each of Quinn's bony hands draped over the armrest of his chair, and Marti's hands resting on the shoulder tote in her lap, Quinn said, "Why did you find it necessary to strike out at me before answering Dr. Lane's question a few minutes ago?"

"I was angry at being put on the spot like that."

"It was a risky thing to do."

"Was it? Are you a man who holds grudges?"

Quinn stared at her without answering, his eyes boring into her. Should she have apologized? Is that what he was looking for? Somehow, she thought not; that he might find backtracking a sign of weakness.

Finally, he spoke again. "In most psychiatry training, the residents must themselves undergo therapy. Was that the case with your program?

"Yes."

"And what did you discover about yourself during therapy?"

"Why is that important for you to know?"

Suddenly, Quinn's deep-set eyes flashed with anger. "I'm not your patient, Dr. Segerson. Stop trying to deflect my questions back to me."

Marti's mind shifted into a gear more suitable to rough terrain. What to tell him? She'd hidden the primary purpose in her life from her therapist and even her closest friends. No one knew how much she was driven by hatred, how she longed to strike back, how she'd waited and waited. And now the opportunity was so near . . . "I learned that my obsession with perfection is a constant attempt to please my father, whose criticism of everything I did as a child came from his wish for a son."

Marti waited to see how Quinn would receive this fabrication. It was exactly the kind of thing most psychiatrists would love to hear. But Quinn wasn't your average psychiatrist.

Quinn mulled her lie over without giving any indication of approval or disapproval, then he said, "Gibson State is an underfunded facility in a rural area of Tennessee that has no cultural amenities. The nearest large city, Memphis, is seventy miles away. The favorite pastimes of most of the local males are drinking beer and shooting animals for the fun of it. The women quilt and gossip. Our existing psychiatry staff consists of the dregs of the profession; licenses restricted because of substance abuse, poorly trained foreigners who can't phrase a question properly, and people who are just not very smart. You come very highly recommended, and all indications are that you could have any job you wish, so I have to wonder, why would you want to work at Gibson?"

Marti wanted very much to ask him why *he* was there, but her behavior had already been far too overbearing. So she let that one go. "I've never liked city life. Rural appeals to me. And, of course, there's your large population of the chronic severely ill. There aren't many places where I could get the kind of experience they can provide."

"They're kept so sedated they're more dead than alive. I don't know what you're going to learn from them."

Marti longed to suggest that maybe these people were being overmedicated, but once again, she kept the thought to herself. "Still, I'd like the experience."

"Dr. Segerson, I don't think you're being totally candid. If it were up to me, I wouldn't hire you, but a copy of all applications to Gibson go to the State Department of Mental Health, where I'm sure they'll see that your credentials are far better than any of our current staff. There's also a statewide initiative in place to give preference to female applicants."

"So you're saying—"

"If I don't hire you, it'll generate a blizzard of paper-work that I don't have time to fool with. So get out the horns and paper hats. We've got a new member of the Gibson family."

CHAPTER 2

GIBSON STATE MENTAL HOSPITAL. Simple black lettering on a white background. And below that, in smaller letters, the firm admonition, DO NOT PICK UP HITCHHIKERS.

As Marti slowed and turned into the hospital entrance, she tried to think how the warning on the sign might have been better conveyed. As it was it made it sound as though the patients were routinely escaping. But maybe they were. Since it was her first day on the job, she had no way of knowing. But God help the people who lived nearby if that was true.

Because of a dense and gloomy woods, the hospital couldn't be seen from the highway. Ten feet from the main road the massive entrance gates stood open and un-attended, the little stone guardhouse between the inbound and outbound lanes, empty. Except for a grassy shoulder, the road onto the property was lined by the same ominous woods that flanked the highway. Even through the window of her car, Marti could hear the croaking of frogs in the wet bottomlands.

The road seemed to go on and on, its edges encroached by fingers of grass, the asphalt full of fissures and potholes. Finally, the road made a gentle curve, and there it was—a looming Gothic four-story brick building with great oval windows and spiked towers topped by metal rods. The only things missing from the scene were flashes of lightning and a crowd of angry villagers with torches. It looked like an evil place. Or maybe it merely seemed that way because she knew what awaited her inside.

She gripped the wheel harder to still her suddenly shaking hands and headed into the ample parking lot, which easily held the ninety or so cars already there. As she pulled into an empty space, she noticed that the one reserved spot, for Oren Quinn, was vacant. Remembering her uncomfortable interview with him in Washington, she was glad she wouldn't have to face him right away.

She shut off the engine, but felt too queasy to get out of the car. So she sat and stared at the hospital through the windshield, her body rebelling at the thought of going inside. As she tried to gather herself, her mind spiraled back to when she was twelve . . . the night she had slept at her sister's beach house . . . the night that made her what she had become.

What was that?

Marti sat up in bed, instantly awake. It sounded like . . . it was . . . the patio door sliding on its track.

She glanced at the open doorway to the hall and saw with mounting fear that it was dark. If Lee was

up, there'd be lights on in the kitchen and they'd il-
luminate the hall.

Unwilling to believe there was a stranger in the
house, Marti leaped off the bed, ran to the doorway, and looked at the mirror on the folding closet
doors opposite Lee's bedroom.

Oh God . . . there she was . . . still asleep.

The slight sound of hesitant footsteps from the
kitchen made her want to pee.

He's coming this way.

She glanced frantically around the tiny room
that offered very few hiding places . . . none of
them any good.

The closet?

No. He'd hear the folding doors rattle when
they opened.

Under the bed?

Too confining and there wasn't time.

The floor on the far side of the bed?

Suddenly, she heard the barely audible rustle of
the intruder's pant legs rubbing together. One more
step and he'd be in the doorway. Praying that she
could move more quietly than whoever was out
there, Marti slid behind the open door.

With her nose practically against the wood and
air hard to come by, she began to breathe through
her mouth.

Then he was in the doorway. She didn't hear
anything that told her that, she just felt it.

What would he do when he saw that her bed was
empty? Would he slam the door against her? Would
he reach behind it and yank her into the open? The
tension was almost more than she could bear.

She heard him breathe . . . a quivering exhalation that made her want to scream.

Marti fought her way back to the present, more distressed now than a moment ago.

"Get control of yourself," she muttered. And with an effort, she did.

She'd been told to arrive for her first day at nine thirty, so the place would already be settled into the morning routine, and she could fit seamlessly into the operation.

She had some books and other things in the trunk that she would want at hand in her office, but there seemed no point in lugging it all in now, so when she got out of the car, she headed directly for the building's front steps carrying only her briefcase.

Inside, she was impressed at the scale and grandeur of what she saw. Under immense Oriental carpets, there must have been an acre of hardwood flooring, glistening in the light cast from the biggest crystal chandelier she'd ever seen. Straight ahead was a double winding staircase right out of *Gone with the Wind.* On the right wall there was a reproduction of Van Gogh's "Starry Night," a painting that always made her think of mental illness. But this one was huge—a hint, she thought, of what lay beyond this deceptive facade.

Her instructions were to report to the office of the medical director, Dr. Howard Rosenblum. Spotting a directory on a chrome stand by the big staircase, she headed that way and looked for his name.

There it was—first floor, but in which of the hallways off the main room, left or right?

Guessing, she went left.

As she crossed the large room, she caught just the

barest whiff of the smell of warehoused humans. Then she began to notice other things that changed her initial impression of the place. When she stepped off the carpeting onto the bare hardwood, her footsteps echoed slightly, making her realize there were no drapes at the window, just some simple, inexpensive fabric treatments. Off to her left, a big water stain had made a Rorschach pattern on the ceiling, and there was some badly damaged plaster on the adjacent wall. The carpets, she now noticed, were worn almost through in spots.

Entering the hall, she discovered from the room numbers that she'd chosen wrong. So off she went, to the other hallway, like a rat learning a new maze.

Certainly no one could accuse the Gibson administration of overspending on their receptionist's digs, for when Marti opened the door with Howard Rosenblum's name on it, she found herself in Spartan surroundings with unadorned beige walls and simple metal furniture.

The woman behind the black desk turned from her computer. "May I help you?"

Extremely thin and stringy, the woman must have been seventy, but she had strawberry blond, twenty-year-old hair that lay in soft curls around her face.

"I'm Dr. Segerson." Marti waited a moment to see if her name meant anything to the woman. Noting no sign of that, she added, "The new staff psychiatrist."

The sun of recognition dawned on the woman's face. "Yes, of course . . . Dr. Segerson." She picked up the phone and punched in some numbers. "Dr. Rosenblum, Dr. Segerson is here."

She hung up, and even while she was saying, "He'll be right—" the door to the inner office flew open and out came a lanky, completely bald man whose black-framed glasses and similarly colored mustache and goatee made him look like the image on a defaced poster.

"Dr. Segerson, so good to see you." He offered his hand and she took it. "So . . . all the way from California. Have any trouble finding a place to stay?"

"I contacted a Realtor on the Internet and located something very quickly."

"Good for you. Sometime today"—he gestured to his receptionist—"give Pat your address and phone number. Pat, will you ask Dr. Estes to join us, please?" While the receptionist picked up the phone, he turned back to Marti. "How much water do you drink?"

"I beg your pardon."

"How much water do you drink?"

Puzzled at the question, Marti answered, "I don't know . . . a glass or two."

Rosenblum wagged his finger at her. "Not enough, not nearly enough. You must do better." Before she could respond, he said, "In the letter you sent Dr. Quinn after your interview, you asked to be assigned to one of our chronic wards, preferably a forensic unit."

This pushed his odd question about her water consumption out of her mind and kicked her heart into a new, faster rhythm.

Here it was . . . the next hurdle. She'd passed the interview and was now on the grounds as an employee . . . closing in. She couldn't come right out and ask to be assigned to Vernon Odessa's unit. That would have created too much suspicion. So she'd tried to pave the way to him by that letter. But had it worked?

"For someone at this stage in your career, you've certainly had a lot of experience with forensic patients," Rosenblum said.

"The criminal mind has always been one of my interests."

"Something you share with Dr. Quinn," Rosenblum replied. "In any event, we don't have a forensic unit. We do have some forensic patients, but they're integrated into the rest of our population. Though I've had to do some shifting of staff responsibilities, I've assigned you to the unit that has the largest number of them, which actually isn't very many."

The unit with the largest number of them . . . Marti was encouraged. The odds of having Odessa on her service were . . . What? She didn't even know how many units they had, so she couldn't calculate the odds. But they must be at least slightly in her favor.

The door to the hallway opened and a woman with a heart-shaped face and the look of a librarian came in.

"Ah, Dr. Estes," Rosenblum said.

He introduced the two women, and Marti learned that Trina Estes was the psychologist assigned to the same patients Marti would be serving and that Trina would be showing her around the place.

"Trina, I've assigned her to Dr. Avazian's old office; two thirty-three. You might want to start by taking her up there." He looked at Pat. "Do you have—"

Even as Rosenblum spoke, Pat produced a plastic ID on a chain from a side drawer of her desk and handed it to Marti.

"You can either use the chain or just clip it on your blouse with that thumb spring," Pat explained.

Marti glanced briefly at the ID and saw that the photo she'd sent at their request in advance of her arrival had reproduced well. Of course, this was no surprise, for she was one of those people who never took a bad picture, always looking in her photos like a model. Over the years she'd learned that when she wore it long, her sandy-colored hair was a man magnet. Tired of fending off the unwanted attention and feeling that she needed to look more professional, two days after starting her residency, she'd had most of it cut off, so now it was about as long as Harrison Ford wore his. And in truth, there was no prescription in the lenses of her dark-framed, Rosenblum-like glasses, those too, being part of her wish to blend into the background. In her estimation these attempts at warding off unwanted male attention had been about 2 percent effective. Unwilling to put any more thought into the problem and figuring that 2 percent was better than nothing, she'd just kept the look.

Pat reached into a different drawer and pulled out two small manila envelopes that she handed to Marti. One was labeled "233," the other "2 East."

"Office key and the ones for the doors to your wards," Rosenblum said. "Your patients' files should already be on your desk." He looked at Pat for confirmation and she nodded.

Rosenblum continued . . . "Since you'll be on one of our chronic units, the files of many of your patients are too voluminous to be kept fully in the metal ward binders. We normally shift the dated overflow to medical records, where everything is transferred to a soft-cover jacket. You'll see both those in your office. So, I guess we're finished here."

As soon as they were in the hallway, Trina said, "Did he ask you how much water you drink?"

"How'd you know?"

"He asks everybody. And no matter what you say, he suggests you should be doing the opposite."

"What's his training?"

"Psychiatrist."

"Is he competent?"

"He must be, he's the medical director."

Trina's comment was loaded with subtext, but Marti didn't feel she should pursue it.

THE OFFICE MARTI had been given contained the same utilitarian furniture she'd seen downstairs. On the desk was a computer and stacks of the two kinds of binders Rosenblum had mentioned. Outlines of pictures that used to hang there were evident on every wall. Next to the baseboard left of the desk lay a couple of dead cockroaches circled with white chalk. Beside each circle was a date; one three weeks earlier, the other, a month.

"Just Dr. Avazian's way of documenting how infrequently his floor got swept," Trina explained.

"Was housekeeping avoiding his office for some reason?"

"He didn't get treated any differently from anyone else around here."

"What happened to him?"

"INS took him away. He was Iranian, apparently here illegally. Ready to see your patients?"

Her patients.

Without warning, the question thrust Marti once again into the past and she found herself behind the door in Lee's beach house, the intruder just inches away.

> She heard him breathe . . . a quivering exhalation that made her want to scream.
> But she didn't scream. She held her ground and

tried to be someplace else in her mind. Then, even though he should have known the room was occupied, he moved on.

Or had he? Though Marti really believed he was no longer right on the other side of the doorway, she couldn't be sure. So she stayed put and prayed that Lee would wake up and call 911, for the only phone in the house was in her room.

After what seemed like the longest time she'd ever stood without moving, she heard a voice, and it wasn't right beside her.

"Hello, Goldilocks. It's Pappa Bear, come to have a party."

He was in Lee's room.

Marti slipped from her hiding place, crept to the threshold of her room, and looked at the mirrored doors in the hall.

The lighting was poor, just the illumination from Lee's night light, but it was enough to see that the prowler was on her sister's bed, straddling her.

"Who the hell are you?" Lee screamed. "Get off me. Get out of here."

Lee was struggling, but the man's weight had her so pinned she couldn't do much of anything.

"Don't be afraid," the prowler said. "This won't take long. But there will be some pain."

Then, Marti saw the guy raise his hand and bring it down hard. There was a thump that sounded like it hit the pillow, and Lee screamed.

When you're twelve, the feeling of being unable to control the events around you is nothing new. But this was worse than that. Her sister was being hurt and she couldn't do anything to stop it because

*she was only a girl . . . she wouldn't have a chance
against a grown man.*

*But she couldn't just stand there. So she crept
from her room and moved quickly to the door
where the prowler had come in. As she fled from
the house, she heard Lee scream again, but this
time it was cut short with a horrible gurgle.*

*Out on the deck, she ignored the steps to the
beach and vaulted over the low railing. When she
hit, she sank into loose sand and lost her balance.
Scrambling to her feet, she took off, running as
hard as she could for the house down the beach,
where she could get help.*

*At any other time she would have loved the feel
of the sand caressing her toes, but now it became
her enemy, shifting under her, preventing her from
pushing off with the force she needed, holding her
back.*

*She couldn't move fast enough. Every second
mattered, but she was moving in slow motion. She
screamed at the sand in frustration.*

"Damn it. Let me go."

"Marti? Are you okay?" Trina asked.

"I'm sorry, I was just thinking of something."

"It must have been pretty important. You were un-
reachable."

"It was. I'm sorry."

"Are you ready to meet your patients?"

"Absolutely."

CHAPTER 3

"THE PATIENT UNITS are in the back part of the building," Trina explained in the hall outside Marti's office. This is the east wing," she turned and pointed to the other hall, "that's west. Our wards are on the second floor of this wing, hence Two East."

"How many patients will I have?"

"About seventy. You'll have a female ward, Two East A, and a male ward, Two East B. And Rosenblum wants you to speak to each of your cases at least once a week."

"How many patients in the entire hospital?"

"Around four hundred. There are four chronic units: Two East, Two West, Three East, and Three West, each with a male and a female ward."

Eight chronic wards, Marti thought. *Four of them male. So my chances of getting Odessa are at worst 25 percent. But Two East has more forensic patients than any other unit. So my odds are actually better than that.*

Trina opened the door at the end of the hall, and they

went into a bare, high-ceilinged corridor with an old, wide wooden staircase that on their right went up and on the left descended, presumably, to the first floor. The smell of incarcerated humans was now perceptibly stronger.

"I guess you noticed all the other smaller buildings around the grounds," Trina said, her voice echoing off the dingy walls.

"Actually, no. I couldn't take my eyes off this one."

"I know what you mean," Trina said, following the corridor as it angled to the right. "It's impressive, in a Transylvania sort of way. There are seven more buildings on the property, but only one of them is occupied, with our acute and intermediate units. The others used to hold children's and adolescent units, but we don't handle those kinds of cases anymore, so they're now full of old furniture and computer equipment. At its peak, the place had two thousand patients, but with budget cutbacks and all . . ."

They had now reached a door with heavy metal mesh across it and a substantial square plate containing a key-hole.

"You've got the keys Pat gave you?" Trina prompted.

Marti produced the envelope labeled "2 East" and shook two keys into her hand, one larger than the other, both medieval looking.

"Let's make sure they work," Trina said. "The smaller one is for this door."

Marti put her key in the lock and turned it. There was a satisfying click that resounded through the hallway as the bolt slid out of its seat. Trina pushed the door open and let Marti precede her. When they were both on the other side, Trina retrieved the key and shut the door.

"It locks automatically," Trina explained, "so always remember to get this back." She handed Marti the key.

"I've never seen it," Trina said, moving on. "but they say there's a tunnel system that connects this building with all the others. I heard they closed it in part because they don't really need it any more, but it apparently also has a bat problem." Noting Marti's expression of amazement, she added, "Oh yes, Dorothy, you're not in Kansas anymore."

"Actually, it was California," Marti said. "But I see your point."

"Well, here we are," Trina said, stopping in front of a wide wooden door about eight feet tall. Stenciled on the chipped and dirty maroon paint was the designation 2 EAST A. "This is your female ward."

"Before we go in . . . Don't introduce me to the group," Marti said. "I'll do that as I meet each of them individually."

"Your call."

Marti unlocked the ward, retrieved the key, and stepped back to let Trina take the lead into what was obviously the ward's dayroom, a sprawling space with the building's usual high ceilings and wooden floors. But the tall windows here were covered with heavy metal mesh like the door in the hall. Now at its source, the smell Marti had detected from the moment she'd walked through the hospital's front entrance made her breathe a little more carefully.

Some of the patients on the ward were pacing, their gaze directed beyond the walls. Others, with the same look, were sitting on the various sofas and chairs provided. A group of three at a small wooden table were playing rock, paper, scissors. At the far end of the room, near a doorway that Marti could see led to the sleeping rooms, was a TV, its picture totally distorted by interference. Despite the malfunction, six women sat in the rows of folding chairs in front of it, mesmerized by the flickering pattern. On the other side of the doorway to the sleeping quarters was a Plexiglas room so filled with cigarette smoke the occupants could barely be seen.

A large woman with a ruddy complexion and thinning, oatmeal-colored hair that she wore tight against her head like an aviator cap came out of the glass-enclosed nursing station beside the entrance. Her white uniform was crisp and clean.

"Good morning, Dr. Estes. Who is this?"

Introductions were made during which Trina validated the nurse's ID that said she was Ada Metz.

"You seem awfully young to be a psychiatrist," Metz observed.

Not knowing how to respond, Marti said, "Well, I was born three weeks premature."

Metz didn't find that amusing. Actually, she didn't seem to get it. Out of the corner of her eye, Marti sensed one of the patients approaching. Turning, she saw a woman with sloping shoulders and a thatch of lifeless gray hair join the group.

"Dr. Estes, I've had the most amazing morning," she said.

"Let me guess," Trina replied. "God has called you to spread the gospel."

"It's the truth. I was over there by the window, and I heard Him say, 'Lessi Gill, I need you to do my work. And as of this moment, all your sins are forgiven.' So you see, I have to leave."

"Lessi, I'm not free to talk just now. We'll discuss this later."

"Promise?"

"Yes."

The woman turned and ambled off.

"How did you know what she was going to say?" Marti asked.

"About ten months ago, she got the idea that if God saved her, we'd have to let her go home. So He's forgiven her sins every day since."

"How long has she been here?"

"Twenty-three years. She's one of our forensic cases, sort of."

"What do you mean, 'sort of'?"

"Before she was committed, people noticed that her husband had stopped coming into town. Curious about the reason, the sheriff went out to their home and found him in bed. He'd been dead so long, he was in an advanced state of decomposition. Lessi refused to admit he was dead . . . said he was just 'doing that' to spite her."

"So she'd killed him."

"There was no real evidence of that, but a few months earlier, when he was in the hospital for a minor surgical procedure, she was caught putting an ice pick in his ear to 'stop the voices he was hearing.' But it was Lessi who was hearing the voices."

"Was she prosecuted?"

"I don't think so."

"But she was committed by a judge."

"The records are murky on that point. In any event, she could never function on the outside."

Trina pointed out a few of the other patients in the room and gave Marti a quick summary of their circumstances. As eager as Marti was to move on to the male ward, she hesitated when Trina suggested they do so.

"Who's that?" Marti said, pointing to a skinny black woman at the water fountain.

"Letha Taylor."

"Has she always been that thin?"

"She used to weigh a little more," Ada Metz said, "but as time passes, some of these people just waste away. Why do you ask?"

"In the few minutes I've been here, she's visited the water fountain three times. Be right back."

While Trina and Metz watched with curiosity, Marti walked over and spoke to Letha Taylor. After a brief conversation, Marti returned to the two women waiting for her.

"Have either of you ever noticed her breath?"

"She always smells a little gamy," Metz said.

"Like acetone?" Marti said.

"Now that you mention it, I suppose that's as good a description as any."

"That's because she's in ketoacidosis. She's starving and burning off whatever fat reserves she has left." Still getting no hint either of them knew what she was getting at, Marti finally said it as straight as she could. "She has diabetes. She needs to have a fasting plasma glucose and a glucose tolerance test done. Do we have an internist on staff?"

"We do, but this is his day off," Metz said.

"Surely there's someone in attendance when he's away."

"Hospital can't afford it."

"Suppose there's a medical emergency on his day off?"

"We call an ambulance."

"Will you bring Letha's problem to his attention to-morrow?"

"Let's talk about that in here," Metz said, gesturing to the glass-enclosed nursing station.

They all went inside and Metz shut the door. "Here's the thing . . . if she does have diabetes, that's just going to complicate her care. We'll have to monitor her blood glucose levels, she may have to take insulin."

"What's your point?"

"I've got all I can handle without that. I've got responsibilities for this ward and the male ward next door . . ."

On the far side of the nursing station Marti caught a glimpse of the other ward through the windows lining the upper half of the wall, and for a moment her mind wandered to what might be waiting for her there. With effort, she refocused her attention on the matter at hand.

"So I'm just saying, why not leave well enough alone?" Metz said.

"Because the woman is ill and it's our responsibility to give her the best life she can have. Now, are you going to take care of it, or not?"

Anger flared in Metz's eyes as she responded. "I'll tell Dr. Wallace what you said."

"He's the staff internist?"

Metz nodded.

"Good. Now let's go next door."

Entering Two East B from the nursing station, Marti's eyes swept the room, looking for Vernon Odessa. It took her a few seconds to assess the population, and when she was finished, two words were branded on her mind in smoking letters.

Not here.

Damn it. Despite the request she'd sent in advance of her arrival, despite being given the units with the most forensic cases, Odessa was someone else's responsibility. Now what?

While she considered the situation, her eyes tracked a little man crossing the room, walking like Groucho Marx.

"That's Carl Woodsen," Trina said, noting Marti's interest. "Everybody calls him 'Chickadee' because of the way he walks."

"What is it, just his thing?"

"No. I didn't work here then, but I heard he used to climb up on anything he could, then he'd jump down. One day he broke both his legs doing it. For some reason no one set the broken bones, but he was just allowed to lie in bed until he could get out under his own power. There's the result."

"The staff should be very proud," Marti said.

"That was a long time ago," Metz said. "Before any of us came here."

"From what I saw next door—" Marti stopped talking in midsentence, her attention shifting to a patient coming out of the dorm wing. He was over six feet tall with long, blond hair and pudgy features. He walked with a swagger and had a self-satisfied look on his face that made her want to rush over and smack him. She could feel her skin flush and her hands began to sweat—for this was Vernon Odessa.

CHAPTER 4

MARTI WATCHED ODESSA cross the room and go to a small table, where another patient was sitting looking at a notebook of some sort. Odessa tapped the guy on the shoulder and jerked his thumb in a gesture telling him to move, which he did without protest. Odessa then sat down and began working in the notebook with a marker he had in his pocket.

"That's Vernon Odessa," Trina said. "If you're interested in the criminal mind, you should love him. He killed fifteen women in your home state about twenty years ago."

Odessa was much older now than the last time she saw him, and his face had fleshed out, but there was no mistaking who he was.

"How is he as a patient?" Marti asked, trying to keep the emotion at seeing him out of her voice.

"Except for an incident last fall, he's been exceptionally well behaved."

"What happened then?"

"Went after Ronald Clary over there with a chair."

"Why?"

"Claimed Clary came on to him sexually. He had to be forcibly subdued."

"I'd like to speak to him."

"I don't see any problem with that. But just to be safe let's get Bobby Ware on standby. That's what I've been doing since he had that episode with Clary." Trina looked at Ada Metz.

"He's in the break room. I'll get him."

Metz went back into the nursing station. Through the glass panels in its walls Marti saw her lean into a room that wasn't enclosed by glass. Her summons brought out a guy with red hair, a full red beard and mustache and an NFL lineman's body.

After Trina made the necessary introductions and told Bobby why she'd asked for him, she looked at Marti. "Let's go talk to him."

"You all stay here," Marti said. "I'd like to do this alone."

Not wanting Odessa to know her name until she was ready to reveal it, Marti turned her ID around so the front was against her blouse. He was so absorbed in what he was doing that he didn't notice her approach, so she was able to look over his shoulder. What she saw made her flush even more. He had drawn a bear standing upright with a hammer in one paw, threatening a cowering young girl.

The years peeled away and she was once more at the beach she had grown to hate, with Odessa in the house behind her, straddling her sister, gloating... *"Hello, Goldilocks. It's Pappa Bear, come to have a party."*

The sand held her back, keeping her from reaching the house next door . . . the sand . . . damn the sand . . .

Finally, she was there, pounding on their sliding door to the beach. "Help . . . Help me. My sister is being murdered."

She pounded on the glass so hard her hand stung, aware that every passing second was hurting her sister even more.

She hit the glass door again and again, until the pain from every blow ran up her arm and set off an explosion in her brain. The light beside the door came on and the drapes were pulled aside. A pair of ashen faces looked out at her.

"Help me. Someone is killing my sister. Hurry. Hurry. Call the police."

The door stuttered open.

"He's murdering her. The house next door. Call 911."

The faces inside belonged to two young women clad only in football jerseys; flight attendants, she thought her sister had said. The blond ran for the phone, while the brunette just stood there and wrung her hands.

Once the call was made, Marti turned and ran back to her sister's house, using a route a few steps farther from the ocean, hoping to find firmer ground. She could see now that the lights were on inside.

When she got there, she would pound on the side of the house, let the killer know someone was there . . . drive him away.

Her course was taking her directly to the tall

*clumps of pampa grass that lined the walkway from
the parking area. Just as she reached them she saw
over the tops of the plants a masculine shape come
out onto the deck and turn in her direction.*

*She ducked behind a clump of grass, where she
could hear the killer's feet heavily on the steps from
the deck. Had she been seen? She wasn't sure.*

*With her breath coming in short, ragged gasps,
her face burning, and her heart a balloon bigger
than her chest, she waited in a crouch for the killer
to pass.*

*Suddenly she felt a sharp pain in her scalp, a
prelude to being pulled to her feet and through the
grass by her hair.*

*The killer had her by his left hand. In the light
from the parking area she saw a raised hammer in
his other hand. The instant before the blow fell, she
stared into a face streaked with her sister's blood.*

Then from far off, the sound of a siren.

*The killer threw her into the grass and ran for
the road out front.*

Sensing Marti nearby, Odessa turned.

She'd only been twelve when he'd last seen her and
the light had been behind her, so *she* had gotten the better look. Because of those two things, Marti had long
been convinced that when they finally met, he would
never recognize her. But now that the moment was here,
she wasn't so sure.

But then Odessa said, "Who are you?"

Looking into his eyes was like staring into the bowels
of hell. She had waited so long for this and now that it
was here, she was suddenly trembling with rage. But it

was all on the inside. Looking at her, there was no evidence of the storm raging through her, for she had learned to hide her hatred of Odessa from everyone around her. Professors, friends, relatives . . . none of them had any idea that every night before she climbed into bed, she held her sister's picture in her hand and swore to her that one day Odessa would pay for what he'd done.

"I asked who you were," Odessa said. "Or don't people like us deserve a response."

Now the next hurdle; the moment he would hear her name. Lee and her husband had been separated, but not divorced when Odessa had killed her, so it was her married name that was in all the papers. In developing her plan for Odessa, Marti had believed that this circumstance would hide her relationship to Lee when she finally stood in front of him again. But just as she had sudden doubts a moment earlier about whether he'd recognize her face, she now became concerned about her name. If he'd been attentive, he could have picked up Lee's maiden name from the few articles that identified her parents. Had he been that alert? Would he remember such a fact after so many years? Nothing to do now but say it.

"I'm Dr. Segerson, the new staff psychiatrist assigned to this unit."

Odessa looked up at her, his brow corrugated, as though searching his mind for something.

The seconds crept by.

"Or don't people like us deserve a response," Marti said, going on the offensive to abort his hunt.

"Sorry. I was just trying to remember . . . never

mind." He stood and offered his hand. "I'm Vernon Odessa."

Quelling her disgust at touching him, Marti willed her hand into his and let him shake it, aware that if he wished, he could break her neck before Bobby Ware could take three steps.

"Our last shrink was a man," Odessa said. "You're a big improvement." His gaze flicked up and behind her. "I see you've called out reinforcements." He looked back into her eyes. "Are you afraid of me?"

"Should I be?"

"I'd never hurt you. At least not here. But on the outside . . . I couldn't make any promises about that."

"I'm just getting acquainted with the hospital this morning. But after that's done and I've had some time to read up on all the cases assigned to me, I'd like to talk to you further. Would that be all right?"

"I'll check my calendar and see if I'm free."

"Do that."

Marti turned and headed toward the nursing station, feeling Odessa watching her. Halfway there an old man with a three-day beard stubble and a profusion of visible nasal hairs approached her.

"I've got a secret," he said.

Marti stopped walking.

"Would you like to share it with me?"

"Maybe. What's tall and fair . . . you think it's here, but it's really there?"

"So it's a riddle."

"Do you know what it is?"

"I'm sorry, I'm stumped. What's the answer?"

The old man raised a cautioning finger. "It's not gonna be that easy. You have to solve it yourself."

Marti reached out and touched him on his bony shoulder. "I'll work on it and see what I can come up with."

Back at the nursing station, Metz said, "Did he ask you his riddle?"

"Does he do that a lot?"

"Every damned day. Sometimes two or three times. He's obsessed with it."

"I guess that's why he's here."

"Just started it out of the blue one day about six months ago. And now he just wears me out with it. When you talk to him, see if you can get him to stop."

"What's his name?"

"Harry Evensky."

"We should move on," Trina said to Marti. "There's a lot more to see."

Marti and Trina left through the hall entrance and headed back toward the mesh door. Though her better instincts told her to leave it alone, Marti found herself saying, "What do you think of the insanity defense for people like Odessa?"

"It's bullshit, if you'll pardon my French," Trina said. "And I don't see how he pulled it off. He killed fifteen women, always at night, under cover of darkness. He never attacked anybody in daylight on a busy street. He waited until he thought he could get away with it. So you tell me how a jury could believe he didn't know what he was doing was wrong or that he couldn't control himself. No, he didn't murder all those women because he was insane . . . he just liked doing it. He shouldn't be here, he should be on death row somewhere or executed already."

Until now, Marti hadn't been able to decide how she felt about Trina. But hearing how Trina's views on Odessa mirrored her own, Marti felt she had found an ally. Not that she was ever going to need one. But it did make her feel less uncomfortable at being there.

"But as long as he's a threat, which he will always be," Trina added, "better he's here than on the street."

Over the next hour, they toured the rest of the main building and the grounds. Returning to Marti's office, Trina showed Marti how to use the hospital's e-mail system and access the Internet, then went off to her own duties, promising to come back at noon and take her to lunch in nearby Linville.

The stacks of files that had been left in Marti's office were arranged in two distinct groups, one at each end of her desk. Discovering that those on the left were for her female patients, she moved down to the male records. Just as Rosenblum had said, there were two kinds of files, some in metal binders, some in soft jackets, each type stacked by itself. Since everything was arranged in alphabetical order, she found Odessa's records with no trouble.

Having four times read the book that had been written about him and possessing a briefcase full of newspaper clippings detailing his grisly career, Marti was already an Odessa expert. Even so, she spent the better part of the next hour reading every word in his files, looking for anything new.

The thickest portion of his records by far was the oldest, dating back to the time he'd spent in the California mental hospital that had allowed him to escape and kill Lee eighteen years ago. The reason he was now in Gibson was not explained in his files, but from conversations Marti had had with a former employee of the California facility when she was trying to track him down, she knew he'd been quietly contracted out to Gibson two years ago under a cost-cutting arrangement.

Among the items in her personal dossier on Odessa was a physical description from the records of the Los Angeles Police Department in which every distinguishing mark on him was cataloged. But it did not mention the scar on his neck that she'd seen when standing behind him earlier that morning. Nor did she find any explanation of it in his files. So the LAPD had either missed it or he'd been injured, probably in a fight, after being confined.

It was interesting that, when he'd been at the California facility, he'd been a real problem, given to violent outbursts on practically a weekly basis, but as Trina had said, the only incident in his Gibson records was the one last September. Why had his behavior improved so much? And why would Gibson want a patient with his background? They couldn't have known when they'd agreed to take him that he wouldn't be the same problem patient he had been. Moreover, there was a note from Oren Quinn in the files prohibiting the staff from giving Odessa any type of neurotropic drug, meaning that even if Odessa *had* continued to be violent, controlling him chemically was not an option.

Her musings on this were interrupted by a knock on the door.

"It's open."

"Hi," Trina said. "Are you hungry?"

"As a matter of fact, I am."

On their way to the parking lot, Marti said, "How long has Oren Quinn been here?"

"About two years."

"So he and Odessa arrived about the same time."

"I think Odessa came around a month after Quinn. Why?"

"No reason, just trying to get a feel for the flow and rhythm of the place."

They ate at a restaurant called The Fishin' Hole, a big log cabin, where the interior walls were covered with dusty taxidermy specimens of items on the menu. Though Marti found the decor a little creepy and was leery of Trina's recommendation that she try the special, the catfish she ordered was excellent. By the time lunch was over, Marti liked Trina even more.

With her review of Odessa's file complete, Marti spent the rest of the day familiarizing herself with her other patients, learning as she did that many of them were layered with so many drugs they were little more than walking zombies. And that caused her to think again about Oren Quinn's note that Odessa couldn't be given any neurotropic drugs. Obviously, Quinn had no philosophical objection to controlling patient behavior that way. Why specifically exclude Odessa? Odd.

IN SEARCHING THE Internet for a place to stay while she worked out her plan for Odessa, Marti had found what appeared to be a wonderful situation: a fully furnished place at Blue Sky Farm, a thousand acres of undeveloped land containing a creek, several ten-acre lakes, and wooded walking trails. It sounded so intriguing she'd immediately contacted the Realtor and snapped it up. What she didn't realize was that the land she'd be living on lay right next to Gibson, so at the end of her first workday, when she pulled onto the highway from the Gibson entrance, she drove only a hundred yards before turning onto the dirt road that led to her new, albeit temporary, home.

Though she would have preferred to live a little farther from the hospital, tonight she didn't mind the short trip, because she had two important phone calls to make, and she wanted to do that where no one from the hospital could see or hear her.

The cottage she'd rented was about two hundred yards from the highway. This distance could have been a problem to navigate, but Clay Hulett, the caretaker and son of the land's absentee owner, kept the road in perfect shape. As she drove deeper onto the property, she saw Clay washing his bronze pickup in front of his own cottage.

Her medical training and obsession with Vernon Odessa had not left much room in Marti's life for romance. The closest she'd come to a serious relationship had been last year with Josh Fellows, a surgery resident who'd finally given up on her because he'd detected that there were other things in her life with a higher priority. And she'd let him go, because he was right. Romance could come later, after she'd settled her score with Lee's murderer.

But that didn't mean she was immune to lanky cowboy good looks, so even though she was eager to make those phone calls, when Clay waved at her, she stopped and rolled down her window.

"Dr. Segerson, how was your first day?" he asked.

"A little uncomfortable, like most first days . . . And call me Marti."

He combed the black hair from his forehead with his fingers. "I've never been on a first-name basis with a doctor before."

"Well, I've never lived on an unpaved road before."

He smiled, showing a set of teeth any cosmetic dentist in LA would love to take credit for. "Looks like your arrival has broadened both of us. Everything okay at the house? I checked it out thoroughly before you got here, but sometimes things still go wrong."

"Haven't had any problems."

"Good. If you're interested in taking a walk later—"

Marti didn't let him finish. "Please don't think me rude, but I need to focus on my work at the hospital just now. I'm not really free to develop any romantic relationships."

"I was just going to tell you that I saw a pair of otters down by the creek yesterday evening and that you might want to go down there and take a look yourself."

Marti felt her face flush. "Oh, I see."

"The creek is on the other side of that big field." He pointed down the road to the right, where the wooded area opposite his house gave way to an expanse of tall grasses and flowers. "The main trail to it is about forty yards from here, just on this side of the little knoll that keeps us from seeing your house. But just off your backyard, there's a path that intersects the main trail, so you could go from there. When you reach the triple fork on the main trail, take the right leg. The creek is about three hundred yards from that point. If you want to see the otters, you'll have to move quietly. I should mention that about eighty yards along the left trail of the fork, just beyond the old barn, there's a quicksand bog. I try to keep a warning sign posted, but kids keep pulling it down. It was there yesterday when I went by, but today, who knows."

Marti's face was still burning with embarrassment when she reached the little brick bungalow she'd rented.

As she went inside, she thought she saw a large bee working the flowering jasmine on the trellis by the door, but then realized with a thrill it was a hummingbird, the first she'd ever seen.

She'd been able to afford a few minutes talking to Clay Hulett because the calls she needed to make were both to numbers in California, where it was two hours earlier. She got out her cell phone and made the first one as soon as she was inside.

She didn't expect the call to be answered by its intended recipient, and it wasn't. It took almost a minute for him to come on the line.

"Hi, this is Marti Segerson. I saw Odessa today and I talked to him. I've got good access, but it'll be a few days before I can figure out how to do it. I just wanted let you know we're on track. But I don't know how much advance notice I'll be able to give you when the time comes . . . I'll do the best I can. Don't let me down. We may get only one chance."

Her second call went to the north end of the Golden State, but the content was almost identical to the first. After she hung up, she stood for a moment, reflecting on all she'd accomplished today. She then let her attention shift to the big picture window and the spectacular view it offered of a distant little lake across the vast field of grasses and yellow flowers Clay had mentioned when he was directing her to the creek.

Over the weekend, she'd laid in a supply of groceries from the Linville Super Saver, so she didn't need to have dinner out. After she'd eaten and cleaned up the little kitchen, she saw there was still enough daylight to visit those otters.

As she followed the path from the backyard of her

house into the fields, she thought about how close she was to the culmination of nearly two decades of work and planning. And for a brief instant, she saw what lay beyond or, more accurately, realized that when this was over, the Marti Segerson she'd become would have no purpose in life. Disturbed by this glimpse of the future, she put it out of her mind by reminding herself that not only was there still a lot to do, the outcome remained uncertain.

Either she made too much noise or the otters were somewhere else when she got to the creek. For whatever reason, she didn't get to see them.

It was a beautiful mild spring night with the most delicious sweet smell in the air, and later, when she was ready for bed, she opened the window and took several deep breaths. Standing there listening to the crickets, she was tempted to leave the window open. Then, shivering at the thought of being so vulnerable, she quickly shut and locked it. Just before turning off the lamp on the nightstand, she picked up the framed picture of her sister she always kept close to her.

"Goodnight Lee. Sleep well. It won't be long now."

AT 2:43 A.M., Marti woke with the sure knowledge she was not alone in her bedroom.

CHAPTER 5

MARTI WAS SO frightened she could hardly breathe. What to do? Should she jump out of bed and scream or pretend to still be asleep? For the moment, she chose the latter.

She was lying on her side, facing the bedroom door, which in the dark room, seemed slightly ajar. She hadn't actually seen anyone, merely sensed another presence. But he was there all right. And she knew exactly who it was. He had recognized her when they'd spoken earlier today and had figured out why she had come to Gibson. Somehow, Odessa had discovered where she was staying and had escaped just as he had the night he'd killed Lee.

And now he was going to kill her.

Her cell phone . . . she could call 911 . . . But where the hell was it? Then she remembered—it was on a chair in the living room, in her handbag. She'd pictured herself as the hunter, but she'd become the hunted, and now she'd screwed up royally.

The injustice of the situation slowly began to nudge her fear into anger.

No . . . it was *not* going to end this way.

She'd get to the door and out of the house. Clay Hulett was only a hundred yards away. And she'd always been a fast runner . . . unless it was on sand.

She leaped from the bed, but her feet caught in the sheet covering her and she pitched to the floor.

Oh God. She was still tangled in it. Any second he'd be on her, straddling her as he had Lee, crushing her skull.

Kicking like a teenager on a bad acid trip, she managed to free herself of the sheet. Then she was up and moving. Her hand scrabbled at the door and she yanked it open.

As she hurtled from the room, she heard a voice behind her say, "I've got a secret."

Marti froze. Then she went back to her bedroom and turned on the light.

And there was Harry Evensky, the old man from the hospital, dressed as he had been earlier, but with muddy shoes and bits of dried weeds sticking to his pants.

"I've got a secret," he repeated.

Marti picked her robe off the chair where she'd dropped it earlier and pulled it on.

"How did you get out of the hospital?"

"I used to be a locksmith. It wasn't hard."

"No one knows where I live."

"The secretary in Dr. Rosenblum's office does. It's on her computer."

"You picked the lock on Dr. Rosenblum's door and then found my address on her computer?"

"Didn't I just say that?"

"Have you ever used a computer before?"

"Not really. But there was a book in her desk on how to work it."

"How did you get here?"

"Came along the creek. I've lived in Linville my whole life, so that was no accomplishment either."

"This is amazing."

"Why?"

"Well . . . I mean you're . . ."

"Crazy? You're a psychiatrist. You of all people ought to know, 'crazy' doesn't mean 'stupid.'"

"I'm sorry, you're right. But you shouldn't be here."

"Nobody back there will listen to me. I thought you might."

"Of course I will. But not like this."

"What's tall and fair . . . you think it's here, but it's really there?"

"I can't deal with that now."

"But you will later? Because I think you should."

"I promise." Now that she'd seen she wasn't in danger, Marti had a disturbing thought. "What door on the ward did you open?"

"The back one that leads to the cafeteria."

"You didn't leave it unlocked, did you?"

"No."

"Did anyone else leave with you?"

"Why would I want to take anybody along?"

"What did you use to pick the locks?"

He reached in his pocket and produced a couple of straightened paper clips.

"That's all?"

"What can I say? I'm good."

"May I have them?"

"Sure."

He gave them to her and Marti put them in the pocket of her robe. "Will you promise me that you'll never do this again?"

"Escape or visit you?"

"Escape."

"*Never* do it again . . . I don't know . . . Never is a long time. Let's start with a month and take it from there."

Marti agreed to his terms because first thing in the morning, she was going to see about getting better locks on all the ward doors.

"How about we get you back to the hospital now, so you can get some sleep. You must be very tired."

"I am. And apparently it was all for nothin'. Sure you don't want to give my riddle a try?"

"I'll think about it. While I try to arrange a ride home for you, how would you like a diet Coke? I've got some in the fridge."

"I wouldn't mind."

"Come into the kitchen and I'll get it."

While Evensky drank his Coke, Marti called 911 and told the county sheriff what had happened. Already alerted to Evensky's escape by the night staff at the hospital, the sheriff had a deputy patrolling the highway looking for him. So help was barely a half mile away.

In less than ten minutes, the only evidence that Evensky had ever been in Marti's home was an empty Coke can and a glass with a couple of half-melted ice cubes in it.

As badly frightened as she'd been, there was no question of getting any sleep, so she sat in the little living room in front of the TV, barely aware of what was flickering across the screen.

Before Evensky's appearance, she hadn't considered that she'd be in any danger living so close to the hospital. But my God. A patient had escaped and come right to her bedroom. Suppose it *had* been Odessa. What would she have done? Could she have made it to Clay Hulett's place? She could be dead now.

She had to take some precautions. Maybe she should move farther from the hospital. But she had a six-month lease here and wasn't so well off financially she could afford to pay rent on two places. One thing she could do was make sure her phone was where she could grab it at night. But it took that deputy at least five minutes to arrive after she'd called for help, and he was only half a mile away. She couldn't count on a car being that close the next time. And even five minutes could be too long. If she ever needed a reason to wrap up her business at Gibson ASAP and get away from there, Evensky had shown it to her. But in the meantime, she needed a contingency plan. There *was* one thing she could do . . .

MARTI HAD NO idea what Clay Hulett's schedule was or even what he did for a living, so early the next morning, as her car topped the hill that hid his house from hers, she was happy to see his pickup in the drive.

She pulled in beside his truck and sat for a moment, worried that he might not even be up yet. Finally, the urgency of her mission forced her out of her car and onto his porch.

He answered the doorbell fully dressed in jeans and a nice olive tattersall shirt with an olive and blue lattice tie.

"Morning," he said brightly. "Did you see those otters?"

"I tried, but I must have been too noisy or something. I wonder if I could ask you a couple of favors."

"Sure, come on in."

He stepped back and Marti went inside.

A man living alone . . . she'd expected to find herself in a sloppy, poorly decorated place, but to the contrary, Clay's living room was warm and inviting with well-blended earth tones and rustic furniture made of tree limbs nailed or twined together and fitted with comfortable-looking cushions. The walls were clothed in wildlife paintings: ducks, a deer with a fawn, a turkey displaying its tail feathers, an eagle plucking a fish from a lake.

"Those paintings are wonderful. Where did you get them?"

Blushing slightly, he said, "I did them. Each one is something I've seen here on the property."

"I'm impressed."

"It is an amazing place."

"I was referring to the paintings."

"Even better."

Marti sensed a little sexual subtext in his reply, but remembering how she'd embarrassed herself yesterday by making a similar assumption, she dismissed the thought.

"Have you had breakfast?" Clay asked.

"I wanted to be sure and catch you this morning, so I guess I just didn't think of it."

"I was about to make myself a mushroom omelet. It's just as easy to make two. Come on back to the kitchen."

Marti followed him to the rear of the house. On the way, they passed a small den whose walls were decorated with paintings of bull riders and other rodeo scenes.

"Are the rodeo paintings in that other room also yours?"

"I'm sort of a professional steer roper. Being at a rodeo inspires me to paint those subjects, so I take my supplies on the road and paint between runs."

The kitchen was small and neat. "Just have a seat there at the table, and I'll whip up those omelets. What did you want to see me about?"

"Last night one of the patients from the mental hospital escaped and showed up in my bedroom."

Clay stopped what he was doing and turned to face her. "That doesn't sound good. Was he dangerous?"

"Fortunately, no."

"How'd he get out?"

"He used to be a locksmith. I'm going to see that we put better locks on the doors, so there's not likely to be a reoccurrence, but it still gives me the willies."

"I'm not surprised. Anything like that happens again, call me. I can be up there before the sheriff could get someone here."

"That's one of the things I wanted to ask you."

"Just put my number on speed dial and keep the phone nearby. What was the other favor?"

"Would you mind putting deadbolt locks on my front and back doors? This patient apparently didn't have any trouble picking the lock."

"I've got a couple of lectures today at Linville Community College, but I believe I'll have time to do that as well."

"What are you studying?"

He grinned. "I teach American history, or at least I try to get some small part of it across to a largely unreceptive audience. Stamping out the fires of ignorance is a bigger job than I thought."

"Sorry, don't know why I assumed *you* were the student."

"Could've gone either way. No cause for concern."

Marti felt that she had stumbled on a rural Renaissance man. College history teacher, painter, steer roper, handyman . . . by now, she would've bet he'd also constructed all the furniture in the living room. And, of course, the omelets he made were the best she'd ever tasted. But he did serve them on mismatched plates, a slip-up that showed he was not perfect. Or, she thought, maybe he did that just to appear more accessible. Psychiatry training . . . sometimes it could be such a curse.

In any event, she left Clay's home feeling much better about living so close to the hospital. Now she could concentrate on the business at hand.

CHAPTER 6

UPON HER ARRIVAL at the hospital, Marti went to her office and sent Oren Quinn an e-mail telling him about Harry Evensky's escape, minus the part about him showing up in her bedroom. She left out the latter because it seemed like more detail than was needed to make the point that the locks needed to be changed on all the unit doors.

She then began to think about how she was going to proceed with Odessa. It would probably have to be done right here in her office. It was the only place with the necessary privacy. But she'd need a couple of tables and more chairs. And where could she put Douglas Packard so he could see what was taking place without Odessa spotting him?

Remembering what Trina Estes had said about the satellite buildings on the property being used for storage, Marti began pulling out the drawers in her desk looking for a hospital telephone directory. She found it on her third try and called the number listed for maintenance.

With each unanswered ring of the phone, it seemed less and less likely that anyone was going to answer. Big surprise. Housekeeping had ignored those dead cockroaches for a month, why should maintenance be any more—

"Hello . . . yes. This is Dr. Segerson. I'm the new staff psychiatrist and I need some additional furniture for my office; a couple of tables, three chairs, and some movable partitions. I was hoping . . . Could we go over there right now? Great . . . Which building? I'm on my way."

THE AMOUNT OF furniture in storage was prodigious, and Marti was able to find everything she needed. Though he seemed extremely put out about the extra work, the maintenance man said he'd probably be able to bring everything up to her office sometime that afternoon.

One step closer, she thought, returning to her office. Then suddenly, she was overwhelmed with all the details she hadn't yet figured out. A major obstacle was the timing. Quinn's office was down the hall from hers in the opposite wing. She certainly didn't want to do it with him in the building. Somehow she'd have to find out when he'd be away. How the hell was she going to do that?

She was generally good at breaking large tasks into manageable pieces. Look down, not up, was the way to go when attacking a major project. But this one . . . all the potential obstacles now stretched before her in a tapestry of depressing complexity. It wasn't going to work.

Who was she kidding? Something would surely happen to make it fail.

Stop it.

She didn't get through medical school and residency by that kind of thinking. Pessimism never accomplished anything. The only certain way to failure is not to try.

Bucked up by her autopilot, her mind turned to Harry Evensky. He was definitely an eccentric character, but from her conversation with him before the sheriff's deputy took him away last night, didn't seem mentally ill. Unable to remember the details of his situation from her review yesterday of the cases assigned to her, she went to the notes she'd made.

It took her a moment to locate what she'd scribbled down about him and when she did, she found it too cryptic to satisfy her. So before doing anything else, she found his records and reviewed them again.

According to his files, sixteen years ago, Evensky had lost his locksmith business in a bankruptcy. His wife, whom he depended on for practically everything, left him shortly after the business failed. These reversals drove him into a suicidal depression that brought him to Gibson for his own safety. While there, he seemed to get better but then began to spend most of each day, cutting all the *R*'s out of the newspaper one of the other patients bought at the hospital commissary every morning. He kept these *R*'s in envelopes stored in a suitcase under his bed, believing that one day there would be a market for "vintage" *R*'s, and he'd become rich. From time to time he still spoke of killing himself.

Not as normal as he appeared, Marti thought, closing his file.

Her review of Evensky's situation was only partially

motivated by an interest in him. It had more to do with delaying her planned talk with Vernon Odessa, for as much as she longed to probe the mind of this monster, she was also afraid of him.

She sat for a few minutes gathering her nerves, then picked up Odessa's file and headed for the ward.

Upon entering Two East B from the hall, Marti immediately encountered Nurse Metz.

"Are you finished with our files?" Metz asked roughly. "Because they need to be in here."

Hiding her irritation at the woman's aggressive tone, Marti tucked Odessa's file under her arm and fished in her pocket for her key ring. There were so many files to read she'd managed only to skim each one for the basics. But Metz was right, they needed to be on the wards. She removed her office key and handed it over. "Feel free to send one of the attendants down to my office to pick them up. And ask them to please take the old files back to medical records as well. I'm in two thirty-three. But don't send Bobby Ware. I want to talk to Vernon Odessa and I'd like Bobby close by. Is he here?"

"In the other ward. I'll get him."

While Marti waited for Ware, Harry Evensky spotted her and came over.

"Have you thought about it?" he said.

"Actually, no," Marti replied. "I've been very busy."

"What's tall and fair . . . you think it's here, but it's really there?"

"I give up. What is it?"

Evensky's brow furrowed. "You *can't* give up. I told you that. If I give you the answer, you'll just wish you'd figured it out for yourself."

"I'll work on it. Now will you do me a favor?"

"What?"

She lowered her voice. "Have you told anyone where I live?"

"No."

"Promise me you won't. I know you like secrets. This one could be just between us."

Evensky beamed. "Then I'd have two secrets."

"But you couldn't go around trying to get people to guess the one you have with me. Do we have a deal?"

"Okay."

"Here's Bobby," Ada Metz said, joining them.

"Something I can help you with Dr. Segerson?"

"Hi, Bobby. I want to talk to Vernon Odessa again." She looked at Metz. "Where's your interview room?"

"It's on the left," she replied, pointing across the day-room. "Just inside the doorway there."

"I don't see him out here."

"He's probably in his room," Bobby said. "Come on, I'll show you which one it is."

Marti followed Bobby into the dorm wing and down the hall to a doorway halfway to the end. "This is it."

Bobby knocked on the door.

"Go away. I'm busy," a voice said.

Bobby opened the door and leaned in. "Dr. Segerson would like to talk to you."

"Some other time."

"Sorry, it's not negotiable," Bobby said, throwing the door open and stepping inside.

From the hall, Marti saw that Odessa was sitting at a small desk, playing some kind of game on a laptop. Un-like the other rooms on the ward, which each held three patients, Odessa appeared to have this one to himself. In addition to his own computer, he had a small bookcase filled with paperbacks. Her fear at talking to him morphed into anger that he was enjoying these small comforts when he should have been dead. Hoping her face didn't show her feelings, she said, "Good morning. It was not my intention to force you to talk. If you like, I'll come back another time."

Odessa perused her from hairstyle to shoe choice, then his eyes stopped at the crotch of her slacks, making her want to slap him. He grinned and looked up. "What the hell, I've got nothing better to do. Interview room?"

"Please."

A few seconds later they were seated across from each other at a long table, Odessa with his back to the wall, Marti on the side closest to the open door, Bobby Ware sitting right outside in the hall.

"Are you menstruating?" Odessa asked. "Because I think I can smell it."

"Was that meant to shock me?"

"Did it?"

"No."

"Why not?"

"I'm a doctor. I'm accustomed to talking about bodily functions."

"But not your own."

"That's true."

"Did you know the average vagina is three inches longer than the average penis? I've always thought that was such a waste of pussy."

His information on this was quite wrong, but rather than correct him and get baited into a discussion about it, she ignored the comment. "You must like it here."

"Why do you say that?"

"According to your records, when you were in California, you were a constant behavioral problem. But since you've come here, except for one incident, you've behaved yourself. Why the change?"

This question obviously caught him off guard because his expression changed from smug to uncertain. "I didn't like the people at the other place."

"What's different about these?"

His face twisted into a scowl. "You know, you're a helluva lot like a detective. You just keep picking and picking at things."

"It's only because I want to understand you."

"I don't want to be understood. I just want to be left alone."

"You didn't answer my question. Why are you happier here?"

"Happy? That's an odd choice of words."

"Perhaps I should have said less discontented."

"Did it ever occur to you that I don't have any choice?" He bit his lip and looked away.

"What do you mean?"

He folded his hands on the table in front of him. "I like Quinn. He's a straight guy. Okay? Let's move on, or better yet, quit."

"Where did you get the scar on your neck?"

He looked at her hard for a beat, then said, "Fell off our garage roof onto some trash when I was a kid."

"Are you sure it wasn't more recently?"

"Which of us is most likely to know when I got it?"

Though his explanation of the scar clearly wasn't the truth, Marti decided to let it pass. "How do you feel about what you've done?"

"You'll have to be more specific."

"The women you killed."

He shrugged. "I don't think about it. What's the point?"

"Are you sorry?"

He shook his head and looked at her like she was someone to be pitied. "You need to hear that, don't you? If I'm sorry, then your tidy little world makes sense. Okay, I'm sorry. Feel better now?"

"Don't tell me what you think I want to hear. Tell me the truth."

His expression hardened. "All right. The truth is, there are only two kinds of people: predator and prey. You're either one or the other. Those women were just in the wrong place at the wrong time."

"So what happened was their fault?"

"What difference does it make? Their fault, mine, yours . . . dead is dead."

"Did you get sexual satisfaction out of what you did?"

"Do you like to watch men masturbate?"

"What does that mean?"

"You don't see the connection with your question?"

"No."

"Then you're not smart enough to be a psychiatrist."

At this point Marti decided to take a big risk. "A few years after you were institutionalized in California you escaped."

"One of the fondest moments of my youth."

"Before you were caught, another woman was murdered at the beach in the same manner as your other victims. Did you do that one too?"

Odessa's eyes rolled up in their sockets and shifted from side to side as if he was searching his memory. "I don't recall."

Marti wasn't surprised at his answer, for he had *never*

admitted to killing Lee. And he apparently was smart enough to know he never should. But soon, it wouldn't matter what he said about it.

As much as she needed to keep him off guard, her loathing of him led her into even more dangerous territory.

"You said people are either predator or prey. Don't you think that's being too simplistic?"

"Why do you say that?"

"Sometimes the roles can be reversed."

"I don't think so. The quail never eats the fox."

"I wouldn't be so sure of that."

"What are you saying? You think you're that quail?"

Damn it. She'd gone too far . . . said too much.

"Because I can assure you," Odessa said, "if I was free, you'd see what the fox can do."

A chill ran from the top of Marti's head down to her toes. He'd just threatened her.

"And quite frankly," Odessa added. "I'd enjoy that very much. But I don't think *you* would."

Marti was caught without a response. She'd pushed too hard, drawn too much attention to herself. Idiot. She combed her mind for a reply that would defuse the situation. But before she could speak, Ada Metz leaned into the room.

"Dr. Segerson, here's your key, and Dr. Quinn wants to see you in his office ASAP."

From the tone of Metz's voice it sounded like Quinn was upset. *Oh no,* Marti thought. *He knows why I'm here.*

CHAPTER 7

HE COULDN'T KNOW, Marti thought, heading for Quinn's office. But what she really meant was "He can't know." *It simply wouldn't be fair after all my preparation, all the years waiting for this. No, it's about something else. It has to be.*

The possibility that she'd been unmasked still loomed large in her mind as she opened the door to Quinn's outer office a minute later and went inside.

She identified herself to his receptionist, a heavy woman with small features set in the center of a large face, and the woman said, "I'm sorry, he's not here. He must have wanted you to meet him in his office upstairs in his lab."

"He has a lab?"

"Fourth floor, west wing of the patient section. They remodeled one of the unused wards."

• • • •

THE WEST WING of the building was a mirror image of the east, and as Marti trekked up the old wooden staircase to the fourth floor, she longed for an elevator. Passing the second floor, she heard a muffled scream coming from one of the other wards.

The trip was long enough that she had time to push her fear of the coming conversation with Quinn aside so she could reflect on her interview with Odessa. She'd made a big mistake by goading him into threatening her. Now he'd be watching her more carefully, thinking too much about her.

But something good had also come from their talk; he'd revealed a weakness—his liking for Quinn. She could use that, providing Quinn wasn't about to throw her out of the hospital.

The only sound as she stepped into the fourth floor was the creak of her weight on the hardwood. The walls here were even dingier than on Two East and there was the usual metal security door halfway down the hall just like all the other patient wings. And her key opened it, as it did all the others.

The receptionist hadn't said which of the wards was remodeled and the door to Four West A gave no indication any work had been done there. Moving down to Four B, she saw that it looked the same. Thinking that the receptionist had sent her to the wrong place, Marti reached out to try the door, expecting that it would be locked.

It wasn't.

Inside was a huge, modern laboratory with many cabinets and work surfaces and bright fluorescent lighting. Glancing around, Marti saw shiny new floor-model centrifuges, fraction collectors, power supplies, computers, and banks of impressive-looking devices whose function was a mystery.

On her left, near the far wall, a slim, dark-haired woman in a white lab coat was working around a large, circular metal tank on a big table. Seeing no sign of Quinn, Marti walked over to the woman and announced herself.

"Hello, I'm Dr. Segerson."

The woman, who had just picked up a white mouse from a cage beside the tank, turned and smiled. "And you're just in time to see something quite remarkable."

"I'm intrigued, but I'm actually here to see Dr. Quinn. Is he in his office?"

"Haven't seen him for an hour. He'll probably be along shortly."

Marti didn't want to keep Quinn waiting, but since no one knew where he was, she couldn't do anything about that. "Guess all I can do then is wait. What did you want to show me?"

The woman had frizzy black hair that contrasted sharply with her almost white skin. She'd chosen to go with a deep red lipstick. The red stitching above the left pocket on her coat identified her as Nadine Simpson.

"Watch this," she said.

She put the mouse into the tank, which was filled almost to the top with murky water that was impossible to see through. The mouse started swimming as though it knew just where it wanted to go. In seconds it found its destination; a platform just below the water's surface, where the mouse could rest. Marti recognized this as the Morris water maze, a classical test to demonstrate learning and memory. The mouse had obviously learned where the platform was through prior training. If he hadn't, he would have wandered all over the tank before finding the platform.

"Are you familiar with this test?" Nadine asked.

"Yes."

"That mouse was trained in this test a month ago, long enough for his training to be consolidated into long-term memory."

Nadine was referring to the well-known phenomenon in which memories exist for a short time in a fragile state where any disturbance such as a severe bump on the head can cause them to be lost. But as time passes, they become fixed, so that they're stored in a form immune to interference.

Nadine put the test mouse back in his cage and reached for a second mouse in a different cage.

"This guy received the same training as the first mouse," she said, dangling the second one by his tail. "Both of them were tested in the tank two days ago to prove that they remembered their training, and both showed they did. But"—Nadine raised her index finger for emphasis—"immediately *after* the refresher test, we gave this guy an injection to block all manufacture of protein in his body. And look at the result."

She put the mouse in the water. Instead of swimming directly for the platform as he apparently had done two days ago, he began swimming aimlessly around the tank, demonstrating no knowledge whatever of his previous training.

This made no sense to Marti. Blocking the shift of short-term memories to long-term by suppressing the manufacture of protein by nerve cells was an old experiment. But once that shift occurred, the drug shouldn't have any effect. "I don't get it. Memories in long-term storage can't be affected by what you did."

"Unless the refresher test made those memories fragile again," Nadine replied.

"You're saying the act of recalling a memory converts it back into the short-term form that once again needs to be consolidated?"

"Can you think of any other explanation?"

Marti couldn't. Then she realized this phenomenon explained why in the sixties, doctors noted that electroconvulsive shock treatments in mental patients produced amnesia for recently recalled memories, but not dormant ones.

"My God," Marti said. "This is a major discovery."

"Nadine." The stern voice came from the doorway to the hall.

Turning, Marti saw Oren Quinn hustling toward them. Talking to Nadine had temporarily diverted Marti's attention from worrying about what Quinn wanted. Now, seeing the stormy look on his face, her concern came back in a rush.

"I'm sure Dr. Segerson doesn't have time for extraneous conversation," Quinn said.

"Actually, what she was telling me is fascinating."

"I'm sorry, Dr. Quinn," Nadine said, cowering like a scolded puppy. "I was just so excited by our results I wanted to share them with someone."

"This is not the time or the place. Get back to work." He turned to Marti. "Dr. Segerson, I expected to meet with you in my administrative office."

"I went there first, but your receptionist sent me up here."

Marti was immediately sorry she'd phrased it like

that. The way he'd jumped all over Nadine for nothing meant he'd probably do the same to his receptionist for this mix-up.

"Well, you're here, so let's make the best of it," Quinn said. "I've got another office in the back."

He took her to a room with an Oriental carpet in vivid shades of blue, and a huge old oak desk with carved gargoyles at each corner. The walls were decorated with slightly water-stained prints of the brain in plain black frames. His bookshelves sagged under the weight of leather-bound anatomy and psychology texts.

"Sit," Quinn said, motioning to the only visitor's chair, a high-backed oak monster carved to match the desk.

Sitting down, Marti discovered that the chair was as uncomfortable as it looked. When Quinn was settled in his own chair behind his oak fortress, Marti pointed to the human brain displayed on his desk in a jar of crystal-clear preservative. "Who did that belong to?"

"Ed Gein."

"The psychopath who was the model for Buffalo Bill in *Silence of the Lambs*?"

"The very same."

"Where did you get it?"

"I rescued it from some misguided scientists who wanted to slice it up in the mistaken belief there would be some obvious gross anatomical correlates to his aberrant behavior. Stupid men. The explanations they seek won't be found that easily. But we're not here to discuss Ed Gein."

Here it comes, Marti thought. She braced for the worst.

"Dr. Segerson, you've been here only one day and

I've already had to deal with two things related to your presence—your orders that Letha Taylor be checked for diabetes and your e-mail requesting that the locks on all the wards be changed."

Letha Taylor and locks. That's all he wanted.

"Both important issues," Marti said, hiding the relief she felt.

"How would you describe life as a patient here?"

"I don't understand."

"Would you want your mother or father to live like that?"

"No."

"So it's a poor existence."

"That's a fair statement."

"Why then would you want to prolong it? Letha Taylor is profoundly disturbed. She'll never get better."

Marti couldn't believe what she was hearing. "You think we should do nothing about her diabetes because she'd be better off dead?"

"Wouldn't she?"

"Of course not."

"You said that very quickly."

"It's an obvious conclusion."

"I disagree. Without the ability to think and reason, we're already dead."

"This is a hospital. We're supposed to care for the sick."

"But not blindly. Some judgment has to be exercised in expenditure of resources."

"I can't think that way."

"Because you don't have to. I do. Take the locks you want changed on all the wards. Do you know what that would cost?"

"How could I?"

"Too much. And it's an overreaction."

"A patient escaped."

"A former locksmith with special abilities and knowledge. If we had a locksmith in every ward it might be
necessary to change the locks, but we don't. So we'll
change them only in the ward with the locksmith. That
not only makes perfect sense, it's fiscally responsible."

"What about Letha Taylor?"

"We'll come back to that in a moment. You probably
aren't aware of this, but I've always been interested in the
phenomenon of close-proximity mind reading; one person thinks of something, another, seated no more than a
few feet away, receives the thought. I know it sounds like
science fiction, but I think there's something to it. In a
way, it's just an extension of the wireless EEG technique
I developed, but in this case, the receiver is another brain,
which, theoretically, should be a far better receiver than
any ever built. We have wireless connections to the Internet, why can't two brains communicate? It's all elec-
tromagnetic radiation."

The thought that Quinn might be able to read her mind
made Marti extremely uncomfortable. But obviously, he
couldn't. Or he'd never have hired her. As much as she
didn't like him she had to admit he was a visionary who
was always on the cutting edge of things. So maybe he'd
make a major contribution in this area too. But why was
he telling *her* all this?

"With your academic record," Quinn said. "I think
you'd make an excellent test subject."

Marti was shocked at his suggestion. "I can assure you
I've never read anyone's mind."

"Maybe that's because the situation was never optimal. I'd like to test you under controlled, very specific conditions."

"I don't know . . ."

During their conversation, Quinn's manner had gradually warmed until it had lost the sharp edge he'd shown during her interview in Washington and demonstrated again when he'd come through the lab door a few minutes earlier. In an instant, he reverted. "I thought you were interested in getting Letha Taylor's diabetes treated."

For a moment, Marti didn't get it. Then she saw what he meant, and it repulsed her. He wanted to arrange a trade—her cooperation for treating Letha Taylor. It was such a monstrous bargain she didn't know how to respond. Finally, she said the only thing she could. "Where and when would this test take place?"

"Up here, in a suite off the main lab. Nadine will conduct it tomorrow at nine o'clock. It's quite an extensive test, so be prepared to spend the morning with her. It was good of you to volunteer. I believe you know the way out."

Nadine didn't even look up from her work as Marti left. But after Marti was gone, she stared at the door to the hall and rubbed at her neck where the high collar on her turtleneck sweater hid a scar—a scar very much like the one Marti had seen on Vernon Odessa.

CHAPTER 8

AFTER LEAVING QUINN'S lab, Marti returned to her office and sat at her computer, still incensed that she'd had to bargain with Quinn to get Letha Taylor the medical care she deserved. But in a way it was good he was such a jerk. If he'd been a decent guy, she might have felt remorse at hoodwinking him to get at Odessa.

But when could she do that?

From the research she'd done on Quinn after he'd interviewed her in D.C., she'd learned that he spoke at nearly every major scientific meeting or congress there was, so he did a lot of traveling. A good place to start would be to see what meetings were coming up.

Ten minutes' work on the Internet located an international congress on advances in EEG technology in Atlanta on Monday and Tuesday of next week. Surely he'd be attending that. But she had to be sure. She spent another few minutes trying to find the speaker's schedule for the conference, but the organizers apparently hadn't posted it. However, there *was* a contact phone number on the site announcing the conference.

She picked up the phone and dialed the number.

One ring . . . Two rings . . . Three . . .

She waited five more, then hung up. Why the devil would they post a useless phone number? That left the e-mail address listed on the site. She hit the hot link for the address and was filling in the message when it occurred to her that the response would come back through the hospital's e-mail system. Would a place that couldn't arrange for the floors to be swept adequately monitor employee e-mails? Very unlikely. But it was a risk she couldn't afford to take. So she jotted down the conference e-mail address, then navigated to her account at HotMail and sent her inquiry through it. Now it was time to act like she was a real employee.

She decided to visit the female ward, primarily because she wasn't in the mood to run into either Odessa or Evensky. But whom should she interview? She got out the notes she'd made when reviewing all the files yesterday and scanned them. Two cases caught her attention: Audry Ewing and Sarah Holman. Those should be enough to finish out the morning.

Happily, Ada Metz was in the male dayroom when Marti arrived at the nursing station, so she didn't have to speak to her. But Bobby was there, standing by the two chart carts.

"Back for more?" Bobby said.

"The fun never stops."

Bobby gestured to the files. "What can I get you?"

"Ewing and Holman, female ward."

Bobby selected the appropriate files and gave them to

her. "What do you think of Odessa's behavior earlier? He got pretty nasty with you."

"I think he's a pig."

"I guess that's a personal view, not a medical one."

"I'm sorry, I shouldn't have said that."

"Doesn't bother me."

"I'd appreciate it if you'd just forget my comment."

"What comment?"

"You're a good man. Now show me who these files belong to."

They stepped into the dayroom and Bobby pointed at a woman with stringy gray hair who was circling the room, trailing the fingers of her left hand against the wall. "That's Ewing. And"—He pointed to a woman with a blotchy complexion slumped in a chair, staring at the floor—"that's Holman."

"Give me a couple of minutes to reread Ewing's file, then bring her to the interview room, would you please? Is it in the same place as on the male ward?"

"Opposite side of the hall."

Audry Ewing, the only child of a prominent local family, had been in Gibson for forty years. When she was a teenager, she'd been vivacious and intelligent but had developed a wild streak. Unable to control her, her parents had sent her to Gibson, where she'd been given a frontal lobotomy, a shameful stain on Gibson's past.

"Here's Audry," Bobby said, gently bringing her into the interview room. With nothing to fear from this patient, Marti was sitting behind the interview table, facing the door.

"Hello, Audry. I'm Dr. Segerson. Won't you sit down?"

Bobby guided Audry into the wooden chair opposite Marti, then withdrew into the hallway.

"How are you feeling today?" Marti asked.

"Today," Audry repeated, her eyes focused on some distant place. "Day is a snow white dove of heaven, give us this day our daily bread, don't put off today what you can do tomorrow, tomorrow is a day that never arrives, daylight comes and me want to go home, today is the first day of the rest of your life . . ."

"Audry, please stop that and talk to me."

". . . Today, I am a man . . ."

"Audry, focus on my face. This is not the way people talk to each other."

"Talk is cheap, all talk and no action, talk up a storm, just talk into the microphone, talk a blue streak, talk and I'll go easy on you . . ."

Okay, Marti thought. *So much for helping Audry.* "Bobby."

Bobby came into the room.

"Would you take her back to the dayroom, please, and in about five minutes, bring Sarah in."

"Will do."

As Bobby led Audry away, she was still doing it. "Talk to the animals, talk to God, don't talk unless you can improve on the silence . . ."

While waiting for Sarah Holman, Marti boiled with anger at what Gibson had done to Audry. A life ruined by a misguided medical procedure. She felt ashamed to be part of the profession. It was a minute or two before she could concentrate on anything else, so she barely had time to skim Holman's file before Bobby reappeared at the door.

"Here's Sarah."

When the woman was seated in front of her, Marti introduced herself and began this interview as she had the previous one. "So how are you feeling today?"

"How should I be feeling? I have no friends, no family, no one cares about me."

"I care."

"Can you smell that? My feet stink horribly. I'll bet I've got gangrene down there. My feet are dead and soon I will be too."

"You don't have gangrene."

"Or some tropical disease that makes your flesh rot. Don't lie to me. I know what's going on. And it's all my fault. If I'd been a better person, this wouldn't be happening. Will it be painful? I'm sure it will be. It's only what I deserve."

"Sarah, listen to me. You are *not* dying."

"Or maybe it's flesh-eating bacteria. You can tell me. I can handle it. God knows, I've had enough practice at dealing with hard times."

Clearly there was no point in spending any more time with this woman either. People can't be talked out of a depression that profound. The Zoloft she was being given was obviously not doing the job.

"Bobby."

"Back to the dayroom?" he asked, appearing in the doorway.

"Please."

Marti wrote a change of medication order in Holman's file, adding Depakote, a mood stabilizer, to Sarah's Zoloft. She alerted Ada Metz to the needed adjustment, then went back to her office, where she headed directly to her computer and navigated to her HotMail account.

Yes. There it was—a response from the EEG conference.

She quickly opened it and scanned the contents.

Dr Quinn is tentatively scheduled to be part of
a panel on Tuesday, but has so far not con-
firmed. Sorry we can't be more help.

Nuts. She couldn't do anything with that information.
She needed to know for *sure* if he'd be there.

She sat for a few minutes trying to figure out what to
do, then got up, walked down to Quinn's administrative
office, and went inside, where she was disappointed to
find his secretary's chair empty. She was just turning to
leave when the door to Quinn's office opened, and he
came out.

"Dr. Segerson, is there something I can do for you?"

Marti's mind went on a wild search for an answer.
Why was she there? Why? Why?

"What time did you say I should come to your lab tomorrow?"

"Nine o'clock."

"I thought that's what you said. Sorry to bother you."

After Marti was gone, Quinn stood for a moment
thinking about her. There was something not right about
that woman. He still didn't understand why she had
wanted a job at Gibson, and that gnawed at him. He
should have turned her application down and taken his
chances with Nashville. Maybe he should just fire her. He
could say her performance didn't measure up. But he had
no proof of that, which would create a worse mess than
having not hired her at all. Better to leave her alone for

now. He could be wrong about her. In any event, he'd be in a better position to assess that tomorrow.

After her close call in Quinn's office, Marti needed some fresh air. So instead of going back to her office, she left the hospital and drove into Linville for lunch.

As she drove, she thought back to her conversation with Bobby Ware earlier and how she'd called Odessa a pig in Ware's presence.

That wasn't smart. She needed to be more careful.

But he *was* a pig . . . and worse. Lee wasn't the only victim in the Segerson family; he'd damaged them all. Before Odessa came into their lives her mother was the story lady at the local library. Each day of the week during the school year she'd visit one of the five elementary schools in the district and read the children there a lovely little story she'd written the week before. She'd try her stories out on Marti, and when she read, Marti remembered there was a sparkle in her mother's eyes that made them look like gemstones.

Before Odessa there would be a different African violet on the breakfast table every morning. And *such* violets . . . each as big as a dinner plate, six weeks between repetition of flower color. Marti loved to see the gemstones in her mother's eyes, and she learned that she could also make them appear by complimenting her on the beauty of her violets.

But after Lee was murdered, her mother never wrote another story, and someone else became the story lady. She lost interest in her violets; and though Marti tried to save them, she didn't have the skill, so one by one, they died. And it seemed that with every plant taken to the trash, she lost a little more of her mother.

Her father was a civil engineer who had once been

able to design, build, and repair anything. She had always believed that if he had just tried, he could have mended her mother's broken spirit; but after Lee's death, he wasn't able to reach beyond his own grief. So not only had Odessa taken her sister, he had robbed her of her parents as well.

Pig? That was a charitable call.

Marti entered the Linville town square and her mind returned to current matters. Circling the court house, she saw an appealing little café with red-and-white gingham curtains hanging in spotlessly clean windows. There were no parking places in front of it, so she had to park on the south side of the square and walk back.

Inside, the place was jammed and noisy with Linvillians enjoying their break from work. There was no hostess and no empty tables. So despite having apparently chosen the most popular place in town, she wasn't going to be able to take advantage of her good judgment. But then someone stood in the middle of the crowd and waved at her. It was Clay Hulett.

He motioned her over.

She made her way through the throng and approached his table, which he was sharing with an attractive brunette in a white short-sleeved knit sweater she filled out nicely.

"Please, join us," Clay said, still standing.

"I don't want to impose."

"Not at all. We'd enjoy the company."

Clay pulled out a chair for her. As Marti sat down, she glanced at the other woman and saw an expression that suggested she wasn't as happy with Marti's presence as Clay was.

Clay returned to his seat and made the introductions. The woman with him was Jackie Norman.

"Jackie teaches English at Linville Community College," Clay said.

"Creative writing," Jackie added, clarifying Clay's description of her.

"That's wonderful," Marti said. "Afraid I'm more of a left-brain person."

"She's a psychiatrist at Gibson," Clay explained.

"Hence the brain reference," Jackie said.

Was that a barb? Marti thought so, but didn't want to jump to any conclusions.

"When psychiatrists go to lunch do they leave their specialty behind or should we worry that you'll be dissecting everything we say?" Jackie asked.

"If you promise not to put me in a story, I won't give anything you say more thought than it deserves."

From the expression on her face, Jackie wasn't quite sure what this meant. Sensing that it might be dangerous to let the two women continue talking, Clay jumped into the breach.

"The special today is glazed ham. It's always good."

"Characters in stories need to be multidimensional," Jackie said.

Clay tapped the menu. "And two vegetables . . . home cooked."

Marti was debating whether she should escalate the hostilities or back off, when the waitress arrived. After their orders were placed it was an ideal time for a fresh start. Deciding to take advantage of that, Marti said her next words to Clay.

"How'd your class go this morning?"

"I was heckled by a forty-year-old female student who

thought my first exam was 'ridiculously difficult' and said so in front of everybody."

"What did you do?"

"I told her that sometimes perception and reality aren't the same. It all depends on where you are on the intellectual spectrum. She had no idea what I was talking about, but that was good, because she couldn't figure out how to reply. Thus goes life at LCC."

"What would *you* have told that woman?" Jackie said to Marti.

"Probably nothing as effective as what Clay said."

"I'm sure you're just being modest."

"Why do you say that?"

"Most likely it's because I hate my mother. Isn't that at the root of all human behavior?"

The waitress arrived with their food, and once again there was a cease-fire. In an attempt to prolong the peace as long as possible Clay chatted amiably all through the meal. At the earliest moment, Marti rose, thanked them for their company, and got out of there.

On the way back to Gibson she found herself wondering if Clay and Jackie were romantically involved. If they were and Jackie perceived Marti as a threat to that relationship, it would explain her attitude. Having arrived at an explanation for an otherwise inexplicable experience, Marti was able to put it out of her mind.

A few minutes after she reached her office, there was a knock at the door. She opened it and saw Mr. Tolbert, the maintenance man she'd met that morning, and a helper. They were accompanied by a flatbed cart piled with the furniture she'd picked out from storage.

"Got your stuff," Tolbert said.

"Great, bring it in."

Feeling guilty about the reason she wanted the items they'd brought, Marti had hoped they could deliver them while drawing a minimum of attention to their destination. But the cart with its load wouldn't fit through the door. So they had to unload each piece in the hall and bring it inside separately, prolonging the evidence of her preparations to anyone who walked by. The first item in was the long table.

"Where do you want this?" Tolbert asked.

"Against that wall." Her plan actually called for it to be in the middle of the room, but she wasn't going to arrange any of it until just before it was needed.

"Next time I change jobs I need to remember not to hire on at any place that don't have elevators," Tolbert complained as he went back into the hall for another item.

In three minutes they were gone and Marti was left to think once again about Quinn and that EEG meeting. She went to her door, opened it, and looked toward Quinn's office. It'd be very risky to try that again. If he saw her this time, what would she say?

She paused in the doorway to devise a cover story.

My car's been running a little rough and I wanted to ask your secretary if she could recommend a good mechanic.

It wasn't inspired, but it would have to do.

With her heart rate shifting to alert status, she walked quickly to Quinn's office and went inside.

This time, his secretary was there.

"Dr. Segerson, what can I do for you?"

Marti glanced at Quinn's door. If he came out in the middle of the tale she was about to spin, her cover story wouldn't wash. So once she started, she'd be out there without a net.

"A former teacher of mine in med school was thinking of visiting me here next week. He's an old friend of Dr. Quinn—" Hearing the door to the hall open behind her, she froze.

Damn it. If that's Quinn . . .

"Sorry, Helen," a female voice said. "I'll come back when you're not busy."

The door closed and Marti relaxed a notch.

"A friend of Dr. Quinn is coming . . ." the secretary said, helping Marti get back to her story.

"Yes. But he wanted to be sure that Dr. Quinn will be here. Is he planning to attend that EEG meeting in Atlanta?"

"He'll be gone all day Monday and Tuesday, but back on Wednesday. Usually after a trip, he's very busy catching up on work that piled up while he was gone. So Thursday or Friday would be the best days."

"Thanks. But don't say anything to him about this. His friend wanted to surprise him."

Helen frowned. "Dr. Quinn doesn't like surprises."

"I think he'll appreciate this one. Do we have a deal?"

While Helen thought it over, Marti silently urged her to make the right choice.

"I don't . . ."

"Dr. Quinn doesn't have to know I told you about it in advance. It could be a surprise to you as well."

"Under those conditions, okay."

And we move one step closer, Marti thought, going back to her office. Surely six days was enough time for the two men she was counting on to arrange their schedules. She'd alerted them yesterday to stay ready.

There hadn't been a single day since Lee was murdered that Marti had been truly happy. And she wasn't happy now. But at least she was excited. Even that was an improvement.

CHAPTER 9

MARTI LEFT THE hospital promptly at five o'clock and drove home. On the leg of the dirt driveway between Clay's house and hers, she met him coming toward her. They each swerved onto the shoulder, stopped when their vehicles were aligned with each other, and rolled down their windows.

"I got your deadbolts installed," Clay said. "Your new key is under the doormat. Same one works both doors."

"Thanks. I know you've been busy today and that wasn't easy to fit in."

"No problem. I realize how important it was to you. Say, I want to apologize for Jackie at lunch this afternoon. It was nothing personal against you. Her sister used to work at Gibson and while she was there, she had a stroke or something. That was last fall, and she's still nowhere near normal. She's had to relearn how to do practically everything. For some reason, Jackie blames

Gibson and takes an immediate dislike to anyone associated with the place."

"I understand. Believe me, I know how close sisters can be and how much pain that's causing Jackie."

"You said that like you've experienced something similar yourself."

"No, I just meant . . . my training gives me a good insight into those kinds of situations and I've seen it happen to others."

He was such a nice guy and had extended himself so much to fix her locks, it made Marti feel bad that she'd rebuffed him yesterday for what wasn't even a pass at her. "You've already done enough for me today, but I wonder if you'd have time after dinner to show me those otters."

Clay grinned, obviously pleased at her request. "How about six thirty? That should give us enough time before dark."

"I'll see you then."

Driving on, Marti wondered why, with all she had on her mind, she'd done that. Probably to show him she didn't harbor any ill feelings toward him for Jackie's behavior at lunch, she concluded.

The new locks worked beautifully and they made Marti feel much more secure. So when she made the first call to California, she felt like everything was falling into place. But she quickly hit a slight snag with Douglas Packard.

She preferred to proceed with the plan on Tuesday of next week, when Quinn would actually be sitting on his panel in Atlanta. But Packard, she discovered, had a commitment that would allow him to be there only on Monday. So Monday it would be . . . unless the second participant couldn't be there then. She punched the number into her cell phone.

"Marti Segerson calling Barry Glaser please."

Glaser promptly came on the line. "It's all set for next Monday," Marti said. "I thought we'd do it around two o'clock. If you can get here in the morning, that should give you enough time to get set up. Can you be here? . . . Great. When you've made your flight arrangements, call me back and we'll iron out the details."

CLAY ARRIVED AT six thirty in jeans and a stone-washed blue denim shirt, not looking at all like a history professor. Seeing his rugged clothing, Marti thought her own blue big shirt with the rolled-up sleeves was an appropriate choice but felt that her white pants with their pink and blue window-pane pattern, might be a little too feminine for the occasion. Too late now.

They picked up the main trail to the creek from the road between their two homes and entered the field of waist-high flowers and grasses.

"I've never seen so many butterflies," Marti said.

"Most of them are a type known as skippers. They're called that because they stay close to the ground and skip from flower to flower."

"Not a bad way to make a living."

A skipper fluttered near and landed on Marti's shoulder.

"A compliment," Clay said, noticing.

"Or it's just tired."

"Then why didn't it land on me?"

"My shoulder's closer to the ground."

"I see you were listening."

"It's one of the things I do best."

The skipper went back to work, and Clay and Marti resumed walking.

A few seconds later, Clay suddenly stopped moving and pointed down the trail. "Look there, on the ground," he whispered sharply. "Left side where the trail turns."

Marti stared hard at the place he was indicating. "I don't see—"

Two little birds suddenly ran across the path and ducked into the weeds on the opposite side.

"What were they?"

"Quail."

Marti looked up at Clay and saw something in him she envied.

"What's wrong?" he asked, brushing at his face. "Can you see what I had for dinner?"

"I was just thinking how comfortable you are with your life. And how much it seems to suit you."

"And you find that unusual?"

"I don't think most people know who they are."

"Do you?"

"Not really."

"And why is that, do you suppose?"

Suddenly realizing she was revealing far too much of herself to someone she hardly knew, Marti pulled back. "Hey, I'm supposed to be the psychiatrist here."

"Look," Clay said, pointing into the sky over the woods just ahead. "It's George."

Marti followed his finger and saw a huge bird land on the highest branch in one of the taller trees.

"Is that an eagle?"

"Yeah. Isn't he magnificent?"

Marti agreed, then added, "But isn't George kind of an

ordinary name? Shouldn't he be called Nicholas the Brave or Eric the Bold?"

Clay looked at her. "Now, how would it sound if I suddenly threw my arm up to the sky and said, 'Look, it's Nicholas the Bold.' Pretty soon they'd have me over there in Gibson as a patient."

"Actually, it was Eric the Bold, but I see your point."

"I named him after George Pickett, my favorite Confederate general."

"You're not still holding a grudge about the Civil War, are you?"

He smiled. "We wuz robbed."

With Clay showing her the way and keeping her from making as much noise as she did on her previous trip, they watched the otters for several minutes, until the sudden intrusive sound of a siren made the animals disappear.

"I have to go," Clay said. "I'm a volunteer fireman and that siren means we've got trouble. Sorry to leave you like this, but I don't think you want to sprint back to the house. Talk to you later."

And off he went, running, Marti thought, like a racehorse.

MARTI OPENED THE door to Quinn's lab and went inside, where Nadine was working at a kneehole desk built into the cabinetry. She looked up at the sound of the door.

"You're very punctual."

It struck Marti that there could be varying degrees of lateness, but not of punctuality, a critical thought no doubt borne of her desire not to be there.

"So how do we go about this mind-reading test?"

Nadine got out of her chair. "We start over here . . ."

Marti followed her to a small room containing an overstuffed recliner chair and a tiny table bearing an iced drink in a plastic glass with a straw sticking out of its lid.

"Dr. Quinn has discovered that the best results are obtained if the test subject is extremely relaxed and is fortified with a high-calorie beverage, in this case, a Coke, before we begin." She turned to a rheostat on the wall and dialed the lighting down. She pressed a nearby button, and the room was filled with the sweet sound of a Tchaikovsky violin concerto. "So I'm going to leave you here for a while to unwind in that big chair."

"For how long?"

"I'm glad you reminded me. I need your watch."

"Why?"

"Worrying about the time while you're here is counterproductive to the test. We want your mind free of all outside influences."

Having no choice in the matter, Marti took off her watch and put it in Nadine's waiting hand.

"We can't begin until you've finished that entire drink. So relax, close your eyes, and enjoy the music. I'll come back and get you when it's time."

Nadine left and closed the door.

Alone in the room, Marti bristled briefly at being coerced into this. How could someone who didn't volunteer for the test be fully relaxed when they took it? It seemed like a real flaw in Quinn's thinking. But she was here and would just have to make the best of it. The thought that she would soon never have to see Quinn again made it all easier to take.

She sat in the big chair and took a sip of the Coke. In a short time, despite her attitude, she felt herself begin to loosen up. The music really was pleasant, and it wasn't as if Quinn were asking her to endure something disgusting or dangerous. So why not just play the game and move on?

Having been tied to a schedule for so much of her life, it was disconcerting at first to be without her watch. But then as she slipped more and more into the mood generated by the music and the soft lighting, she ceased to care about its absence.

As the minutes slipped by, the music spun a web around her that made Vernon Odessa and her plans for him seem as far away as they had when she was still in medical school. This was actually quite nice. Maybe she ought to try this a few minutes every day on her own. So good to be free of the guilt for running out on Lee that horrible night . . . so good.

"DR. SEGERSON, WAKE up."

Marti's eyes opened to see Nadine standing over her in the glare of the room's lights, now on full blast. Tchaikovsky was no longer in evidence.

"I see you didn't have any trouble relaxing," Nadine said, smiling.

"I can't believe I fell asleep."

"You must have been worn out."

"I didn't think so. How long was I asleep?"

Nadine wagged a warning finger at her. "Remember, we're not going to worry about time while you're here this morning. The test will be conducted in the room next door."

Nadine led Marti to a room with a long table bearing

a pair of computer monitors arranged back to back with a rolling chair in front of each of them.

"You sit over there," Nadine said, pointing to the monitor on the far side of the table.

When Marti was settled in her chair, Nadine said, "We're going to look at many sets of items in which six images at a time will appear on both monitors. For each set, I'll concentrate on one of the images on my monitor. When you're ready, you pick the image you believe I've chosen."

"How do I do that?"

"Each image will have a number under it. To choose an image, just hit the corresponding number on your keyboard. That's all there is to it. Let's try a practice set."

She worked a few keys on her keyboard, and a set of six simple drawings appeared on Marti's monitor: a cone, a boat, a dog, a bird, a cube, and a car.

Nadine came around the table to Marti's side. "If you believe I'm focusing on the bird, you just hit key number four. Go ahead."

Marti tapped the appropriate key, and an asterisk appeared by the number four on the screen.

"How do I change choices?"

"The delete key. Then, when you're ready to proceed, you just say so and we'll move on. Shall we start?"

"Why not?"

There were thirty image sets in the initial batch. For the first few, Marti really tried to concentrate and figure out which one Nadine had selected. But then the whole thing became so tedious she started picking images at random, until Nadine gently said, "Dr. Segerson, I don't think you're trying."

"Why do you say that?"

"Your response time has decreased significantly from the first ten sets."

"Maybe I'm just getting the hang of it."

"That's not usually the case. If you don't cooperate, Dr. Quinn will blame me."

Not wanting to create any trouble for her, Marti went back to doing her best on each set of images.

After the first batch, Nadine offered to give Marti a break.

"I'm fine. Let's just keep going."

They did another block of thirty. And then another. This time Marti accepted the offer of a short break. "How many more of these things are there?"

"You'll just get upset if I tell you."

The blasted test went on and on, until Marti had lost all track of time. Was it eleven, twelve, or two o'clock? She had no idea.

Finally, Nadine said, "You'll be glad to hear that we're finished."

"How'd I do?"

"We won't know until the computer analyzes your responses."

When Marti was given her watch back, she discovered that it was five minutes until twelve, the entire morning shot.

She left Quinn's lab and went to her car, intending to find a place for lunch. But first, after checking to make sure she wasn't being followed, she drove to the Best Western Inn and went up to the desk, which was staffed by an attractive young blond.

"I'd like to reserve two rooms for next Monday night. The occupants will be arriving early on Monday and will

need to be in them well before the normal check-in. Will
that be possible?"

"We're never full, so I'm sure that won't be a problem."

As the girl spoke, Marti saw the flash of a silver stud
in her tongue. "One reservation will be under the name
Douglas Packard, the other, Barry Glaser."

The clerk jotted down the names. "Will you be using
a credit card?"

RETURNING TO HER car in the Best Western parking
lot, Marti reached for the Hampton Inn directory in the
glove box, looked up the number for the Memphis inn
closest to the airport, and called it. When they answered,
she reserved a room for each of the same two men and
one for herself for Monday night, because right after
they'd finished their business with Odessa, they were all
clearing out.

Though she fully understood that Jackie Norman was
merely sublimating her anger about her sister to anyone
associated with Gibson, that didn't mean Marti wanted to
chance running into her again. So today, Marti chose to
eat at the Linville Burger King. Just as she carried her
food to a table, her phone rang.

"Marti Segerson."

"This is Barry Glaser. I'll be arriving in Memphis at
seven-forty Monday morning."

Marti glanced at the people eating at nearby tables and
lowered her voice. "Okay, thanks for the news. I haven't
heard from Packard yet, but I'll figure out how to pick
you both up." She scrambled in her bag for a pen and
held it over a napkin. "What airline?"

"Not necessary. A friend from Memphis is going to meet me at the airport and we're going to have breakfast together. I'll just rent a car afterward and drive there myself. Just tell me where to go."

"You're registered at the Best Western in Linville. I figured you could do your prep work there and go over to the hospital just before we do it. They said you could get into your room early. You can't miss the motel. It's right on the main road to town. Do you need driving instructions from the airport?"

"I'll get a map from the rental car company. How long's the drive?"

"A little over an hour. When do you go back?"

"Tuesday morning."

There wasn't any need now to tell him he wouldn't be spending the night in Linville, so she simply said, "Okay, see you Monday."

The second call Marti was waiting for came right after lunch as she was pulling into a parking slot at the hospital.

"This is Packard. I'll get there Monday at nine twenty-eight on Northwest Airlines, flight eight forty-four."

"I'll pick you up."

"Everything else all set?"

"Ready to go."

After putting her phone back in her bag, Marti sat for a moment reflecting on the one possible hitch in the plan. It wasn't anything that could be dealt with in advance. It had to be done at the last minute. And if it didn't go well . . . shivering at the thought, she filed the worry away for now and went back to work.

•   •   •

OREN QUINN SAT in his car and watched Marti walk toward the building. He didn't know any more about her motives for being at Gibson now than he did yesterday. That had always been a possibility. But the other thing that had happened was totally unexpected. And it had the potential to harm him. But would it? He'd just have to wait and see and make sure he didn't allow things to progress that far.

CHAPTER 10

FROM THE PARKING lot, Marti went to her office and reviewed her notes on some of the patients she had not yet interviewed. She then went up to the wards to continue the charade.

A few minutes later, as she was opening the door to Two East A, she heard a scream.

Rushing inside, Marti saw a crowd of patients looking down at the floor. From the center of their circle, a geyser of blood shot into the air in rhythmic spurts.

She dashed to the crowd and pushed her way through. There, sitting slumped against a chair, was a woman with an ugly gash across the left side of her throat. Lying beside her was a shard of broken mirror. The blood spurting from her wound was already diminishing in force, a sure sign that she would soon go into shock. And no one was doing anything, including Bobby Ware and one of the other orderlies, both of whom were just standing there as if this were some kind of entertainment.

"Bobby, give me your T-shirt," Marti yelled. "Now."

Bobby tore off his white coat and his outer shirt and pulled his T over his head. He gave it to Marti and she dropped to the wounded woman's side, where she pressed the balled-up fabric against the woman's throat, ignoring the blood that splattered her own clothing.

Because of the victim's falling blood pressure, it would have been best to lay her down, but Marti was afraid that would cause the wound to gape and make it harder to stop the bleeding, so she left her sitting up. Regardless of her position, she was going to need some decent collateral circulation from her other carotid if she was going to avoid brain damage, which, considering her status at Gibson, would be like throwing water in the face of a drowning woman.

"Has anyone called nine-one-one?" Marti shouted.

"I did," the third orderly assigned to the floor said, joining the crowd. "They're on their way."

"Who's responsible for this?"

"She did it to herself," Bobby said.

Marti held the bloody T-shirt against the woman's wound for the entire twelve minutes it took for the ambulance to arrive. When she was finally relieved by a paramedic, her legs were frozen in a kneeling position, so that Bobby had to help her up.

Looking at the blood on her hand and arm and splattering her clothes, she turned to Bobby and voiced the concern that hadn't even occurred to her before this moment. "She didn't have HIV or hepatitis, I hope."

"No problem there, Dr. Segerson. Nice job. You probably ought to wash up in the ward bathroom. I'll get you some fresh towels and soap." He turned to the other two orderlies. "You guys better get started on this mess."

The ward door had barely closed behind the paramedics taking the injured woman away when it opened
again and Ada Metz arrived. Seeing the blood on the
floor and on Marti, she hurried over to the scene.

"What happened?"

"Lois Wilkie broke a mirror in the bathroom and cut
her own throat with a piece of it," Bobby explained.

"She was catatonic," Metz whined. "She never did
anything, but stand in one spot and stare at the floor."

"Well, she did something today," Marti said, heading
for the bathroom. As she went, she heard Metz berate
Bobby for not paying more attention.

After washing up, Marti left the hospital and drove
home to change clothes and take a shower.

When she was once again clean and had dried her hair,
she called the local hospital on the bungalow's phone,
identified herself, and asked about Lois Wilkie's condition. They told her that Wilkie would live and likely not
be any the worse for her injury. Rather than feel good
about saving the woman's life, it just made her wish she
also knew how to fix Lois Wilkie's mind.

That call reminded Marti she had another one to
make; to Delta Airlines. Having saved their number on
her cell phone, she went to the kitchen table and got her
bag. Standing there, poised to make the call, she thought
about the one-way ticket she was about to buy for next
Monday—or more precisely, her destination.

For now, it would have to be LA, because there would
be things to do there in the aftermath of what was about
to take place here. But when that was done . . . where was
home?

Her father was gone from a heart attack, and her mom
was in the final stages of Alzheimer's disease, didn't

even recognize her when she visited. She didn't really have any friends. Where *was* home?

That question still haunted her after she bought her ticket, so instead of going back to the hospital, she took a walk, following paths she hadn't yet explored.

She found a weathered old barn that looked like those she'd seen in watercolors, and a blackened, shattered tree that appeared to have been struck by lightning. She saw a bird the most incredible color of blue, and a black one with bright red patches on its wings. Entering a small clearing, she surprised a rabbit that wiggled its nose at her, then darted away. In the woods, she saw vines as big around as her wrist, and a lovely little brook that rippled and splashed over a rocky bed that created dark little pools dappled by the leaf-shaded sun. There were large stands of primeval ferns and stretches of soft green moss that looked as though it had been growing there forever. The area had apparently experienced a major windstorm because a number of big trees in the woods had been blown over. But even uprooted, the fallen giants were still part of a harmonious natural tapestry. It was a place where everything she saw, even if damaged, seemed to belong.

But where did *she* belong?

In her present frame of mind, the woods and fields seemed a better place to be than the hospital, so she took the rest of the afternoon off and roamed the property's many paths.

BY THE NEXT morning, Marti was in a better mood and ready to return to work. Arriving at her office a little before nine, she found a message on her answering machine.

"Dr. Segerson, this is Pat, Dr. Rosenblum's administrative assistant. It's now eight thirty-five A.M. Thursday morning. Dr. R would like to convene an inquiry this morning into what happened yesterday with Lois Wilkie. The meeting will begin at nine-fifteen in Dr. R's office. Please be prompt. The necessary records are already here."

In addition to Marti, the inquiry participants included Ada Metz and Trina Estes. The meeting lasted less than half an hour and ended with Rosenblum concluding that Lois Wilkie had given no prior indication she was capable of what she'd done and no one was culpable for what had taken place. On the way out, Trina and Marti walked down the hall together.

"I hope yesterday wasn't typical around here," Marti said.

"Events usually don't get quite that dramatic. Wouldn't you know, I take the day off, and all kinds of things happen."

"What do you mean?"

"Harry Evensky escapes. If he had shown up in *my* bedroom, I would have freaked."

"Why did you say that?"

"Didn't *you*?"

"Trina, I'm lost. Didn't I what?"

"Freak when he came into your bedroom the night he got out."

Marti was so shocked at what Trina had just said, she stopped walking. "He didn't."

"The report in his file says the sheriff picked him up at your house."

This conversation was becoming surreal. "I can't imagine why that's in there. Someone got the story wrong."

Trina looked at Marti as though she were a creature from another planet. "The report was written by Olivia Barr, the senior night floor nurse. Unlike a lot of the folks around here, she's an extremely meticulous person. She would have included that detail only if she knew it to be true."

Somewhere deep in her brain, Marti felt a sensation like a downed wire snapping and fluttering on the ground, its circuit disrupted.

Locks . . .

She had new locks installed on her bungalow because . . .

Why had Clay done that?

"Marti, are you all right?"

"I'm not sure. Come on, I need to check something."

Marti started walking, much faster than before, so that Trina had trouble keeping up. When they arrived at Marti's office she went inside, picked up the phone, and dialed information. "County Sheriff's Office, please."

They answered on the first ring.

"This is Dr. Segerson at Gibson State. One of your officers brought an escaped patient back here Monday night. Could you check your reports and tell me where he was found?"

Marti and Trina waited while someone went through the records.

A couple of long minutes later, the female voice at the other end came back on the line. "Dr. Segerson, he was picked up at your home."

Trina could tell by Marti's shocked expression what she'd just been told. "I guess that's where Olivia heard it."

"There's something very wrong here," Marti replied, putting the phone down and grabbing her handbag. She got her cell phone out and called Clay Hulett.

"This is Clay."

"It's Marti. Why did you change the locks on my doors?"

"Because you asked me to."

"Why did I do that?"

"You said a patient from the hospital got into your house."

"When did I tell you this?"

"The next morning . . . Tuesday."

Marti let her arm with the phone drop limply to her side. Then, regaining her composure, she put the phone back to her ear. "Thanks. I'll talk to you later." She put the phone down and looked helplessly at Trina. "That was my landlord. He said I told him Evensky broke into my home the night he escaped."

"And you don't remember that?"

"I absolutely have no knowledge of such a thing happening."

"Have you had memory lapses before?"

"Small things, sure; the occasional name of someone I met a long time ago, a phone number, a star in an old movie. But nothing like this. This was a major event. How could I forget it?"

"If you were asleep when it happened, maybe you dealt with the whole thing in a stupor."

"But I apparently told my landlord about it the next morning."

"Or that old man frightened you so badly, you're suppressing the memory."

"I don't scare easily, and I'm not that fragile."

"Could you have scuffled with him and hit your head? That could have disrupted the memory so it got lost before being stored."

"An injury severe enough to cause memory loss should have left some lasting physical evidence. I've felt fine. No headaches, no contusions."

Trina took a breath as though she was about to say something, but then didn't.

"What?"

"I was thinking you might have had a tiny stroke, but the brain isn't so discretely organized that one memory and nothing else would be affected. So I don't think that's the explanation."

"Trina, I need to sit by myself and sort this out. Do you mind?"

"Not at all."

"I'd appreciate it if you wouldn't say anything about this to anyone."

Trina put her hand gently on Marti's shoulder. "I understand. You can count on me. I'll see you later."

Marti could think of only two other possibilities for her memory loss: transient global amnesia or a spontaneous subarachnoid hemorrhage. The former was the most innocuous of the two possibilities because it often occurred only once in a person's life and wasn't a harbinger of something worse. The other condition could signal the existence of an aneurysm in a cerebral blood vessel that had developed a small leak. And if that aneurysm should burst big time . . .

Marti was not prepared to accept the diagnosis of an

aneurysm. It just couldn't be. Her problem had to be TGA. But how could she verify that?

There was one way.

She left her office and headed for the wards. As much as she didn't want to believe she had an aneurysm, she found herself moving more slowly than usual to keep her blood pressure down.

Reaching the second floor of the patient's wing, she went to the male ward and let herself in. She made a quick scan of the dayroom looking for Harry Evensky. At first she thought he wasn't there, but then she spotted him sitting in front of the TV, which in this ward had a fairly good picture.

She walked over to him and leaned close to his left ear. "Mr. Evensky, could I speak to you in the interview room please?"

He jumped in surprise and looked to see who was there. Then he grinned. "You figured it out."

"Let's talk in private."

When they reached the interview room, she let Evensky go in first and she shut the door behind them.

"Okay, what's tall and fair . . . you think it's here, but it's really there?" he said.

"I need to ask you about the other night . . . when you came to visit me."

"I haven't told anyone about that, just like you asked."

"When we spoke, did I appear . . . normal? By that I mean did I seem to know where I was?" As worried as she was about her loss of memory she could still see the irony in this, asking a mental patient to vouch for her own behavior. It was bizarre, but necessary because Evensky was a better witness to what happened than she was.

His brow furrowed, Evensky said, "You're spookin' me, Dr. Segerson. That's not the kind of question we expect from our doctors."

"Frankly, it's spooking me, too."

"Well"—He rolled his eyes in thought, then said—"You were more concerned about how I got there instead of how you did."

"So our conversation focused on you?"

"Pretty much."

"Did I move around my home as though I were familiar with every part of it?"

"Seemed that way to me. You gave me a diet Coke. Went right to the fridge and got it."

"Did I give you a glass?"

"Yes."

"Did I have any trouble finding one?"

"I didn't think so."

"Thanks. You've been a big help."

"I could do more if you'd just work on that riddle."

In the hall outside the ward, Marti took stock of what she'd just learned. One of the hallmarks of TGA is incessant questioning by the victim about their immediate circumstances while it's happening. From what Evensky said, she had been in complete control of herself that night, which left the more ominous possibility.

THE CT SCANNER began to move smoothly and Marti slid from its confining cave into the open, where a nurse helped her up. The neurologist on call at Linville Methodist Hospital, a silver-haired fellow that looked like he'd fought many a brain war, came out of the control room.

"Dr. Segerson, I see no blood on your scans and the contrast study showed no evidence of an aneurysm. So I don't believe you've had a hemorrhage of any kind. We could do further tests, of course, if you wish."

"What are the chances that would change your opinion?"

"I'd be very surprised."

Knowing that one of the other tests he might do was a spinal tap, Marti said, "That's good enough for me."

On the way to her car, Marti mulled over the situation. Patients who've had an episode of TGA usually have a headache that persists beyond the acute onset into the phase where normal mental function is restored. A subarachnoid hemorrhage causes an even worse and longer-lasting headache along with mental confusion that persists for days. She'd had no headaches and no mental confusion, so there was no question she had reached the correct conclusion about those two conditions. She hadn't been a victim of either one.

Then why the hell had she lost the memory of Evensky's visit? Even if it never happened again, this one incident could come back to harm her later when she would have to appear perfectly healthy in front of a jury.

The question of her memory loss remained foremost in her mind as she drove back to Gibson, for the moment pushing aside all thoughts of Vernon Odessa. By the time she arrived at the hospital, she found herself focusing on the mind-reading test she'd been given the day before, and the unexpected nap she'd taken after drinking the Coke Quinn's assistant, Nadine, had given her. If there had been any other explanation for her loss of memory, she'd never have questioned that event. But now, left with no other possibilities, she decided to go up and have a talk with Nadine.

CHAPTER 11

MARTI TRIED THE door to Quinn's lab, but found it locked. She knocked and waited for an answer.

No response.

It was a little after two o'clock, so it seemed too late for Nadine to be at lunch. Not in the mood to wait around and see if she'd show up, Marti hiked back down to Quinn's administrative office and went inside.

"Dr. Segerson, good morning." his secretary said. "What can I do for you?"

"Helen, I need to speak with Nadine, Dr. Quinn's lab assistant, but she's not there. Do you know if she took the day off?"

"I don't handle any of her scheduling. Dr. Quinn does that himself."

At that point, Marti thought about asking for her telephone number, but she didn't want to talk to Nadine on the phone and didn't want to give her any advance notice of their coming conversation. "Do you have her address?"

Helen looked at her with such an expression of surprise, Marti wondered what she'd said that was so startling. "Have I said something odd?"

"I thought you knew. Nadine is a patient here."

"A *patient*?"

"She suffers from bipolar disorder, or at least she did before Dr. Quinn took over her care personally. She seems to be doing much better now. In fact, she doesn't even live on the ward anymore."

"Where *does* she live?"

"In an apartment Dr. Quinn had built for her in the vacant ward next to his lab."

"What did she do before she came here?"

"I believe she was a lab tech at St. Jude Hospital in Memphis."

"Does the state know he's spending the hospital's money that way?" It was a dumb thing to say aloud and as soon as she'd said it, Marti wished she had it back.

"That's between Dr. Quinn and them, I'm sure."

"Of course," Marti said, trying to back and fill. "It's none of my business, I agree. Thanks for the information."

As Marti headed back upstairs, she mulled over what she'd learned. A patient . . . during the mind-reading test, she'd been in the hands of a mental patient and had even taken a nap. Boy, was this getting weird.

NADINE ANSWERED THE door to her apartment in jeans and a paint-spattered T-shirt with black lettering across the chest that said: WHAT ARE YOU LOOKING AT? She was obviously surprised to see who had come to visit.

"Dr. Segerson. What's wrong?"

"What makes you believe something's wrong?"

"I thought . . . I mean, no one comes up here to see me just to be social."

"You're right, there is a problem and I was hoping you could clear it up for me."

Nadine looked behind her, then said, "I'd invite you in, but I'm painting and the place is kind of a mess."

"You don't work in the lab on Thursdays?"

"On most days Dr. Quinn lets me set my own hours. As long as I put my time in, he doesn't care when I do it."

"Nadine, this morning I realized I've lost the memory of something that occurred just a few days ago. As far as I can tell this memory loss is very specific . . . for just that one event, and I was wondering if you had any idea how this might have happened to me."

On Nadine's pale complexion the flush that now crept over her face was not a subtle change.

"What makes you ask *me* that question?"

"I can't come up with any explanation for why I have this gap in my memory. As I was thinking about it, I remembered falling asleep next door just before the mind-reading test . . ."

"And you think I did something to you while you were asleep?"

The normal reaction to being wrongly accused of something is anger. What Marti now saw in Nadine's eyes was worry.

"I didn't even know you were asleep until I came back in to start the test," she said. "And I woke you right away."

Marti had no idea what Nadine might have done to her, but she continued to press the point. "Did you?"

"I said so, didn't I? Look, I've got paint drying in my brush. I can't talk any more. I'm sorry."

And bang . . . she shut the door in Marti's face.

Marti stood for a moment staring at the chipped paint on the old door. She hadn't come up there on anything even as strong as a hunch, more a desperate gamble, and now it seems it had paid off. But instead of clearing things up, she was as confused as ever.

Turning, she started for the stairs, trying to figure out what Nadine was up to. By the time she'd reached her office, she'd remembered the first time she met Nadine, and the mice she was testing—in a *memory* experiment.

Jesus. Had Nadine done some kind of experiment on *her* while she was asleep? Suppose she had? Wouldn't that mean Quinn was also involved? Assuming for the moment Nadine was acting under Quinn's orders to do whatever she'd done to her, would pursuing this be wise? Creating any kind of disturbance could jeopardize her plans for Odessa.

But if she were right, they'd done something to her brain. No one should be allowed to get away with something like that.

All this was so confusing, she felt she needed some fresh air to sort things out, so she bypassed her office and headed for the stairs to the front exit.

Less than a minute later, as she descended the hospital's front steps, she heard a wild fluttering of wings. Looking up she saw a flock of pigeons heading west, apparently leaving the comfort of the hospital roof. Not interested enough in the birds to strain her neck to see more, she continued down the steps.

Perhaps it was a shadow or it might have been another sound. Whatever the cause, she had a premonition something was coming toward her from above. Before she could react, a body hurtled past her and hit the steps head first, shattering the victim's head so that the steps were awash with blood and bits of brain. Though the victim lay face down, the black hair against the white T-shirt told Marti instantly who it was.

CHAPTER 12

MARTI STOOD THERE as though she were catatonic, looking at the carnage in front of her, her mind replaying the last few seconds . . . the sickening sound of skull against concrete . . . white matter and gray torn apart . . . splattering the concrete, wetting it with hopes and worries, dreams and memories. It played like a slide show in Marti's own brain, a series of before and after shots . . . Nadine in her T-shirt . . . WHAT ARE YOU LOOKING AT? . . . her body hurtling past . . . Nadine excited over that mouse experiment the day they met . . . bits of her brain drying onto the steps . . . brain drying . . . Nadine . . . then it was Lee's face . . . Lee's brain, drying on the bedroom walls, becoming part of the paint. Nadine . . . Lee . . . they spun past her mind's eye, blurring, running together.

Behind her, a scream from someone who'd just come out of the hospital brought Marti out of herself. "Call an ambulance," Marti shouted without even looking to see who had screamed. She went to the body, knelt and even though she knew it was a useless gesture, picked up a limp arm and felt for a pulse.

Nothing.

As she was kneeling there, her eyes went to Nadine's neck, where she was shocked to see a familiar-looking scar. It was very much like the one Odessa carried.

The next fifteen minutes were a blur. In keeping with people's need to maintain some kind of barrier between themselves and death, someone brought a sheet to cover the body. A crowd gathered.

The ambulance arrived and the attendants verified that Nadine was dead. Realizing the body shouldn't be moved until the sheriff gave the okay, the ambulance paramedics moved back and waited like everyone else for the grisly event to play out.

Marti soon found Trina Estes beside her.

"Who is it?" Trina asked.

"Nadine Simpson . . . Quinn's protégée."

"Why do you say protégée?"

"She worked for him, and he was handling her case himself. Even built her an apartment near his lab . . . Did you know all that?"

"I'd heard about her, sure. What happened?"

Even though she viewed Trina as a potential friend, Marti had no intention of telling her about the conversation she'd had earlier with Nadine. She shouldn't have even said what she did when Trina had joined her. "I was coming down the steps and she fell out of the sky. I guess she jumped."

"That's horrible. I feel so sorry for her. It must have been awful for you too, to have it happen right in front of you."

"I expect I won't sleep very well tonight."

"Appears it wasn't such a good idea after all to give her the free run of the hospital."

Over Trina's shoulder, Marti saw Oren Quinn working his way around the crowd, conferring briefly with one or two in a group, then moving on. Finally, he spoke to someone who pointed in Marti's direction.

"Here comes Quinn," Marti warned.

"He probably wants to see you," Trina said. "So I'll just leave you two alone."

As Trina slipped away, Quinn took her place.

"I hear you witnessed this," he said.

"She fell right in front of me."

"Jumped?"

"I don't know. I didn't see her until she was at eye level."

"Trouble seems to follow you."

"What do you mean?"

"First Lois Wilkie, now this."

Marti's heart began to thump. Had Nadine called Quinn after their conversation? "Are you implying this was my fault?"

"It was just an observation, no need to get defensive."

"What are you going to do now?"

"About what?"

"Your research."

"I don't know. Hire someone else, probably. No one is irreplaceable. But this is hardly the time to be thinking about that. There's a woman dead under that sheet. We should be mourning her loss instead of figuring out how to minimize the inconvenience her death caused us. Dr. Segerson, you have a cold streak in you."

Marti was shocked to hear him say that . . . the same

man who suggested that Letha Taylor would be better off
dead than treated for her diabetes was lecturing her on
compassion. It was incredible, especially since he didn't
seem all broken up about Nadine's death himself. Marti
took a moment to frame a suitable reply, but she never
got to deliver it because seeing the sheriff arrive, Quinn
left her and headed in that direction.

"What did he want?" Trina Estes said, coming back to
stand with Marti.

"To show me once again what an ass he is."

"You should be careful about saying things like that,"
Trina whispered. "I don't disagree with you, but he has
spies on staff who will run right to him with any dirt they
hear."

The sheriff was tall and trim with a full head of wavy
blond hair and a brush mustache. The man in a white shirt
and bow tie who was riding with him was a bald head
shorter, at least fifty pounds heavier, and about thirty
years older. Marti assumed the civilian was the medical
examiner.

Quinn greeted the two men, spoke with them a moment, then they all headed for the body. When they
reached it, the sheriff removed the sheet and he and the
ME took a quick survey of the remains, then both of them
looked up at the point where Nadine had gone off the
roof. Marti expected at any moment that Quinn would
point to her and they would all come over and she'd get
to say once again that she didn't actually see anything.

Surely there'd be no reason to ask her if she'd talked
to Nadine earlier. But if they did what would she say?
She'd about decided to lie if the conversation went that
way, but then she remembered . . . she'd asked Quinn's
secretary where Nadine lived. If they caught her in a lie,

it would create more of a disturbance than if she just admitted they'd spoken. Okay, then she'd admit to the conversation, but say she just went up there to find out how she did on the mind-reading test.

As it turned out, all her concerns about saying just the right thing when she was confronted were a waste of time, because Quinn didn't point at her or even look at her. Instead, the sheriff re-covered the body with the sheet and all three men went into the hospital, presumably to check out the roof.

They were gone about ten minutes, during which Trina and Marti just stood around without saying much. When the three reappeared, the sheriff spoke to the ambulance attendants, and they loaded the body and drove away. Then the sheriff and the ME left as well.

Quinn raised his arms and waved his hands for attention. "Okay, everyone, it's all over. There's nothing more to see. Go on with your day."

"I was expecting to see the ME take Nadine's file with him," Marti said to Trina as the crowd dispersed. "But he left empty-handed."

"Guess they don't have any questions about what took place."

"Where *are* her records?"

"I don't know. Maybe Quinn has them. In any event, I expect they'll be in his office tomorrow morning for yet another inquiry. But this time, since the patient in question *succeeded* in killing herself, I'm sure the hospital's attorney will be there to make sure we're legally in the clear for what happened."

"You don't think Rosenblum will chair this one?"

Trina shook her head. "Too important. It'll be Quinn."

Going back into the building, Marti and Trina found

themselves behind Quinn and Meredith Chapman, head of the psychology department, from where they overhead Quinn say to Chapman, "I need you in my office at nine tomorrow morning to review what just happened."

At this validation of her prediction, Trina nudged Marti and nodded as if to say, "See, I told you."

Inside, as everyone dispersed and Quinn and Chapman moved out of earshot, Marti said to Trina, "I guess when the inquiry is over, Nadine's file will go to medical records."

"I'm sure it will. Why all the interest in this case?"

"No special reason, I'm just still trying to get a feel for how the place operates."

From the look on Trina's face, she didn't find that explanation totally believable, but she let it pass. "I know you've just had a bad experience, but do you feel up to discussing some of our patients this afternoon? I thought we could review the status of those who are scheduled for treatment team meetings next week."

"Sure. When would you like to do it?"

"In about half an hour?"

"My office or yours?"

"I'll come to you."

DURING HER MEETING with Trina, Marti's mind was in two places at once because she couldn't get Nadine out of her thoughts. Right after she had practically accused Nadine of experimenting on her, Nadine had jumped off the hospital roof. Could there be any clearer indication of a guilty conscience? But guilt over what? It was such a drastic reaction Marti believed that whatever they had done to her could be a thread that, if picked at, might lead to something much bigger. And what about the scar on Nadine's neck . . . in the same place and about the same dimensions as the one Odessa carried? What was that all about?

As intriguing as these puzzles were and as angry as she was at having been taken advantage of while she slept, she knew it would be wise to ignore it all and stay focused on her primary objective. But emotion doesn't always follow wisdom, so even though she knew what she *ought* to do, she was also aware that as soon as possible she was going to try to get a look at Nadine's records.

CHAPTER 13

THE NEXT MORNING Marti got to the hospital early and kept a watch on Quinn's administrative office as discreetly as she could from her own doorway.

Around nine o'clock she saw Howard Rosenblum and his secretary arrive and go inside. They were followed a few minutes later by the staff internist and Meredith Chapman, the head of psychology. The last to arrive was a man in a well-cut gray-pinstripe suit. Marti surmised that he was likely the hospital's legal counsel.

While the meeting was under way, Marti thought about what she could have told them regarding the cause of Nadine's sudden need to kill herself. And for a brief time, she fought with her conscience about keeping it to herself, which, considering the stakes involved in keeping quiet, didn't make much sense. Finally, reason prevailed and she let the meeting go on without her input.

The inquiry into Nadine's death lasted nearly two hours, so by the time everyone emerged from Quinn's office, Marti was extremely weary of leaning out her door and peeking down the hall. The most significant thing she saw as the participants dispersed was Rosenblum's secretary, Pat, carrying a set of patient records still in the metal binder used on the wards. There was little doubt that this file had Nadine's name on it.

With everyone walking toward her, Marti couldn't continue her clandestine behavior, so she just came into the hall and headed for the big front stairway. Medical records occupied much of the hospital's third floor, so as she and Pat drew nearer to each other, Marti silently urged the other woman to go up the stairs, not down.

And that's exactly what happened.

Pretending to be off on an errand of her own, Marti went down the stairs to the lobby, turned right, and moved along the east hallway on the first floor, where she kept walking until she reached the door to the patient wing. She keyed that door, went inside, and hurried to the old staircase that served the east wing wards. Taking the steps as fast as she could, she went up three flights and unlocked the door to the third-floor administrative hallway. Checking before darting into the open, she saw Pat, now without the file she was carrying, going down the front steps.

As Marti moved quickly to her destination, two plans for getting a look at Nadine's records competed for her acceptance. In one, she would just tell the records clerk she was a member of the inquiry team and needed the file back for a few minutes to verify something to go in their report. The down side there was the clerk might realize she was lying and, in any event, would then know of her interest in Nadine. Should the clerk mention that to the wrong people . . . Marti would take that chance if necessary, but there might be another way.

Standing now at the entrance to medical records, she opened the door and went in.

She'd been there briefly once before when Trina had shown her around the hospital on Monday. So she knew that in front of the many rows of file folders in oak bookcases that ran from the front of the room to the back, there was an old oak counter across which much of the department's business was conducted. The first thing she looked at when she stepped inside was that counter.

And there was the metal binder with Nadine's name on it. With the binder so accessible, Marti decided to go with plan B.

Between the counter and the bookcases a small woman sat at an oak desk punching holes in records and threading them into a binder like those on the shelves. It wasn't the woman she'd met on her previous visit, which was a disappointment, for where the other woman seemed like someone who'd take things at face value, this one, with her squinty eyes and thin lips, looked like she was suspicious of everything. Her appearance almost made Marti turn and leave without putting her plan into action.

But ultimately, her anger at whatever had been done to her while she slept in Quinn's lab during her mind-reading test stiffened her resolve.

"Good morning," Marti said, taking the offensive. "I'm sorry to bother you, but I need to see the overflow records of several of my chronic patients."

"And you are . . .?" the woman asked from where she sat.

"Dr. Segerson, the new staff psychiatrist."

The woman got up from the desk and came to the counter, where she leaned over and inspected Marti's ID. Satisfied she was legit, the woman said, "And you'd like these records when?"

"I'd really appreciate it if you could pull them while I wait."

"Is it all that urgent? I've got a lot of other work to do."

"Please . . . it would mean a lot to me."

The woman hesitated, then said, "I'll do it this time, but in the future, you need to give us a little breathing room."

"I will, I promise."

The woman got a pen and a scratch pad from her desk. "Who are the patients?"

Marti rattled off the names of five patients she remembered as having overflow records in the stack of files she'd reviewed when she'd first arrived. She was about to add a sixth name for good measure, but, noting the increasingly unhappy expression of the clerk as she wrote, decided against it.

The records here were arranged by number, not patient name, which meant the clerk had to find each name in the computer data base, write down the identifying number, then pull the file. The good thing about this procedure for Marti was that the required computer was not on the desk out front, but was somewhere in the back, out of sight.

Marti had just about decided this was going to work, but as the clerk turned to go, she picked up Nadine's file and carried it to her desk, where she left it.

Damn it.

If the clerk had caught her reading the file when it was

left on the counter, it wouldn't be such a big deal . . .
something she'd done out of boredom while waiting. But
now . . .

As the clerk disappeared into the stacks at the far left
end of the room, Marti's heart, already clipping along at
a rapid pace, accelerated, for she had a decision to make.
To her right, the counter had a gap in it and its top was
hinged so it could be lifted, creating a walk-through.

Go or stay . . .

Go or stay . . .

Unable to walk away after coming this far, she ducked
under the counter and hurried to the desk, where she
pulled Nadine's file around and flipped up the cover.

Aware that at best she had only minutes before the
clerk returned, she looked at the document that lay on top
of the file's contents and read it in snatches with her eyes
flicking between the words and the aisle where the clerk
had gone.

The document turned out to be Nadine's death certificate, which surprised her. Even though she believed Nadine had committed suicide as the certificate stated, it
seemed like there should have been at least the sem-
blance of an investigation. But the sheriff and the ME had
apparently thought mental patients didn't warrant that
kind of time.

She flipped first to the tabbed section labeled HISTORY
and ripped through the contents using the speed-reading
skills she'd taught herself to get through medical school.

There she read that before Nadine had come to Gibson
she had been a research tech at St. Jude Children's Hospital in Memphis, just as Rosenblum's secretary had said.
She had been committed as a severe bipolar who was sui-

cidal when she was down, and unable to control her anger when she was up, a lovely combination.

What she was really looking for was a note explaining the scar on Nadine's neck. So she turned next to the section labeled MEDICAL, where she quickly found an entry indicating that around eighteen months ago, Nadine had experienced a bout of appendicitis and had had the organ removed at Gibson.

Appendicitis . . .

Now *that* was interesting . . . and curious.

She made a mental note of the date the operation took place, then moved on.

She skimmed the rest of the medical section, then, even through she knew she needed to get out of there, turned to PROGRESS. There she found a copy of a letter from Quinn, dated a year after Nadine's admittance to Gibson. Apparently intended for the judge who'd signed Nadine's commitment papers, it said that Nadine continued to be a danger to herself and others.

Considering how normal and functional Nadine seemed that day in the lab, Marti found this conclusion a bit surprising. But the letter *was* written nearly ten months ago, so maybe she'd improved in the interim. But if that were true, why was she still at Gibson?

Feeling it was just too risky to continue reading, Marti closed the file and ducked back under the hinged section of counter, standing up just as the clerk returned with the records she'd requested.

Marti was very lucky not to have been caught, but her visit was actually a failure, as she'd found no explanation for that scar.

She did, however, carry with her a question that sent her first to her office to dump the unneeded files she'd acquired, then up to Two East, where Sandi Cooper, the ward's junior nurse, was making up the afternoon pill dispensation. Sandi was concentrating so much on her work Marti made it to the chart cart without having to engage in any conversation beyond tossing off a cheery good morning as she passed.

Picking up Odessa's file, she thumbed through it until she found the entry she'd remembered from her review of the contents the first day she'd arrived for work. Odessa, too, had been operated on at Gibson for a case of appendicitis. And his operation had taken place a mere two days before Nadine's.

Both with a case of appendicitis . . . both with unexplained scars on their neck. The correlation between these two things couldn't be just coincidence. But what did it mean?

These links she'd discovered between Nadine and Odessa made it difficult to give in to the little voice that kept telling her if she persisted in this Nadine fixation, it could put next Monday's plans for Odessa at risk. So she let her mind go where it would.

In med school, because she had an uncanny ability to pick the correct answer from the distracters even when the topic was something she knew little about, Marti always tested better than her fund of knowledge would have predicted. Today, the part of her mind responsible for that sent her back to her office, where she picked up the phone book and took it to her car.

From Nadine's death certificate she had learned that the medical examiner's name was Frank Nichols. After driving to the In and Out Mart two miles from the hospital, she looked him up in the phone book and found that the only Nichols listed was a pediatrician.

ME and a doc for kids . . . odd combination.

She had no idea how medicolegal investigations were conducted in this county, but because the only listed phone number for Nichols was his private medical practice, she concluded that when an autopsy was required, the body was probably sent to some central facility, maybe as far away as Nashville. But Nichols had signed off so quickly on Nadine's death, Marti doubted he'd even considered an autopsy. He might not have even removed her clothing for a complete examination of her injuries. All of which meant he probably wouldn't be able to answer the question she was wondering about.

And how was she going to ask it anyway? It was going to sound really strange. "Yes, Dr. Nichols, I'm calling from Gibson State Hospital about the incident that happened there yesterday. . . . We were wondering . . . did Nadine Simpson have an appendectomy scar?"

And suppose Nichols mentioned the call to Quinn? Even though she'd be using a pay phone, Quinn might somehow link her to the inquiry.

No, she couldn't do it that way. But she could ask . . .

Having decided on a plan, she got out of the car and punched Nichols's number into the pay phone keypad. A female voice answered even before Marti heard it ring. "May I speak to whoever handles the medical examiner records, please."

"Hold on . . ."

Another female came on the line. "Karen speaking. How may I help you?"

"This is Gibson State Hospital calling. One of our patients, Nadine Simpson, committed suicide yesterday at the hospital. Dr. Nichols has already signed off on the death certificate and we were wondering where in the process the body is at the moment."

"Let me check."

After a short interval, Karen returned. "It's been sent to Edwards Brothers for cremation, just as Dr. Quinn instructed."

Marti thanked Karen for her help, went back to the car, and picked up the phone book again.

Edwards Brothers . . .

It was a funeral home on Clifton Street. Where the devil was that?

Two minutes later, having obtained the directions to the funeral home from the clerk in the store, she returned to her car, fired up the engine, and left the parking lot faster than she'd entered it, hoping she wouldn't arrive at Edwards Brothers too late.

She'd never have considered making a personal appearance at Nichols's office to inquire about Nadine, but the funeral home, being once removed from the action, was a different matter. Still, she felt very uncomfortable just walking in there looking like she normally did. So, despite the need to get there ASAP, she sped into Linville, grabbed a few things from the Super Saver drugstore, and hurried home. There, she blackened her eyebrows, applied a dark lipstick, hid her short hair under a slouchy hat she'd brought from California, and donned a duster that would make it difficult for anyone to guess her weight.

EDWARDS BROTHERS FUNERAL home was in an old Queen Anne four-square house whose columns and trimwork needed paint. Half the yard had been converted to

an asphalt parking lot. If their sign were to be believed,
the brothers were A PILLAR OF STRENGTH IN A TIME OF
NEED. Prospective customers were also advised that the
place was AIR-CONDITIONED, and there was a PAYMENT
PLAN AVAILABLE.

Preferring not to go in the front door, where she would
likely encounter someone practiced in the art of visitor
scrutiny, Marti followed the asphalt around to the rear of
the house.

The brothers might be a pillar of strength, but they
were also an untidy pair, for the back of the place was a
mess. The cedar fence around the parking lot was falling
over, there was a big pile of old lumber near the rear
property line, and there were bits of Styrofoam everywhere. The parking lot itself had sunken in several places
and the low areas were full of water that glistened with
an iridescent gasoline slick. Through a sagging gate in
the rear of the fence, Marti saw a separate weed-choked
enclosure that contained stacks of rusting fifty-five-gal-
lon drums. Reminded of the crematorium in Georgia that
had been running a little behind and was discovered to
have hundreds of bodies stacked around the place, Marti
briefly wondered if Nadine might be in one of those
drums.

She parked her car in a spot that was dry, then, in one
more attempt to look like someone else, she took off her
glasses and put them on the seat. Leaving the car, she
walked up to the big metal door that seemed to serve as
the funeral home's rear entrance, where she turned the
door handle and pushed.

As the door opened, she paused, expecting to hear an
alarm go off. But all remained quiet. Inside, she found
herself in a well-lit storeroom shared by more fifty-five-

gallon drums, a lot of cardboard litter, and caskets; some in crates, some ready for occupancy.

She made her way across the storeroom and went through the door at the opposite end, entering a white tile-lined room that smelled faintly of embalming chemicals. There were three gurneys in the room, each bearing something lumpy covered with a heavy cotton sheet.

Could she be that lucky?

She walked over to the nearest gurney, took hold of the smallest bit of the covering sheet she could get between her thumb and forefinger and pulled, uncovering the cadaver's head.

It was an old woman with drool dried on her cheeks.

Oh this *is fun,* Marti thought sarcastically as she recovered the woman and moved on to the next gurney.

This time she found a young man with a head wound so horrible he was probably going to need a closed-casket funeral.

One left . . .

She gripped the sheet and pulled. At practically the same instant she realized she was looking at the remains of an ancient black man, she heard the door on the far side of the room open.

"Who the hell are you?" an angry voice said. "Get away from there."

The man who'd caught her looked like Uncle Fester from the *Addams Family* TV show, only Fester's face was never as red as this guy's. He had on a rubber apron and was pushing a blue furniture dolly that Marti thought he might use to drive her from the building.

Marti launched into the story she'd made up on the way over. "I'm Lori Simpson, Nadine Simpson's sister. They told me her body was here. I haven't seen her in years. When I heard she was dead, I came right away, hoping to see her one last time."

If this worked, she was going to ask if she could be left alone with Nadine for just a minute or two to commune with her departed spirit.

"What's wrong with our front entrance?"

"Didn't want to make a fuss. I just wanted to see my sister."

Fester's manner suddenly softened. "Honey, I'm sorry to say, you're too late. She's already been cremated."

Marti's heart sagged with disappointment. "I was afraid that might be the case."

"Since you're her sister, you might be able to explain something to me. It's in here . . ."

Fester pushed his dolly to the side and motioned for her to follow as he went back the way he'd come in.

The next room was similar to the one they'd just left, but in an alcove straight ahead, Marti saw the crematory, a long, blue metal structure about six feet high with some data-recording equipment attached to it.

Fester went to a stainless-steel bench against one wall, picked up something, and brought it back to where Marti waited.

"I found this in the crematory after the burn. It's not uncommon for there to be metal surgical objects among the cremains, clips, screws, mending plates . . . but I've never seen anything like this. Do you know what it is?"

Fester held out a black object about an inch long and a quarter of an inch wide that had a melted appearance.

Marti took it from him and looked at it more closely.

"I'm puzzled too. May I keep it? Just to remind me of her?"

A door to the right opened and a slim, blond man with the tallest forehead Marti had ever seen came in.

"What's going on, Jonathan? Who's this woman?"

"The sister of the suicide from Gibson. I was just showing her that odd thing I found. She'd like to keep it as a remembrance."

"I have no problem with that as long as you've established her identity and kinship to the deceased."

Jonathan looked at Marti. "Do you have anything you could show us?"

Marti's mind suddenly felt like one of those phony cans of peanuts whose lid had been removed, releasing a bunch of spring-loaded worms. All she could think to say was, "Afraid I don't. I discovered on the way over here I'd left my wallet back in my room at the motel. I'll go get it and come back."

She turned to leave the way she'd entered.

"Where's the black object?" tall forehead asked.

"Miss, I'm afraid until you prove who you are, you'll have to leave it here," Jonathan said.

Reluctantly, her face burning at having been tripped up, Marti gave it back.

"See her out, Jonathan," tall forehead said, with an inflection that made it clear he knew she wouldn't be returning.

A minute later, as she pulled from the funeral home parking lot onto Clifton Street, Marti hoped the Edwards brothers hadn't called the cops. All the way back to her cottage to remove her disguise, she kept checking the rearview mirror for flashing lights.

By the time she finally reached the Blue Sky Farm driveway, she'd decided it was far too risky to pursue her suspicions that Quinn was up to something sneaky with his purported mind-reading test. Leave it alone, accomplish what you came here to do, and leave, she told herself.

THAT SAME AFTERNOON Oren Quinn walked along the sidewalk of a strip mall in Jackson, Tennessee, the tiny hole in his briefcase aligned with the young girl in the short skirt a few feet in front of him. Inside the briefcase, positioned so its lens was peering through the hole, a digital movie camera recorded every sensuous movement of her legs and thighs as she headed for her car after her shift at the Radio Shack.

His little film was a work in progress. And no part of it had been easy. First, he'd had to find just the right subject; he preferred to think of her as a subject rather than the term outsiders might use. To qualify, she had to be blond, between eighteen and twenty-five, with long hair, and, of course, she had to be attractive. Just as important, she had to live alone in a place with the appropriate geography.

He would have preferred not knowing her name, but in order to determine exactly which of the units she occupied in the quadriplex where she lived, it had been necessary to learn who she was. It was something that, when it was over, he would try hard to forget.

Just fulfilling the selection criteria had taken a month. Then he'd started on his film. He couldn't risk her realizing she was being followed, so he'd been able to capture only a single angle and a few seconds of footage on each trip. It was all so tedious that were it not for the fact this was definitely going to be the last one, whatever the outcome, he might have packed it in.

Today, he managed to get about twelve seconds of footage before she reached her car, not a bad day's work. One or two more trips and they should be ready to proceed.

CHAPTER 14

FRIDAY EVENING MARTI closed the door on the bungalow's dishwasher and was wondering whether she should run it for such a small load when she heard the sound of a car engine approach the house. The engine stopped and a door slammed. Going to a front window, she saw Clay Hulett walking toward the porch. She had the door open even before he knocked.

"I see you still have your eyebrows," she said. "So I guess you handled that fire the other day successfully."

"A couple kids set the inside of a junked car on fire. It wasn't much as fires go."

"I guess you're wondering about my phone call to you yesterday."

"It did rouse my curiosity."

After a lifetime of hiding who she was from people, there was no way she was going to tell Clay about her memory loss or anything else that had been happening. Why should she? They barely knew each other. So she had decided to do what, by now, came naturally . . . she'd lie.

"One of my colleagues at the hospital didn't believe me when I told her the patient who escaped showed up in my bedroom. I called you to prove it. She was listening in when we spoke."

Clay's face took on a troubled look. "Isn't that illegal . . . violation of a wire tap law or something?"

Marti sensed her face flush. "I'm sorry. I didn't think you'd mind . . . you didn't say anything sensitive about yourself . . ."

Clay grinned. "Just kidding. Why would I care about that?"

The last few days at the hospital had been so intense, Marti had felt at times as though she was drowning in a vast and violent sea with no help in sight. So it wasn't surprising she seized on Clay's smile as a life preserver.

"So you're a prankster in addition to your other qualities."

"I have qualities?"

"'Quality,'" Marti recited, "'any trait or characteristic by which a thing may be identified.' While in some usage it implies excellence, that's not always the case."

"Perhaps I'd better not explore the point any further."

"A perceptive decision," Marti said, playing along.

"Interesting you should mention the fire . . . that's actually why I'm here. I feel bad for running off when we were down at the creek."

"You didn't really have any choice."

"Still, I'd like to make it up to you. How about I take you to lunch tomorrow and show you where my brother, Burke, and I practice our roping skills. If you'd like, we could even arrange for a little demonstration. If you're interested, that is . . ."

Marti should have realized her flirtation with Clay might lead to something like this. But she hadn't. She'd just enjoyed the moment. Now, her first reaction was to make up some reason to beg off. But then she thought about the long weekend she was facing. With nothing to do, she'd spend the entire time worrying about how things were going to go on Monday. So why *not* do something to take her mind off that? And a steer-roping demonstration sounded like just the thing.

"You're on. What time?"

"I'll pick you up at noon."

As Marti watched Clay's truck head down the drive toward his own house a few seconds later, Marti's inner voice issued a stern warning. "Do not become involved with this man."

"Don't be ridiculous," she responded. "He's only a diversion to help the time pass, nothing more."

And with this assurance, the voice was stilled.

LUNCH AND AN afternoon of steer roping . . . even though she wouldn't be the one doing the roping it sounded to Marti like she ought to wear something she wouldn't mind getting dusty. So when Clay picked her up on Saturday, she was wearing a pair of boot-cut khaki stretch twills over a pair of brown boots and a beige short-sleeved drifter, an outfit much better than she should have been able to come up with, considering she'd left most of her clothes in storage in LA. Since Clay was accustomed to seeing her in glasses, she made sure she was wearing them as well.

Adding to his growing mythology with Marti as a man with few peers, Clay said just the 'right thing when he first saw her.

"I don't know if we can do any roping today. The horses see how good you look, they aren't gonna pay any attention to me or Burke."

"Yes, I have quite a following among horses. They just seem to sense that I'm oh so country."

They ate lunch at The Happy Pig, a barbecue place that seemed willing to barbecue anything. They even had barbecued baloney on the menu, although Clay said he couldn't recommend it.

"I like their retro fifties look," Marti said, as they showed themselves to a chrome dinette table and chairs.

"It's not retro," Clay replied. "It's the same furniture that's been here since they opened."

Marti shrugged. "Why mess with something that's working."

"Exactly."

"But the name . . . The Happy Pig—"

"Yeah. The customers are happy, but I'm pretty sure the pigs have been working on a list of grievances."

Clay's comment about the pigs personified them in Marti's mind, so when it came time to order, she got the barbecued chicken. When the waitress brought their iced tea it came in plastic glasses so big Marti could barely get her hand around hers, so she had to hold it with both hands like a little kid.

"I guess I didn't make it clear to her that I wanted a *large* tea," she quipped.

"The next size comes in a twenty-gallon keg," Clay replied. "Be glad to get you one."

Clay was sitting facing the door with Marti opposite

him. Had their positions been reversed, she would have seen Oren Quinn come in. As it was, Quinn crossed the room and slid into one of the high-backed booths along the left wall without seeing her either.

When it came, Marti's food was wonderful, but so spicy she knew why the drinks were huge. Even so, unsure of when she'd next have access to a bathroom, she rationed her tea.

On their way out, when Marti and Clay stopped at the counter by the door to pay the bill, Quinn spotted her for the first time. Just before they left, he managed to get his server's attention. "The couple by the register," he said in a confidential tone. "Do you recognize the man?"

She looked in that direction. "Sure, it's Clay Hulett. He's the caretaker of Blue Sky Farm, that big piece of land next to the nut house. He lives there, just off the highway. Beyond his place there's a cute little cottage they rent out. I heard it's been leased to a new psychiatrist over at the hospital. You know, I wouldn't be surprised if that's who's with him. I've never seen her around, so that could be who it is."

That Clay lived close to the newest member of the Gibson staff was information currently of no use to Quinn. But great minds do not gather data only when the need is obvious. They collect and store facts constantly so they may respond more rapidly than the unprepared to changing conditions. It's not the meek who shall inherit the earth, but the flexible and quick. And there was still something about Marti Segerson that just didn't add up.

"He do anything other than manage the farm?" Quinn asked.

"Teaches history at the college and he's a volunteer fireman."

"Interesting."

As Quinn turned his attention back to his food, he decided that some night soon, late enough that he wasn't likely to run into anyone, he'd drive over to Blue Sky Farm and check things out.

THE VENUE WHERE Clay practiced his roping skills was on the far side of Blue Sky Farm, where he and his brother had a twenty-acre compound devoted to the sport. As they drove up to the large, well-maintained barn, Clay's brother, Burke, was waiting for them. Shorter than Clay and stockier, Burke looked as sturdy as a concrete fence post.

As they pulled to a stop, Burke headed for Marti's side of the truck, so when she got out, he was right there to meet her.

"Burke Hulett," he said, thrusting out his hand. "You must be Marti."

Taking his rough hand, Marti admitted she was.

Turning to Clay, who was coming around the truck to join them, Burke said, "Little brother, I thought you were exaggerating when you described her, but you weren't."

Marti looked at Clay and said, "Have I been the subject of rodeo gossip?"

That actually made Clay blush.

"Don't be upset with us, Marti," Burke said. "When God is good to someone, like he was you, it ought to be commented upon."

Generally, Marti's scarred psyche would have caused her to silently challenge a statement like that, but remarkably, today, it never crossed her mind.

"There's no shade out by the corral," Clay said, producing a wide-brimmed straw hat he'd apparently brought along. "So you'll probably want to wear this."

"You bought this for me?" Marti asked, taking it from him.

"Nah, it belongs to one of the horses. I just borrowed it."

Marti looked the hat over. "So where are the ear holes?"

Burke grinned and said, "See, that's what happens when you keep company with an educated woman."

"Don't assume from my comment about the hat that I know anything about what you guys do."

"Let's head out to the corral and we'll show you," Burke said. "Best way is through the barn."

They all went into the barn, which had many horse stalls and was as clean as Clay's house. Halfway down, they exited by another big door into a fenced area well trampled by hoofed animals. Straight ahead and through a gate Marti saw a dozen steers standing head to tail in a narrow chute that led to a big corral. In the corral, two saddled horses stood waiting.

When they reached the horses, Marti found a nice clean folding metal chair waiting for her inside the fence.

"Usually Burke is the header," Clay said. "It's his job to rope the steer around the horns. I'm the heeler. I'm supposed to keep the steer running straight. Once Burke gets his rope on the horns, I put a loop on the hind legs. We pull our ropes tight, the steer is immobilized, and the event is over." He looked at Burke, who was already mounted. "You ready?"

"That's why I'm up here."

Clay gracefully swung up into the saddle of the other horse and he maneuvered the animal around to the far side of a chute that held one steer apart from the others. Clay pulled a rope and the door of the chute clanged open. Apparently eager to be free of its confinement, the steer bolted from the chute. With a surge of rippling muscle, its hooves throwing up dirt, Burke's horse shot forward, after the steer. At the same instant, Clay's horse bolted into the fray.

In seconds, Burke threw a perfect loop from his rope over the steer's horns. Marti had imagined that Clay would have to dismount to do his part, but he made a magician's throw from the saddle and somehow got his loop around the animal's hind legs, so it was all over so fast it didn't seem possible.

The two men dismounted and freed the steer. Both then climbed back on their horses. While Burke herded the animal out a gate into an adjacent pasture, Clay rode back to where Marti waited.

"How did you ever got that rope on his hind legs?" she said.

"I ought to quit right now, so you'd think it always goes that well. And I would, but I promised Burke we'd do all ten steers. Do you mind?"

"Not at all. You keep these steers just for practice?"

"No other way to do it."

"Doesn't that make it easier than when you do it in competition? I mean you get to know these animals and how they behave."

Clay shook his head. "Makes it harder. They get to know us too and they learn when to duck. Kind of makes you wonder which of us is smarter."

Clay and Burke performed just as flawlessly with the rest of the animals, but they let one bolt from the chute without pursuing it. When they were finished, that was the first thing Marti asked Clay about when he led his horse over to where she was waiting.

"When we do these practice trials we're training the horse as well as ourselves. In competition, there's a laser that shines across the path of the steer a few feet from the chute, and another that shines across the ropers' paths. If we cross our line before the steer crosses his, we're disqualified. So we can't have the horse deciding when to go. By letting an occasional steer loose without chasing it, we teach the horse to wait for our signal."

"Is it okay to pet him?"

"Sure."

Marti reached up and stroked the neck of Clay's horse, which looked down at her with its big brown eyes. "I've never been this close to a horse before."

"Would you like to ride one?"

"Could I?"

"It'll take a few minutes to get one saddled." He looked at Burke, who was closing the gate after herding the last steer into the holding pasture, and shouted, "Marti wants to ride."

"Let's give her Sammy," Burke called back. "I'll get him ready."

Ten minutes later, Clay and Marti were riding side by side on a trail that led through a woods that made the rest of the world seem very far away.

"You can't really appreciate how powerful an animal a horse is until you're on one," Marti said.

"When you consider how much they can carry on their back and that they even sleep standing up, they're pretty incredible."

"Do you and Burke usually win when you compete?"

"I just had a good day. Burke's always nearly perfect.

I'm off and on. He wants to do it professionally . . . to make his living at it. I'm not as serious about it. He has another partner he competes with a lot of the time. Those two eat and sleep roping. That's all life is to them. I don't think either one of them has had a date in the last six months."

Before Marti could censure herself, she said, "Have you?"

Clay blushed. "Now that you mention it . . . except for today, no."

Until that moment, Marti hadn't considered what they were doing was a date. Of course it wasn't. It was just . . . two people passing some time together. That's all.

The thought that Clay had the wrong idea about it almost made her want to suggest they turn around and go back to the barn. But this was so preferable to being alone with her thoughts, she said nothing.

CHAPTER 15

IT WOULDN'T BE accurate to say that over the weekend Marti didn't think at all about the effect Nadine's suicide might have had on Quinn's decision to attend that EEG meeting. The worry just didn't hit full force until she was waiting for Douglas Packard in the Memphis airport concourse. It was true that Quinn didn't seem overly upset by Nadine's death when they'd spoken on the hospital steps right after it happened, but he could have been more upset than he let on. And maybe he'd somehow found out she and Nadine had spoken shortly before Nadine jumped, or that she'd gone to Edwards Brothers and posed as Nadine's sister. Any of those things might have caused him to cancel his trip.

Stop it, rational Marti ordered. *You're just jumpy because the day you've waited for so long is finally here.*

No further thought on the matter was possible because Douglas Packard came into the airport lobby looking even heavier and less fit than when Marti had last seen him, so that the collar of his white shirt seemed to have a death grip on his throat. When he spotted her, he barely showed any sign of recognition, about what you might expect from a man who'd lived the life he had.

She moved toward him and met him halfway. "How was your flight?"

"We all walked away from it, so I'd rate it a big success."

"Are you hungry?"

"I'm always hungry. That's why I have to buy my suits at a tent store. But I already had breakfast, so I don't need another one."

"You've got the pictures?"

"Doctor, I didn't come all this way just to leave the photos at home. Where's Glaser?"

"Don't know. But his plane got in nearly two hours ago."

"You didn't see him arrive?"

"He said he was meeting a friend for breakfast. He'll join us at the motel."

"He better."

Marti took Packard to her car and he hoisted his small bag into the trunk. When they were settled in their seats and he pulled his seatbelt across his suit coat, she could clearly see the outline of a gun in a shoulder holster. Even though it was a tool of his trade, she was surprised they'd let him on the plane with it.

Neither of them spoke again until they were on the expressway heading east.

"How far is it?" Packard asked.

"About seventy miles."

"Never been in Tennessee before. We gonna see any cotton fields?"

"Can't say. I have no idea what it looks like when it's young."

"How's our boy?"

"Odessa?"

"Yeah."

"Far too healthy for me."

"Hopefully we can do something about that."

They reached the Best Western in Linville a little before eleven o'clock and got Packard's room key.

Marti then asked the desk clerk, "Did Mr. Glaser arrive yet?"

"About ten minutes ago. I believe he's in his room. It's three eighteen, right next to Mr. Packard, as you requested."

They went first to Packard's room, where he dumped his bag on the bed and got a nine-by-twelve manila envelope from one of the outer compartments.

"Are those the photos?" Marti asked, growing queasy at the thought.

"Yeah. You gonna watch when we do it?"

"Are they bad?"

"Some of them."

"I'll try, but I don't know . . ."

They left Packard's room, went a few steps down the hall, and knocked on Glaser's door. It was opened by a lean guy with a long face that gave him the look of a greyhound.

"Dr. Segerson . . . Douglas . . . good to see both of you. Come in."

He stepped back and they could see he was already at work with a laptop and a scanner set up on the writing desk.

"How are we doing on time?" Marti asked.

"You wanted to begin testing at two?"

"Yes."

"Shouldn't be any problem . . . if Douglas has the—"
Packard showed him the manila envelope.

"That's all I need," Glaser said, reaching for the photos.

"How long will it take to set up this afternoon?" Marti asked.

"No more than thirty minutes."

"You saw the hospital on the way in, so you know how to get there. Come in the front door of the main building, go up the big set of stairs directly in front of you, and take the left hallway on the second floor. I'm in two thirty-three. I'll be waiting for you. When we're ready, I'll go get Odessa."

"Where's a good place to eat?" Packard asked.

Marti gave him directions to The Fishin' Hole, then left and drove to the hospital, where the first thing she did was cruise by Quinn's parking place to be sure his car wasn't in it.

Satisfied he really was on his way to Atlanta, she parked her car and went inside, too nervous to even think about lunch.

MARTI CHECKED HER watch for the fifth time. Twenty-nine minutes after one; a minute later than the last time she looked.

She paced the floor. Soon she'd find out if this was going to work. She still had done nothing to prepare Odessa, because she didn't want to give him any advance warning. If he resisted . . . the thought made her sick to her stomach. Beyond the fact it would ruin everything, she didn't want to tell Packard his trip had been a waste of time. Glaser, she could handle, but Packard was a tough old bird who—

Someone knocking . . .

They're here.

She opened the door and froze.

It was Oren Quinn.

Jesus. And with Packard and Glaser arriving any minute. Why the hell wasn't he on a plane to Atlanta? Fearing that he could hear her heart hammering in her chest, she tried to appear calm. "Dr. Quinn. I was just on my way to the restroom. What can I do for you?"

His eyes traveled to a point over her shoulder as he apparently inventoried the furniture she'd obtained from storage. "Some of the staff are calling you a hero for saving that patient's life last week. Do you feel like a hero?"

"No. My response to the situation was simply a reflex action."

"And now she can return to her rich existence as a human manikin."

"What would you have had me do?"

"I suppose what you did was necessary."

"I don't mean to be rude, but I really need to make that trip I mentioned."

"I'm leaving for the airport in just a few minutes. I'll be back on Wednesday. I'd like to see you sometime Wednesday afternoon to discuss the amount of time you've been absent from the hospital during working hours. Make the appointment with my secretary. Have a nice day."

Then he turned and headed for his office.

To keep him from becoming suspicious, Marti followed him as far as the women's restroom, where, before

ducking inside, she took a quick look at the main stairs.
And sure enough, there were Packard and Glaser, coming
up to the second floor, carrying the equipment they'd
need.

Damn. Damn. Damn.

Seeing them, Quinn paused.

Immobile, with her hand on the restroom door, Marti's
heart was now about to rip from its moorings. If Quinn
questioned those two . . .

Quinn called out to them. "May I help you?"

"We're looking for Dr. Segerson," Glaser said.

And there it was . . . right out in the open.

Marti did the only thing she could. She took two steps
toward the stairs and said loudly, "My office is two
thirty-three, down this way. Just go inside. I'll be with
you in a minute." Though she was dying to see what
would happen next, she thought it would look suspicious
if she stayed in the hallway any longer. So she retreated
to the restroom and went in.

She remained beside the door and looked at her watch.
Two minutes should be long enough to make her trip
there appear genuine.

While she waited she listened hard to determine if
Quinn was still talking to Packard and Glaser, but, of
course, she couldn't hear anything. Then one of the toi-
lets flushed.

Not wanting the occupant of that stall to see her with
her ear pressed to the door, she hurried to a sink and
began washing her hands.

In a few seconds Howard Rosenblum's secretary
emerged from the stall and went to the adjacent sink.

"Dr. Segerson, how are you doing?"

"I'm adjusting quite well, thanks."

"We don't usually have as much excitement around here as we had last week. You just never know what these people are going to do next."

Marti's mind was so focused on what was happening in the hall she could barely think of a response. Finally, she managed to say, "It's best to always expect the unexpected."

"Yes, I suppose that's true."

Marti didn't want to leave the restroom first, so she fiddled with her hair until the other woman said, "See you later."

Marti waited about five seconds after the woman was gone, then she went out into the hall and looked toward the stairs.

No one was there.

As she hurried to her office, she was convinced Quinn had thrown Packard and Glaser out and that everything was ruined. But when she pushed her door open, there the two men were, setting up the necessary equipment.

"Do you know who that was at the top of the stairs?" she asked. She answered her own question without waiting. "Oren Quinn, the superintendent of the place. And just the guy I didn't want to know you were here. Did he ask you anything?"

Packard shrugged. "Didn't seem to care who we were."

"Well, it's not a good start."

"It's not how you start, but how you finish that matters," Packard said.

They had pulled the long table to the center of the room and had two laptops sitting back to back on it the same way Nadine had arranged their computers for Marti's mind-reading test.

"Are those partitions for me?" Packard asked.

"I figured we could arrange them so you could see what was going on, but he couldn't see you."

"That'll work."

Packard set about moving the partitions into place.

Barry Glaser was the chief technician from Brain Fingerprinting Laboratories, Inc., a firm that had developed a technique for determining if the brain of a criminal suspect contained any memory of the crime he was accused of committing. Though quite new as an investigative tool, the test appeared to be 100 percent accurate in linking a criminal to his crime, even if he was trying to conceal his participation. The test consisted of showing the suspect crime-related images his brain would recognize only if he had been at the scene. And it didn't matter how many years had intervened between the commission of the crime and the brain fingerprint test. Not only had the test been ruled admissible in court, it had recently been involved in exonerating a man serving a life sentence in Iowa for a murder he was accused of committing decades ago.

Douglas Packard was the LA detective who had worked the murder of Marti's sister. He, along with Marti and her parents, had been incensed when the LA district attorney had declined to prosecute Odessa for that murder, citing a lack of evidence, even though Marti had *been* there. So Odessa had simply been returned to the mental hospital from which he had escaped.

A year ago, in reviewing the case at Marti and Packard's insistence, the current LA district attorney had agreed to take the case to a grand jury if any new evidence linking Odessa to Lee's murder could be produced. Today, with the help of Glaser's company, which was donating their services for the publicity that would be generated when the case came to trial, Marti would get that evidence. And this time, with the tougher standards in California for copping an insanity defense, Odessa would receive the death penalty he deserved.

There wasn't much for Packard to do to get ready, so he slouched in one of the chairs at the long table and read a paperback he'd brought. Glaser likewise didn't need any help.

With nothing else to occupy Marti's mind, she worried. What if Quinn returned to his office in the middle of the test? What if Trina came to see her? Suppose Odessa refused to cooperate? All this made her want to get started as soon as possible.

Finally, sitting at the keyboard of the control computer, Glaser typed in a few last commands and stood up. "It's showtime."

CHAPTER 16

INSTEAD OF GOING right up to the ward and getting Odessa, Marti first went out to the parking lot and checked Quinn's slot.

It was empty.

At least now she didn't have to worry about him.

Two minutes later, she paused at the door to Two East B, calmed herself, and went in.

Odessa was not in the dayroom, but Bobby Ware was over by the smoking enclosure talking to Chickadee.

Before she could head in that direction, Ada Metz came out of the nursing station.

"Good afternoon, Doctor."

Her emphasis on the word *afternoon* made Marti think it was probably Metz who had called Quinn's attention to her irregular work hours.

"I'm going to take Vernon Odessa down to my office for some psychological tests."

Metz's face looked as though Marti had slapped her.

"That's very irregular. He's usually not allowed to be in that part of the building."

"Nevertheless, that's where we're headed."

"I don't think Dr. Quinn would approve of that."

"He already has."

"Then you won't mind if I call him."

Knowing that Quinn was out of the building, Marti cavalierly said, "Not at all."

But then she thought, suppose Quinn had a cell phone? He almost certainly did. If his secretary relayed Metz's call to him . . . Or maybe Metz had his cell phone number and could call him directly. Sensing everything starting to unravel, Marti said, "But I should tell you that I saw him a few minutes ago and he was in a particularly foul mood."

It wasn't a very creative ploy, but it was all she could think of.

Metz looked at her for several seconds without blinking, then said, "I don't know why I'm bothering myself over this. It'll be your skin if anything goes wrong. But we've got orders that whenever he leaves the secure part of the facility, he's to be shackled. Bobby knows how to do it." Then she went back into the nursing station.

Marti was burning a lot of bridges, but since she'd be leaving the state for good in just a few hours, what did it matter?

She walked over to Bobby, took him aside, and explained what she wanted. He then went to the nursing station and got a drawstring bag containing the necessary restraints.

They found Odessa in his room at his computer.

"Sorry to bother you," Marti said, "but Dr. Quinn would like for you to take a short psychological test."

"When?"

"Now."

"He didn't say anything to me about that."

Odessa's comment made it sound as though he and Quinn were old friends who chatted on a regular basis. As ridiculous as this was, Marti went along with it. "He's away at a conference, so he probably had a lot on his mind the last few days getting ready."

"How long will this take?"

"Just a few minutes."

"I'm not a trained animal that's here to perform for you anytime you feel like it."

"I understand. But the doctor who will administer the test has come a long way and I'd hate to tell him we can't proceed. And of course, Dr. Quinn would be very disappointed."

When she mentioned Quinn, she could see Odessa's resistance weaken.

"All right. Let's get it over with."

"We're going to do it in my office."

Odessa's lips curled in a malevolent grin. "We're going to do it? I can't wait. I'll bet you're a tight fit."

Then Bobby spoke up. "Since you'll be going into an unsecured area, you'll have to be restrained."

A storm gathered in Odessa's face. "I won't be paraded through the dayroom like that."

Marti was surprised he would care what a bunch of mental patients thought about him. But then, in this situation, they *were* his peers.

"I know," Bobby said. "We'll go out the back way."

In the bag was a waist chain with cuffs to hold Odessa's hands at his side. There was also a set of ankle chains that would restrict the length of his step. Despite his obvious anger over being shackled, Odessa didn't resist as Bobby locked him in.

"Regs state that we need another orderly to go along," Bobby said to Marti when he was finished preparing Odessa for the trip.

"I'll get someone."

Marti turned to leave, but met Ruben Hernandez, one of the other orderlies, at the door. He wasn't nearly as big as Bobby, but still looked as though he could handle himself.

"Nurse Ratchet told me you need some help," Ruben said, grinning at his own joke.

"We're going to take Mr. Odessa downstairs to my office," Marti said.

"Then let's go."

The rear door to the dormitory hall and the back stairs was the way the ward's occupants went to the cafeteria on the fourth floor at mealtime. But there was also a corridor connecting to the front hallway. With Odessa jingling at each step, they made their way to that hallway, through the metal security door, and to the administrative access, where Marti called the parade to a halt.

"Bobby, you do have the key to his cuffs don't you? Because he's going to need one hand free to take the test."

"I have them, but is that a good idea?"

"We don't have any choice."

"Don't be afraid," Odessa purred. "I would never hurt you . . . much."

Marti hadn't considered it might require two orderlies to take Odessa out of the ward. In constructing her plan, she had anticipated it would just be Bobby escorting Odessa to her office and she had spent more than a few minutes trying to figure out what to do with him during the test. At first it seemed obvious he shouldn't be there to witness what was going on. But without him, she thought Odessa might try to take advantage of the situation. Packard would be there for damage control, but she didn't want Odessa to know of his presence. So she'd decided that the only thing she could do was let Bobby watch. Faced with this necessity, she'd realized it didn't really matter if Bobby was there. So it likewise wouldn't matter if Hernandez was also present. Once the test was over, nothing about Gibson would matter.

Marti opened the door to the administrative area and took a quick look into the hall. Seeing no one around, she stepped out and held the door for the others.

They made it to her office unseen and Marti went inside first to alert Packard to conceal himself. Then she let the three men waiting come in.

She introduced Glaser as though this was some kind of social event, and Bobby unlocked one of Odessa's handcuffs. Bobby guided Odessa into the chair in front of the test computer and stood beside him. As Ruben hovered nearby, Glaser explained what was going to happen.

"Mr. Odessa, we want to test your memory for complex events with an emotional context. So I'll be showing you a number of photographs on the screen in front of you. Each of these images will involve a homicide."

"Sounds like fun," Odessa said.

"We'll begin by showing you six photographs you'll be asked to identify during the test as one of those you've just seen. To do that you'll press the left button on the mouse when one of those images appears. I've taped a small note to the table there to remind you that left means it's one of those six, which we'll call targets.

"Mixed in with the targets will be many other images. When you see an image that is not a target, press the right mouse button. Each image will be flashed on the screen for a short time then there will be approximately a three-second delay before the next image appears. The test will consist of two blocks of seventy-two images with a short rest period between the two blocks. In each block you will see a given image more than once.

"We'd also like to see how your brain processes the images you recognize, so you'll need to wear this . . ." Glaser picked up a headband connected by a bunch of wires to a four channel EEG amplifier. "May I put it on?"

"Sure, but don't you think *I* ought to be the one to wear it?"

Glaser grinned amiably. "That's what I meant."

Glaser put the headband on Odessa, pulling it down until the frontal electrode made contact with Odessa's forehead, and all the other electrodes across his scalp were equally secure. Glaser fiddled with the knobs on the amplifier, then asked, "Do you have any questions?"

"So where are the six target pictures?"

Glaser picked up a different manila envelope than the one Packard had brought and put a small stack of black-and-white eight-by-ten photos in front of Odessa. Marti was standing on the opposite side of the table so the photos were upside down. Even so, she distinctly saw that the first picture was of a woman with her face mutilated by knife wounds. Disgusted and sorry she'd looked, Marti averted her eyes and moved away.

As Odessa looked at the target photos with obvious interest, Marti wondered if they were teaching him some new tricks. Then she thought about the photos of her sister's murder that Glaser had scanned into the system that morning and which would soon be flashing onto the monitors. Just being in the room with them was starting to make her sick to her stomach.

Packard had not brought all the available photos of Lee. Some would be held back so they could be pressed into service during an official court-ordered brain finger-print test of Odessa after he'd been indicted. A part of Marti found this parading of Lee in front of her murderer profane and a violation of her memory. But it was the only way she knew to bring her sister—and herself—ultimate peace.

After spending what seemed like an inordinate amount of time examining each target picture, Odessa looked up at Glaser. "Can I keep these?"

Glaser stepped in and picked up the stack. "Sorry, no. Are you ready to begin?"

Odessa's eyes flicked from Glaser to the partitions on the opposite side of the room, and Marti wondered if he'd spotted Packard back there. She looked in that direction trying to see Packard herself, but the opening between partitions was too small to give him away. When she glanced back at Odessa, his eyes were riveted on her, as though he were wondering what *she'd* found so interesting on the other side of the room.

"Mr. Odessa . . . are you ready to begin?" Glaser asked a second time.

Suddenly looking ill at ease, Odessa didn't answer. He looked again at the partitions, then did a general fidgety survey of his surroundings.

Marti's heart moved into her throat for fear he was going to balk at continuing. But then he looked at Glaser and said, "Can't wait."

Marti made it a point not to watch the monitor during

the test, but she did keep her eyes on Odessa's face, which grew flushed as he viewed the carnage flashing past him. And he gradually began to breathe harder. Seeing his excitement grow as one victim after another sped by, Marti felt like picking up a chair and bashing him in the head with it. Fortunately, the only one that was unoccupied was the one behind her desk, and it was too heavy to lift.

So she endured and did nothing.

Finally, when she felt she couldn't take another minute of seeing Odessa wallowing in the horrors they were showing him, Glaser said, "And we're finished."

He went around to Odessa's side of the table and removed the EEG headband.

When Odessa stood up, Marti saw that there were now large sweat stains under the armpits of his shirt. He looked at her and shook his head. "Great show, Doc. Anytime you want to go again I'm available."

"Good," Marti replied. "Because I'm sure you'll be doing it one more time."

Sensing there was some hidden meaning in her comment, Odessa's brow knitted as he tried to figure out what it was. But the moment was cut short by Bobby moving in to recuff his free hand.

"Bobby, would you take him back?" Marti said. "I need to stay here and discuss some things with Dr. Glaser."

"No problem." He put a hand on Odessa's shoulder and pushed gently. "Let's go home."

"Ruben . . . thanks for the help . . . you too, Bobby," Marti called out as the group moved away from the table.

With his chains clanking, Odessa short-stepped to the door and Ruben opened it for him. Before leaving,

Odessa looked over his shoulder. "Don't talk about me when I'm gone. And that goes for you too, whoever's behind those partitions."

When the door closed, Packard came into the open. "Have I mentioned how much I hate that guy?"

"Not nearly enough," Marti said. She looked at Glaser, who was working the keyboard at his computer.

"What's the verdict?"

"I'll need just a few minutes to collate the data."

"I think he was getting off on those pictures," Packard said.

"No question about it," Marti replied.

While Glaser worried his keyboard, Marti wandered over to her desk chair and sat down. Packard leaned against the wall and tended his fingernails with a clipper from his pocket.

With each second Glaser worked, the tension in the room mounted until Marti's nerves were sizzling. Packard, though, didn't seem fazed by the wait.

Unable to sit still, Marti got up, walked over to where Glaser was sitting, and tried to decipher the data on his monitor herself. But it was all unintelligible.

She turned to say something to Packard, then, thinking it might disturb Glaser's concentration, she kept quiet and returned to her chair, where she sat back with her feet up on her desk.

Exactly twenty-eight seconds later, Glaser announced, "Well, we got a brain wave recognition signature on each of the six targets."

Marti rocked her chair forward and stood up. Packard put his clippers in his pocket.

"What about Lee's pictures?" Marti asked.

"Negative. Absolutely no sign of recognition."

Marti came around her desk fast. "That's impossible. He did it. I know he did. I was there."

"I'm sorry," Glaser said, pushing his chair back and standing up, "but the data we just generated don't support that."

Marti steamed over to confront Glaser. "You said this test was infallible."

"I've never known it to be wrong."

"So how do you explain what happened?"

"I can't. All I can say is his brain isn't carrying the fingerprint of that event."

Marti was so devastated she didn't know what to say. Years of planning . . . washed away in an instant. There was nothing now to take to the Los Angeles DA. Lee's murderer would go unpunished.

"He must have found a way to beat the test," Marti said.

"He'd be the first," Glaser replied.

Packard came over and put his hand on Marti's shoulder. "That's the way it goes sometimes, kid. You think you've got your man in the bag and he wiggles out of it."

"I feel like hell," Marti said. "Not only because we didn't get him, but because of all the time you two put it into this. And with nothing to show for it."

"Never count on anything until it's in your hand," Glaser said, starting to pack up. "I learned that a long time ago."

Though her mind was reeling, Marti was still able to address the last remaining threads of the disaster that had just taken place. "Since I arranged this without permission, I figured we'd need to get out of Linville right afterward, so I made motel reservations for you both at the

Memphis Hampton Inn on Millbranch Road. It's the closest one to the airport."

She went to her desk and got the map she'd drawn for
them. "Here's how to find it. Douglas, I was thinking you
two could ride back together."

"What are *you* gonna do?" Packard asked.

"At the moment, I just don't know."

Five minutes later, with the two men on their way to
Glaser's van, Marti stood in the middle of her office,
arms folded across her chest, eyes closed, trying to shut
out what had just happened. But it was a pain she
couldn't avoid.

Odessa had escaped her trap. How had he done that?
But more importantly, what was she going to do now?
She couldn't simply walk away, but what other option did
she have? Tears welled behind her closed eyes and she
opened them and looked at the ceiling.

"Lee, I am so sorry. I was sure this would work."

She shuffled to the chair behind her desk and dropped
into it, where she sat tilted forward, elbows on her thighs,
staring at the floor.

Then, like a bubble escaping from the slimy bottom of
a stagnant pond, an idea slowly began to work its way
from the darkest recesses of her brain into the light. She
fought its ascent, but it was so buoyant it eventually
slipped around her attempts to constrain it.

When it reached the surface, it popped, expelling its
repulsive contents in a gaseous belch.

Kill him yourself.

CHAPTER 17

KILL HIM . . .

At first the idea seemed too monstrous to consider, but then, what other options were there? Odessa had to die. There was no other way to satisfy the fire that had raged within Marti for nearly two decades. But being the instrument that funneled him onto death row legally was a far different thing than ending his life with her own hand.

Could she do that?

Wouldn't she be as evil as he was if she did it herself?

Of course not, emotional Marti argued. *You'd simply be ridding the world of a plague. It would be an act no different than those that had cleansed the world of smallpox. Odessa was just a different kind of pathogen.*

Very different, objective Marti said. *He's a human being, not a microbe.*

He may not be a microbe, but he's not human either. So why give him that consideration?

But what would happen to her if she killed him? She'd

be arrested and likely either be executed herself or sent to prison for the rest of her life.

Do you really care about any of that? emotional Marti sneered. *You had one chance of snaring him legally, and he beat you. Now you have to put up or shut up. You promised Lee you'd see that he would pay for killing her. Are you going to break that promise? Are you going to fold like a paper hat or will you keep your word? Are you strong or weak?*

Suppose I did want to kill him myself? How could I do it?

Her mind now turned to possible courses of action.

What about poison?

Very complicated. She'd have to slip it into his food, which would not only be difficult to do, but he might survive. It should be a way that leaves no chance for error.

She could get a gun somewhere, walk right up to him in the ward and blow him to hell. But then he wouldn't know why it was happening. She wanted him to see it coming and know who she was before he died. She needed to see that smug look change to fear, needed to see him know what it was to face death the way Lee had.

She'd had no trouble getting him down to her office for the brain fingerprint test. She could probably do that again. Bobby Ware could shackle him to a radiator and then she could send Bobby and Ruben, or whoever came along, out of the room on some pretense. It wouldn't take more than a minute or two.

But where could she get a gun? Didn't it take seven days for some kind of background check before a dealer would sell you one?

A pawnshop . . .

Surely you could buy a gun in a Memphis pawnshop

without a background check. She could be there and back in just a few hours. Then, tomorrow . . .

What? What exactly would she do?

Her mind took her back to her med school rotation in the emergency room and she remembered the frightful damage gunshot wounds to the head inflicted . . . how they blew away huge pieces of skull as they exited, carrying away pieces of the victim's brain. Damaging him as he had done to Lee was undeniably appealing, but regardless of how much she hated Odessa, she could never cause something like that.

Seeing what she was planning in such stark terms, she realized she couldn't kill him at all. It just wasn't in her. And that made her miserable, because she had no other way to make him pay for what he'd done.

She began to pace the room, at a loss for what to do. If only the brain fingerprint test had worked. Why the hell hadn't it? Why wasn't the memory of her sister's murder there?

Then she began to think of how she had lost the memory of Harry Evensky's visit the night he escaped. Two memory losses by people associated with the hospital . . . could that be mere coincidence?

Wait—

Clay Hulett had said Jackie Norman's sister, who used to work at Gibson, had experienced some kind of brain trauma that caused her to forget *everything* she once knew. Three people in one hospital experiencing memory loss . . . no way that was coincidence.

She hurried to her desk, grabbed her cell phone from her bag, and punched the preset for Clay's number.

"Clay . . . this is Marti. Do you know where Jackie Norman's sister lives?"

"Right after her illness she was staying at a school for the retarded in Jackson, where they could watch her and teach her how to feed and dress herself and things like that. I don't think she's there anymore. But I can find out."

"Do you have time to do it now?"

"Sure. I'll call you right back."

"Use my cell number." She gave him the number and stood with the phone in her hand while her mind tried to fit the three cases of memory loss into a workable hypothesis that would explain why they had occurred. But it was like trying to spin flax into gold with no flax. There was simply no raw material to work with. But if she could talk to Jackie's sister or maybe Jackie herself about the circumstances surrounding her sister's trouble . . .

Marti's thoughts were shattered by the sound of her cell phone.

"Okay, I found out where she lives," Clay said. "Did you want to see her for some reason?"

"As soon as possible. Is there a problem?"

"I'm not going to ask you why you want to see her, although that question *is* burning a hole in my brain. But I learned that she lives with Jackie now. And Jackie just left the college to go home . . . so if you go over there now—"

"I'll run into her too."

"Exactly. So maybe I should go along . . . just to sort of act as a referee."

Marti wasn't prepared for Clay's suggestion, and her first reaction was to tell him she didn't need his help. But that could turn out to be wrong. Jackie's resentment against Gibson was so strong there was a good possibility she'd be extremely uncooperative. In that case, Clay could make the difference.

"Good idea," she said. "Where are you?"

"My office at the college. Do you know where the campus is?"

"No."

"It'll be easier then if I pick you up."

"I'm at the hospital now, but I'm going to leave and drive right home."

"See you there in ten minutes."

AS HE DROVE, Clay remained true to his word and at least outwardly, let the reasons for Marti's interest in Molly Norman go unclarified. But from his silence, Marti felt he was actually waiting for her to volunteer an explanation. A part of her wanted to tell him everything, but she had lived privately for so long, it was hard to suddenly go public with the secrets she had protected for most of her life. So she said nothing. With neither of them speaking, the trip took place in an awkward silence that made Marti hope it would soon be over.

Jackie Norman lived in an old two-story farmhouse that needed paint even more than the Edwards Brothers funeral home.

"This isn't what I expected," Marti said as Clay stopped his truck in the dirt driveway and cut off the engine.

"Why not?"

"Jackie seemed more like the upscale chic apartment type."

"If they ever build any places like that around here, maybe she'll move."

They got out of the truck and went up on the wooden porch, where Clay knocked on the door. Jackie answered, looked briefly at Clay, then leveled her dark eyes on Marti.

"Why are you interested in my sister?" Jackie asked.

"I told her I was inquiring about Molly for you," Clay said. Then, obviously feeling that Marti might be miffed at his disclosure, he added, "Couldn't be avoided."

"Clay told me she experienced some sort of brain trauma while she was working at Gibson," Marti said. "And as a result, lost all her memories."

"What is that to you . . . you want to study her, so you can write a paper about her . . . pad your bibliography at her expense?"

Marti had anticipated this moment and had considered the effect what she was about to say would have on Clay. She'd lied to him when she'd explained her call from the hospital asking why he'd changed her locks. Now she was going to tell Molly the real reason behind that call. But if she kept her response generic, Clay wouldn't catch on.

"The same thing happened to me a few days ago," Marti said to Jackie. "Not to the same degree, of course. I just lost the memory of one event, but I have to think your sister's problem and mine are related."

Marti could see by Jackie's expression she had lowered her defenses.

"You think there's something in the hospital that causes memory loss?"

"I know of at least one other case in which it happened, so yes, I believe it's likely."

"I've always thought Gibson was at fault. I mean, she was a healthy young woman when she went to work there. And look how she came out. What do you think's going on?"

"I have no idea. I was hoping by seeing your sister and talking to her, I might pick up a clue."

"She's still struggling with relearning language as well as a lot of other things. So I don't think she's going to be much help."

"I don't know where else to turn."

"Then you better come in."

The living room of the farmhouse was comfortably decorated but largely unremarkable except it contained a sofa and a chair made of the same tree limb construction she'd seen in Clay's house. Evidence Jackie and Clay were once more than just friends? Maybe.

"As I understand it," Jackie said, "there are two kinds of memory. One for facts and one for skills like typing, or riding a bicycle. Even people with nearly total amnesia always retain their skills. But that wasn't the case with Molly. She used to be an excellent tennis player. After her . . . I don't even know what to call it. After it happened, she was worse at tennis than I am, which means she was horrible. So she lost both kinds of memory . . . the first case like that in history, I guess. And there were no physical findings to account for it . . . nothing on CAT scans, nothing on MRI."

"My loss was a minor one, but I didn't have any physical findings either," Marti said. "What was Molly's job at Gibson?"

"She was a nurse."

"Do you know on what wards?"

"I'm sorry, I don't."

"May I see her now?"

"She's in the dining room with Mrs. Martin . . . she's

the retired schoolteacher I hired to work with Molly after I took her out of the home for the retarded." Jackie's eyes grew flinty. "Molly's *not* retarded and doesn't belong with those who are."

Jackie went to a tall pair of sliding doors and parted them to reveal that the dining room had been converted to an elementary school classroom; a big rolling blackboard on the far side of the dining table, a long bulletin board bristling with tacked-up sheets of paper on the left wall . . . a playhouse in one corner with lots of stuffed animals piled into a container made of black fishnet.

An older woman, who reminded Marti of Aunt Bea on the *Andy Griffith Show*, was standing behind a young woman working in a notebook at the dining room table. Both looked up at the interruption.

"Mrs. Martin, I'm sorry to disturb you," Jackie said, "but this is Dr. Segerson. She'd like to talk to Molly for a few minutes."

"Of course. I'll just make myself some tea in the kitchen."

Marti pulled a chair over to Molly and sat down. "Hello, Molly. My name is Marti. What are you working on?"

Molly had all the same general features as Jackie, but they didn't fit together in quite the same way, so that where Jackie was beautiful, Molly was not. But there was a peacefulness and innocence in her face that made her look ageless. She turned her notebook so Marti could see she had been practicing writing the numbers from one to a hundred.

"That's very good," Marti said. "Do you like school-work?"

"It's not fun, but Jackie says it's—" Molly's smooth brow furrowed and she looked at Jackie for help.

"Nece . . ." Jackie prompted.

"Necessary," Molly said.

"Molly, do you remember when you were a better tennis player than Jackie?"

"They said I was, but I don't think so."

Marti looked at Jackie. "Has she been back to Gibson since this happened—driven by it, or seen it in any way?"

"Absolutely not."

Marti turned back to Molly. "If I asked you to draw something for me, would you try to do it?"

"Okay." Molly turned to a fresh page in her notebook and picked up her pencil.

"Draw me a picture of the Gibson State Mental Hospital."

Molly set to work and Marti's hopes rose that Molly had retained some thread of a recollection for the hospital she could use as a link to other memories. But Molly's sketch quickly turned into a generic drawing of a house a six-year-old might make.

"May I draw something?" Marti asked.

Molly gave her the pencil, and Marti stood up. Moving to Molly's right, Marti turned the notebook so she had the length of the paper to work with. In broad strokes, she drew an outline of the mental hospital then sketched in the main entrance and the windows, finishing with the lightning rods on each spire.

"Do you recognize that?" she asked Molly.

"Is it the place you wanted me to draw?"

Marti's hopes rose. "Yes, do you remember being there?"

Molly shrugged. "I just figured since you asked *me* to draw it, that must be what it is."

Marti looked at Jackie. "Can she read?"

"Not very well. I think she's only worked her way up to third-grade material so far."

Though it seemed like a long shot, Marti decided there was nothing to lose in trying the next thing she had in mind. She leaned down and wrote Oren Quinn's name in large block letters under the drawing she'd made.

"Molly, do you know who that is?"

Molly put her index finger under the letters and tried to sound out the name. "O . . . rrr . . . eeee . . . nnn."

"Oren . . ." Marti said, helping her along.

"QQQQQ . . . iiii . . ."

"Quinn," Marti said. "Oren Quinn."

Molly just looked at Marti with a blank expression. Marti sat down again beside her. "Molly, do you remember anything at all about when you were a nurse?"

"I know people say I was one, but I can't picture that at all."

Marti looked at Jackie, shook her head, and turned her hands palms-up in surrender.

"Molly, why don't you go into the kitchen and ask Mrs. Martin for some orange juice."

Molly nodded and headed for the kitchen.

"I admit I could have come better prepared," Marti said, "but I don't think it would have mattered. She seems to have no trace of a memory of her former life."

"And she's been difficult to teach too."

"Children are sponges for information while they develop. When we become adults and much of our neural wiring is already formed, we're less receptive to learning new things. But I think she's going to be fine. Did you notice how she figured out what I drew must be the hospital? So she's capable of deductive reasoning."

"Who is Oren Quinn?" Jackie asked.

"The superintendent at the hospital. I figured if she remembered any name from there, it would be him."

"What do you make of *this*?" Clay said, from the bulletin board.

Marti and Jackie walked over to see what he was talking about.

"Look at these pages where she was practicing writing the months of the year," Clay said, pointing. "Every time she writes September it's twice as big as all the others. And over here, where she's written the numbers from one to a hundred on three different sheets, the number twelve is always the largest."

Marti looked at Jackie. "Was that the day she lost her memory; September twelfth?"

"No. She was fine on the twelfth. She was found wandering around the highway outside of town where it goes through Gwatney swamp on the fourteenth. There was a big truck accident out there. The driver said she caused it, by just standing in the road."

"Can you think of any significance the twelfth would have to Molly?"

"You really think those large numbers mean something?"

"There has to be some reason why she's emphasizing them."

"Well, I certainly can't think of any reason."

"You said she was fine on the twelfth," Clay said. "How do you know?"

"We had lunch together. We always did that a couple of times a week."

"Did she say anything at lunch to indicate why that day was special to her?"

"It's been eight months. I can't recall exactly what we talked about."

"Why don't we ask Molly about the number?" Clay suggested.

"I'll get her," Jackie said, heading for the kitchen.

The two returned a few seconds later and Jackie took her over to the bulletin board. "Molly, we've noticed that every time you write the month September and the number twelve, they're always larger than the other months and numbers. Can you tell us why?"

Molly shrugged. "It just seems like that's the way it should be."

"I think we're finished here," Marti said.

"Go tell Mrs. Martin our visitors are leaving," Jackie said to Molly. Obediently, Molly did as Jackie asked.

Back in the living room, Jackie looked at Marti and said, "I'm sorry we couldn't have been of more help."

"It was worth the try."

A few seconds later, as Marti and Clay walked to his truck, Jackie came back onto the porch. "I do remember one thing Molly and I spoke about at lunch."

Marti and Clay returned to the porch and stood at the bottom of the steps. "I don't see how it has any bearing on what happened to her," Jackie said. "but we talked about the young woman who was found murdered over in Blake earlier the same morning. I didn't know anything about it, but Molly had heard the news on the radio as she drove to the restaurant."

"Was she acquainted with the victim?"

"I can't remember the details of our conversation, but I don't think so. That kind of thing just doesn't happen around here, so I suppose the rarity of the event is what kindled her interest. It did mine."

"Did they ever catch the killer?" Marti asked.

"I think it went unsolved."

"If she didn't know the victim," Clay said. "Why would the date of the crime survive the loss of memories that were a lot more personal?"

"We don't know it did," Marti responded. She looked again at Jackie. "But thanks for telling us about that."

Marti and Clay went to his truck and Jackie returned to the house.

"Where to now?" Clay said, firing up the truck's engine.

"How far away is Blake?"

CHAPTER 18

"BLAKE IS ABOUT thirty miles west of here in McNairy County," Clay said. "You're thinking of going over there?"

"I'd like to know more about that murder."

"So you *do* think that's what Molly's remembering from the twelfth."

"I don't know what to think. But it's the only thread I have to follow at this point. Don't feel you have to go too. That's certainly way beyond what you thought you were getting involved in today."

"I don't have anything else to do. Might as well take a ride."

"Is Blake big enough to have a police department?"

"I think we'll be wanting the county sheriff's office."

THE SHERIFF'S NAME was Billy Ray Banks. Marti saw it stenciled on the frosted glass panel of his door just before the deputy showing them in opened it. Marti was prepared for a redneck with a big belly that threatened to pop the buttons on his uniform. Instead, they found that Banks was a slightly built black man with short white hair. And his uniform fit him just fine.

As they entered, he looked up from where he was pouring himself a cup of coffee and said, "Either of you want a cup? It's not nearly as bad as you might imagine."

Both Clay and Marti demurred.

Banks brought his coffee to his desk, a big golden oak structure of utter simplicity like a couple of those Marti had seen in storage at Gibson, and said, "Too much of this job is done standing up, so I think we all ought to sit while we talk."

When they were all settled and Banks had sampled his coffee, he set his cup down on a stone coaster, leaned forward, and folded his hands on the desk. "Now, who are you?"

Since it was Marti's show, she did the introductions. Curiously, when she mentioned her affiliation with Gibson, Banks's eyes seemed to shift from polite tolerance to sincere interest.

"And you're here for what reason?" Banks asked.

"I'm interested in the murder you discovered in Blake on September twelfth."

"Do you have information to offer on the case?"

"Actually, I know nothing about it except the date it occurred and that the victim was a young woman."

Banks's brow furrowed and he shook his head in confusion. "I don't understand."

"An employee of Gibson acquired a severe case of amnesia a few days after the murder. We just visited her and noticed she seems to have a fixation on the date

September twelfth. Her sister doesn't know of anything significant in the patient's life from that date. But she did remember the Blake murder was on the news that morning."

Banks took a pen from his shirt pocket, clicked the tip, and pulled a notepad in front of him. "What's this amnesiac's name?"

Alarmed that she might be creating trouble for Molly and Jackie, Marti said, "Her name is Molly Norman, but there's no point talking to her. She doesn't remember anything before September fourteenth, the day she was found with total memory loss."

Ignoring Marti's last comment, Banks said, "What's her address?"

Because she hadn't bothered to note it, Marti looked at Clay, who hesitated. Realizing he was waiting for her permission to divulge where the Normans lived, she nodded.

Banks jotted down the address.

"Sheriff, we came here to *obtain* information, but so far we've been the ones giving it."

"Why are you so interested in Molly Norman you would drive all the way over here from Linville?" Banks asked. "Are you treating her?"

"No. I went to see her because I recently experienced some memory loss myself and I was hoping by talking to Molly I might be able to figure out why it happened." This would have been the time to mention Vernon Odessa's memory loss, but there was no way Marti was going there.

"How long have you worked at Gibson?" Banks asked.

"A week."

"And you came from . . ."

"California."

"Just before you started at Gibson?"

"Yes. I assume from your interest in Molly Norman that the Blake murder is still unsolved."

"No one at Gibson has spoken to you about the case?"

"No. Why would they?"

Banks sat back in his chair, folded his arms across his chest, and stared at Marti for awhile before speaking. Finally, he said, "Because our best suspect is a patient there."

Marti couldn't believe what she was hearing. "One of our patients? Who?"

"A man named Vernon Odessa."

Marti nearly gasped aloud.

"Is that a familiar name?" Banks asked, noting her reaction.

"He's on my ward. I'm his psychiatrist."

"Then you know his history."

"Of course, but why is he a suspect?"

"There were certain features of the crime that fit his pattern."

"You mean the use of a hammer?"

"I didn't say that."

"You didn't have to. But how can he be a suspect? He's locked up. He's not free to roam the countryside."

"So the superintendent over there pointed out to me. He also called my attention to the book that had been written about Odessa." Banks pulled a book from one of his desk drawers and dropped it on the table. "I bought this copy and read it twice. And frankly, it disgusted me both times. Dr. Quinn believes we're dealing with a copycat killer who also read the book and who knows

Odessa is being held at Gibson. Quinn suggested that this hypothetical alternate suspect arranged for the murder scene to resemble Odessa's work to confuse the investigation."

"Did you personally go over to Gibson and check out the situation?"

"Yes."

"And you still refer to Odessa as your best suspect. Why?"

"I've been in police work for thirty years. After that long, you develop a good feel for the truth. And the truth is, Odessa did it."

"So why hasn't he been indicted?"

"I don't have any proof. And he has Gibson as an alibi. He couldn't have been in Gibson and in Blake at the same time."

"People have been known to escape from Gibson."

"There's no indication he did."

"So what are you going to do?"

"Go over and see what I can find out about Molly Norman."

"I don't think that's going to help you."

"So you said earlier. Is there a better number to reach you than at the hospital?"

Marti gave Banks her cell number then said, "Will you keep me informed of anything you learn that might be important?"

"Maybe . . ."

"BOY, WE REALLY stepped into something, didn't we?" Clay said when they were back in his truck and heading home.

Marti didn't answer because her mind was grappling with what she'd just learned. If Odessa had committed the Blake murder, he could be executed for that. She wouldn't have to prove he murdered Lee. At the moment, she had no idea how Odessa could have been in two places at once, but she liked Banks and felt his police instincts were reliable. But mostly, she believed Odessa had committed the Blake murder because that would give her another shot at him.

But where to begin . . . she could call Barry Glaser at the Hampton Inn in Memphis and coax him back to Linville. Then she could arrange another brain fingerprint test using photos Banks must have from the Blake killing.

But if Odessa had no memory of killing Lee, he likewise might pass a brain fingerprint test of the Blake murder. And there was no time . . . Glaser was booked up for weeks . . . he couldn't just come back and wait for her to arrange another test, even if he was willing to do another one for free, which he might not be.

"I'm sorry, did you ask me something?" Marti said to Clay.

"It was just a comment of surprise about what we just learned. Whether Odessa did the Blake murder or not, I never did like the idea of having him around here. He should be in a California facility where he belongs."

"You know who he is?"

"Jackie mentioned it once when he first arrived."

"Was it common knowledge . . . I mean, did the local paper cover the story?"

"No. I think Jackie learned about it from Molly."

Marti thought about this a moment, then got out her cell phone.

"Who are you calling?" Clay asked.

"Someone at Gibson. . . . Dr. Estes please . . ."

She wasn't in her office, so Marti had her paged.

"Trina . . . hi, this is Marti. Did you know a woman named Molly Norman who worked at Gibson?"

Clay glanced at Marti and saw her brows lift in apparent surprise at the response she got.

"What did she say?" Clay asked as Marti put her phone away after thanking Trina for the information.

"Before she had her problem, Molly Norman worked on Odessa's ward as the junior nurse."

"So maybe that's why the date of the Blake murder is still fixed in her mind . . . she thought Odessa did it too."

"The bastard . . ." Marti muttered.

Realizing she'd said that aloud, she looked at Clay, who was obviously surprised at the anger she'd expressed.

Suddenly, Marti was tired of carrying the burden of Lee's death all by herself. She was sick of being two people and lying to practically everyone she met. It was just too much and had gone on too long. She couldn't be that person anymore.

"Do you remember when you were apologizing for Jackie's behavior at lunch and you asked me if I'd experienced a similar kind of pain with my sister? Well, I lied when I told you I hadn't. Odessa killed my sister practically in front of me eighteen years ago. He was never prosecuted for her murder and I came to Gibson to see that he pays for what he did. So I'm a fraud in almost every way."

She hadn't cried since she was twelve, but now that she'd revealed her secret, she felt tears welling up in her eyes. She fought to hold them back, but the years of liv-

ing as a clandestine shadow culminating in the shattering
results of Odessa's brain fingerprint test came crashing
down on her.

Clay drove the truck off the road onto the shoulder,
switched off the engine, and turned to look at her. Marti
braced herself for his reaction. As the first words of her
confession had poured out of her, she'd been convinced
he'd be sympathetic, but hearing herself talk, she realized
how natural it would be for him to feel she'd played him
like a fool. In fact, that was the more likely reaction.
Looking at his face, which was locked in an inscrutable
expression, she was now sorry she'd spoken.

Then Clay unbuckled his seat belt and got out of the
truck. He went around to Marti's door, opened it, and un-
hooked her seat belt.

Marti was stunned. Was he going to leave her here to
find her way home alone? Was he that angry at being
misled? He motioned her out of the truck. Okay, if that's
the way he wanted it, she'd go. She didn't want to be
where she wasn't wanted.

She slid out of her seat and stepped onto the grassy
shoulder. Then suddenly his arms were around her,
pulling her close. Instead of resisting as the old Marti
might have, she let herself go to him.

"No one, let alone a kid, should have had to see what
you did," Clay whispered against her hair. "And to know
he was never punished for it makes it even worse."

Marti's last resistance crumbled under Clay's sympathetic words and the tears began to flow unrestrained.

"It's okay," Clay murmured. "I understand."

And so there they stood, beside the road, cars passing,
the occupants gawking at them, neither of them caring.

Finally, Marti gently pulled back and wiped her tears away with her hand. "This isn't me. I never cry."

"It's not a sign of weakness. It just means you're human."

A passing car honked at them. When Marti looked that way she saw the driver give them a thumbs up.

"Could I be human now in the truck, where the rest of the county can't witness it?"

Clay grinned and released her.

Back in the truck, Clay handed Marti a small pack of tissues from somewhere on his side, and she wiped her eyes.

"I can't imagine going through what you did," Clay said. "How does a twelve-year-old kid deal with something like that?"

"Therapy," Marti replied. "Lots of it. That's what gave me the idea of becoming a psychiatrist so I could get to Odessa."

"What did you mean when you said you came to Gibson to see that he pays for what he did?"

Marti explained about the brain fingerprint test and what she'd hoped to accomplish with it.

A look of relief appeared on Clay's face. "I was afraid *you* might have been thinking of killing him."

"Believe me, when he passed the fingerprint test, I thought about it."

Clay's face lit up with an idea. "If he did kill the girl in Blake and it could be proved, that would get him fried."

"But from what Banks said, it doesn't sound as though that's going to happen."

"Didn't seem optimistic, did he? What now?"

"Go back to Gibson and see if I can figure out how he could have done it."

"I don't know what help I could provide, but if you can use me, I'm available."

"Right now, it's a one-person job. But I appreciate the offer."

Clay started the truck and pulled onto the highway.

VERNON ODESSA SAT in the Gibson cafeteria, ignoring his food, his mind burning with the images he'd seen in the brain fingerprint test. Except for a single night eight months ago, when he had even been stripped of the pleasure that could have brought him, he'd been denied the one thing that defined him, that made life worth living. He'd succumbed to incarceration and accepted being treated like a zoo animal. But now those sleeping urges, roused by thoughts of what must have happened on the trip to Blake and fueled by the pictures Glaser had shown him, were awake and demanding to be satisfied . . . on his own terms, not on someone else's whim.

But how to do that? His hand went to the scar in his neck and he ran his fingers over it. Then he looked at the plastic fork in his hand.

Useless.

He picked up the thin, blunt plastic knife next to his plate and considered that.

Far too flimsy.

Damn that veg in the women's ward. If she hadn't cut herself with that piece of broken mirror, they wouldn't have replaced all the mirrors in the place with unbreakable glass and he'd have something he could work with.

Screw the lousy luck.

Finished with the slop the cooks called food, Odessa got up, carried his tray to the garbage cans, and dumped all the paper and plastic from his meal. As he moved down and slid his tray into the rolling cart with the stacked shelves, he noticed in the food line a case knife sitting next to a tray of dinner rolls. And with all his ward served, no one from the kitchen staff was nearby.

He didn't have to turn around to know at least one of the two orderlies that had accompanied his ward to the cafeteria was watching him. So he made no attempt to get the knife, but instead walked back to where most everyone else was still eating and took a seat next to Chickadee.

"Chick, how would you like to earn some cigarettes," Odessa said under his breath.

"Doin' what?" Chick had an irritating speech impediment that sent everything he said through his nose, and you could barely tell one word from another.

"Go over to that rolling tray cart and push it over."

"Why?"

"It'll be fun."

"I'll get in trouble."

"That's why I'm willing to give you three cigarettes to do it."

Chickadee looked at the cart then back at Odessa. "Five . . . I want five cigarettes."

"Done."

"I want them now."

"Three now, two after we get back the ward."

"Okay."

Odessa passed Chickadee three cigarettes under the table and Chick put them in his shirt pocket, using a napkin to hide the movement.

"The wheels are probably locked. If not and it starts to roll, you'll have to put your foot behind one of them so it'll tip. Can you do that?"

"Why couldn't I?"

"You haven't noticed your pins are messed up?"

"Don't you worry about me. I'm no cripple."

"After you do that, go into the kitchen and yell at the cooks about how bad the food is. I mean scream at them, and keep it up until you're forced to stop."

"You didn't say anything about yelling."

"I'll give you an extra cig for that."

Chick got up and reached for his tray.

"Not now. Wait until I move to a new table."

Odessa got up, went to the front of the room, to the row of heavy oak tables closest to the serving line, and slid into the attached picnic-bench-type seat, where he pulled a paperback from his pocket and pretended to read. But he was actually watching the two orderlies over the top of the pages.

Bobby Ware was leaning against the wall to Odessa's left about halfway between the front and back of the room. Eddie Greer was on the opposite side of the room closer to the back. Both were looking right at him.

From the corner of Odessa's right eye he saw Chick get up and head for the front. *Don't screw up, you fruit,* he thought. Keeping his eyes on the pages in front of him, he waited for the crash.

A few seconds later, there was a sound that had to be the cart rocking once, then it went over with a shattering of plates even louder than Odessa had imagined it would be. Eddie Greer bolted for the front of the room, but Ware stayed where he was.

Odessa silently urged his puppet into phase two. *Don't forget the kitchen, moron.*

Then he heard a string of incomprehensible bellowing.

This sent Ware into action and he too, headed for the serving line.

Odessa waited until Ware had passed behind him, then he stood up and followed. While the two orderlies were dealing with Chickadee's diversion, Odessa plucked the case knife off the dinner rolls and slid it up his sleeve.

BACK IN HIS room a few minutes later, Odessa turned on his radio and began sharpening the blade on the case knife by sliding it over and over along the rough surface of his radiator.

CHAPTER 19

THOUGH MARTI WAS eager to get back to the hospital and take another look at Odessa's records, she agreed when Clay suggested they stop and have dinner at a little café on the outskirts of Linville, where there were a lot of cars in the parking lot. She didn't have much of an appetite but figured eating now would get that out of the way and clear the rest of the evening for thinking. The delay meant she didn't reach the hospital's front entrance until a little after six o'clock.

The good part of her late return was she arrived after the shift change, so when she went up to the ward to get Odessa's files she didn't have to deal with Ada Metz. Instead, she met for the first time Nurse Olivia Barr, a sweet-tempered woman with a sparkle in her eye and a pin on her uniform that was a tiny picture frame containing a photograph of her pet Westie. Happily, she didn't see Odessa anywhere in the dayroom.

The major impediment to Marti's belief that Odessa

had committed the Blake murder was the same one that had stumped Sheriff Banks. The night rules for Odessa at the hospital called for an orderly to physically make sure he was on the ward every three hours. The orderly was supposed to actually look at his face, not respond to a lump under the blanket that looked like a person. The orderly was then required to sign a check sheet indicating Odessa was there.

It didn't seem likely he could have escaped from the ward, make his way thirty miles to Blake, find a victim that fit his criteria, get cleaned up, and come back, all without transportation, in just three hours. And if he did escape, why come back to the hospital at all?

The murder in Blake had been discovered on the morning of September 12, so when Marti reached her office, she riffled through Odessa's logbook, looking for the check sheet entries for the night of September 11. When she found them, she got a surprise, because in the blanks where the orderly was supposed to sign off by writing his initials, someone had written *patient in seclusion.*

Seclusion . . .

September 11 must have been the night Odessa attacked Ronald Clary.

Marti cross-checked the nurse's notes for the date, and saw she was correct.

She found these circumstances more than interesting. The one night when Odessa's presence in custody was crucial to establishing an alibi for a murder, his usual routine had been altered. She picked up the records and headed back up to the ward, where she found Olivia Barr just coming back to the nursing station from the dayroom.

"Olivia, were you working on this ward last September when Vernon Odessa was put in seclusion?"

"Yes. Why do you ask, dear?"

"I was just looking at the logbook for him and noticed that instead of checking on him every three hours that night, the orderly on duty just indicated he was in seclusion. Did no one actually verify he was there the whole night?"

"That's the same question the sheriff from Blake asked me when he came to investigate the murder they had. No, we didn't bother because seclusion is more secure even than the ward. There's just no way anyone could escape from there."

"I don't understand. Don't you closely monitor patients in seclusion? I thought that was standard procedure across the country."

"Usually, yes . . . when we use the seclusion room on the ward, but Odessa was in the old facility where there's no wiring for cameras."

"Where is the old facility?"

"There's one in the basement of both wings at the bottom of each front stairwell . . . relics from the past. Dr. Quinn specifically ordered him put there because they're so nasty. Odessa has the potential to be such a behavioral problem Dr. Quinn wanted to impress upon him that we simply will not tolerate violent behavior. As I understand it, the use of an unmonitored facility is perfectly acceptable if it's part of a specialized individual behavioral program."

"If no one was watching him, how can you say he couldn't have escaped?"

"It's physically impossible. Were you thinking Odessa might have been responsible for that murder?"

"It occurred to me."

"The sheriff was thinking the same thing until he saw the way seclusion is laid out. Then he just went away. So you know if it satisfied him, it's very secure."

"Were any other patients there at the same time?"

"I don't think so. Like I said, it's not a place we normally send people."

"Which one was Odessa in?"

"The one in our wing. Are you going down there?"

"Is that a problem?"

"No, it's just dirty."

IN HIS ROOM, Odessa stopped stroking the stolen case knife on the radiator and examined the blade. It wasn't ready yet, but it was coming along nicely. When it was finished, there'd be no more flashlights shining in his eyes every three hours at night while he was trying to sleep, no one telling him what he could do and what he couldn't. All that would be over.

THE MESH METAL door at the head of the basement stairs clanged shut and Marti started down the steps on the other side. Accompanied by the most awful creaking noises that made her worry about the safety of the staircase, she descended into ever-increasing darkness. By the time she reached the foot of the stairs, she could see almost nothing in the gloom ahead.

She stepped tentatively forward and paused to let her eyes adapt to the poor light. As they did she saw across a rough concrete floor an old steel door with huge strap hinges that looked as though it had been made in a medieval metal foundry. Instead of a doorknob, there was a metal ring welded to it above a large keyhole.

She pulled on the ring.

Locked.

A quick inspection of the old brick walls surrounding the door revealed a filigreed iron rectangle with a large key on it hanging from a big nail with a square head.

She took the key down and put it in the lock. From the ancient appearance of the door, she figured the lock mechanism would be hard to move, but it rolled over with oiled ease, making hardly a sound. When she pulled on the door's metal ring, the door moved ever so slightly. Bracing herself, she put her back into it and the door swung open, again smoothly and without a whimper from the hinges.

The space beyond was a cave as dark as the inside of a coffin and she could see not one inch of its contents. She fumbled to the right of the entrance for a light switch and eventually found one; an old-style push button on a raised round base. It turned on the power to a string of what seemed to be forty-watt bare light bulbs wired to a low, curved ceiling made of the same old brick that lined the walls. With the lights on, feeble as they were, she could now see that water laden with calcium had dripped through the mortar in many places, studding the ceiling with small, white stalactites, which gave the space the appearance of a great mouth filled with teeth.

Along the right wall were five metal doors, which looked to be of the same construction as the one behind her, but were smaller. Each one had a rectangular slit covered with metal mesh in it near the floor, presumably for passing a food tray. Remembering Trina's warning about getting her key back before going through the metal

doors upstairs, she turned and reclaimed the big key that
had let her in. It was then she realized there was no keyhole on the inside. Once the big door was shut, there
would be no way to open it from the inside. That must
have been what the night nurse meant when she said it
was physically impossible to escape from here.

Worried that the door might shut behind her, Marti put
the key in her back pocket and looked around for a loose
brick or something else she could use to make sure the
door couldn't fully close. But there was nothing available. She turned to the door and pushed hard on it, swing-
ing it to its full open position. Then she stood and
watched it carefully to see if it would stay put.

After ten seconds of close scrutiny with no movement
of the door, Marti decided to trust it.

She then went into the cellblock, where on a scarred
old wooden trestle table, she saw another rectangle and
key similar to the one in her pocket, but slightly smaller:
apparently the key to the individual cell doors. She
picked up this key and approached one of the cells, suddenly aware that she was merely assuming none of them
was occupied.

"Is anyone here?" she said softly.

No answer.

"I'm Dr. Segerson," she said, a little louder. "If you're
behind any of these doors, please say so."

Once again she heard no response. But considering
whom she might be dealing with, that didn't mean much.

Located at eye level on the door in front of her was a
small metal disk free to pivot on the rivet holding it in
place: the cover for an observation port. She shifted the
disk upward and looked through the quarter-size hole

under it. But there was no light in the cell, so she could
see nothing.

Noticing another old-style black button switch to the
right of the door, she pressed it and looked again through
the observation port. But the cell was still dark, so if the
switch was meant to operate a light in there, it wasn't
working.

Then, realizing if the cell were empty, the door might
be unlocked, she put the key from the table in her other
back pocket, grasped the hand ring just above the keyhole, and pulled. With a rusty squeal that made her
wince, the door inched open, then stalled. She let go of
the ring, put both hands on the now-exposed edge of the
door, and pushed it open another foot, causing the hinges
to make a horrible din.

With the door open, a dank, musty stench rolled over
her. Enough light now filtered into the cell for her to see
it was an inhospitable place. Lined with the same bricks
as the main chamber, the small cell also had a curved
ceiling, which limited the space in which an occupant
might stand. Though the sides of the cell were shrouded
in darkness, she could see on her right the edge of an iron
bed with a stained mattress. On the floor to her left,
nearly lost in the shadow, she saw the toilet facilities: a
dented galvanized bucket and a roll of moisture-rippled
toilet paper. She thought it an inhuman place to keep
someone until she remembered that this cell or one of the
other four had once held Vernon Odessa. Then it seemed
far too good for him.

She turned to examine the cell door and found that
like the main door, there was no keyhole on the inside.
She went around and checked the tray pass-through,
which was covered by a mesh grid fitted with a latch on

its upper edge and hinges on the lower. With the grid locked in place, it would be impossible for an occupant to reach through the slit. She looked up at the keyhole. Even if the occupant had the key, no one possessed an arm long enough to reach the keyhole through the pass-through.

Wondering if the cell might contain a hidden escape passage, she went inside and started checking the walls for loose bricks.

Eight minutes later, she came back into the staging room confident the cell she'd just examined was structurally sound. But maybe that wasn't the one Odessa had been in. She didn't want to do it, but all the others would have to be examined too.

She found each of the other cells empty, unlocked, and without a working light. Despite the lack of decent illumination, her efficiency at examining the cells improved as she went along so she finished the entire job in less than thirty minutes. All the cells were equally sound.

Then how the hell did Odessa escape?

Even if he had somehow stolen the keys necessary to unlock his cell door and then the main door, there was no keyhole on the inside of either door.

And . . .

Thinking about how the unlocked cell doors opened without the key she'd found on the trestle table, she left the cellblock and shoved the main door closed. Just as she'd now suspected, that door didn't lock automatically either. It had to be done with the key.

This seemed to negate the possibility that whoever had locked Odessa up had forgotten to lock both doors. If that's what had happened, how did Odessa lock himself back in after the murder?

Or maybe he didn't.

If the person who put him in seclusion *had* forgotten to lock the doors and had discovered the mistake in the morning, wouldn't it be best to just keep quiet about it? Especially since Odessa was suspected of committing a murder that night. Whoever might have forgotten to lock him in could probably be charged with criminal negligence or some other crime.

But she still had no explanation for why Odessa would come back to the hospital after the murder.

Deciding to worry about that detail later, Marti put the cell key back on the trestle table where she'd found it. Returning to the hall, she closed the big door, locked it, and hung that key on its nail.

Her thoughts then turned to how Odessa might have gotten out of the building once he left the basement. All the doors leading from the patient wings to the administrative part of the hospital were kept locked. And all the exterior doors were likewise to be locked after five o'clock . . . so how . . . ?

As she crossed the basement's concrete floor on her way to the stairwell, she saw through the gloom another metal door on her right. Approaching it, she saw that this one was secured with a hasp locked in place with a padlock.

Remembering something Trina Estes had said about the hospital on her first day, Marti wanted very much to see what was on the other side of this door. But a search of the surrounding walls revealed no key.

Now what?

In a clear indication of how badly she wanted that door open, she decided she needed a pair of bolt cutters.

But where could she get one? There was probably nothing open this late locally that sold hardware.

Clay . . . He might own a pair. Then she remembered seeing a gas station just west of the hospital that sold trailer hitches and various kind of animal pens. They should have some kind of cutters for metal.

FIFTEEN MINUTES LATER Marti once again stood in front of the locked door, a little ashamed at having used her feminine wiles to talk a horny young guy at the gas station into lending her just what she needed. Realizing she was just getting herself in deeper and deeper trouble, she put the jaws of the borrowed bolt cutter on the padlock blocking her way and sliced it off with surprisingly little effort.

The door made no noise when it opened and she found herself staring into another black space. Fumbling around the wall just inside, her fingers felt a light switch like the one on the cellblock. But when she pressed this one, nothing happened.

Having anticipated something like this, she flicked on the flashlight she'd had the foresight to bring from the trunk of her car and played it into the darkness.

It was just as she'd thought. This wasn't a room. It was the tunnel Trina had mentioned. As she stepped through the door, she hoped the story about it being infested with bats wasn't true.

CHAPTER 20

BEFORE MOVING FORWARD, Marti examined the tunnel with the beam of her flashlight and saw that the walls here were lined with the same old brick as she'd seen in the cellblock. Though this ceiling was slightly higher, it too, was studded with toothy stalactites, but the tips of these glistened with the water forming them. She couldn't see very far ahead because the tunnel seemed to turn to the left, just beyond the reach of her light.

Wondering how much time had passed since anyone else had been in here, she crouched down and played her flashlight along the floor so the beam raked the concrete at a shallow angle. Despite the ability of such a technique to reveal details normally invisible to casual observation, she saw no signs of footprints in the dust. But with her nose down near floor level, she caught the distinct and unpleasant odor of ammonia. And she could now hear the far-away sound of what seemed to be little voices chattering in earnest conversation.

She stood up and started walking . . . and immediately thrust her face into a spiderweb. Flailing at the gossamer strands that seemed to be all over her, she danced forward another couple of steps, wondering if the spider responsible for the web might now be in her hair. Shuddering at the thought, she brushed violently at her scalp with her free hand, worried that if the creature *were* there it might jump on her hand and run up her arm. All this kept her working on her hair like an obsessive–compulsive.

Finally, wiping at a strand of web that had somehow gotten into her mouth, she got control of herself and calmed down. Once again moving with deliberation, she found that as the tunnel turned to the left, it also began a gentle descent to a deeper level. The ammonia odor was now so strong she could smell it even standing erect. And the little voices were louder too.

She moved cautiously forward, the beam of her flashlight darting from floor to wall to ceiling. She'd gone about fifteen yards when her flashlight suddenly lit up a furry patch on the ceiling. The beam had no sooner fallen on the fuzzy growth than it burst apart, sending a dozen chattering bats in all directions.

One came directly at her face, and she threw up her hands for protection. As she did, the flashlight slipped from her fingers and clattered to the floor. She felt a rush of air against her hands, but the bat made no actual contact. Dropping to one knee, she recovered the flashlight and shot the beam at the ceiling, where the bat colony was now in full pandemonium, furry bodies flying everywhere, filling the air with urine and screeches of protest.

Something wet hit her on the shoulder.

Crouching there in this circle of hell, Marti's thoughts ricocheted back to a lecture she'd had in medical school on rabies, and she remembered that most human cases in this country in the last ten years had come from bats. And there was some evidence you could get it even if you weren't bitten. Saliva or urine in your eyes, aerosol transmission . . . nobody knew exactly how, but at the moment the mechanism didn't seem important.

She felt another spray of liquid soak into her shirt.

Most women, and men too, would have retreated and called it a night. But that wasn't the way Marti was constructed. Obstacles in her path just made her more determined to succeed. If she had not been so stubborn she might have realized that even though she hadn't seen their escape route, the bats would probably soon be leaving on their nightly search for food. As it was, she had decided from the moment she went on a search for bolt cutters she was going to explore that tunnel . . . from start to finish. And no colony of flying mice was going to stop her.

With that decision already made, she got to her feet, lowered her face so the bats couldn't urinate into her eyes or mouth, and started forward at a brisk clip, the beam from her flashlight trained on the floor.

She saw her next problem and then was into it at almost the same instant: bat guano at least an inch deep on the floor. She was now directly under the densest part of the colony so she couldn't slow down and choose the best route through it. Straight-ahead as fast as possible was the answer.

She tried to pick up the pace, but her left foot slipped

on the wet droppings, sluicing to the side so she almost went down into the disgusting carpet of filth. She pulled her errant foot back under her, but just as she felt she was regaining control, her right foot went AWOL.

Slipping and sliding like a kid on ice skates for the first time, she fought her way down the tunnel, wings brushing her hair and face, mad rodent chatter so loud it seemed to be coming from inside her head, a steady shower of urine fouling her clothing. This had definitely been one of the worst decisions she had ever made. But there was no way she was going to retreat now.

She pushed herself forward, knowing this had to end soon.

Or did it?

Maybe the colony occupied the entire remaining part of the tunnel. If that was the case, every slimy step she took was just taking her farther away from sanity.

Then suddenly, she was once again on solid footing. The rush of wings around her dropped off noticeably and she could hear that the center of the lunatic squealing was definitely behind her.

Wanting to get completely away from the horror she'd just been through, she kept moving at a brisk pace, thinking about what the bats had done to her. Her hair and shirt were wet with bat piss, her shoes were caked with bat shit, God knows if any of them had bitten her. Bats had very small teeth and their bites weren't often obvious.

What was the percentage of bats with rabies? She couldn't remember . . . pretty low, she thought.

After Lee's murder, she had replayed the night many times in her mind, thinking about what she should have done differently, how she might have stopped what had happened. The only thing that had saved her from descending into madness herself was the realization there was no way to change the past. Dwelling on it accomplished nothing. What mattered afterward was how she would deal with her new reality. Acceptance of that proposition had given her life purpose, and she had moved forward.

While much of her momentum had been aimed at Vernon Odessa, she began to apply the lesson she'd learned to other aspects of her life, so now she spent very little time lamenting things in life that went haywire. This meant her mind quickly moved from her ruined clothing and the possibility she had been infected with rabies virus to refocusing on the task at hand.

With her sights reset, she immediately had an idea.

She stopped, turned around, and played her light on the floor, looking for bat guano footprints. Not even seeing her own, she slowly made her way back toward the colony, which by now, she had left well behind her.

Finally she saw the faint imprint of a shoe and another close by. Fitting her own foot into the first print, she saw that these were the ones she had made. She then looked carefully all around the area to see if there were any others.

After a minute or so in which she found nothing, she moved a little closer to the colony. There she saw more of her own prints even more clearly outlined.

She shifted the light closer to the wall and . . .

She knelt and looked closer.

More footprints . . . and definitely not hers. Someone else, with much bigger feet, had also walked through the guano, going the same direction as she was. But when?

No way to tell. Nor were the prints distinctive. Unlike

the tread marks her shoes had left, these were smooth and featureless.

At first it seemed like an important discovery, but then she realized that the other prints could have been from anyone: a security guy, a biologist interested in bats, someone working for a pest control firm . . . possibly even Sheriff Banks.

Disappointed because there were so many explanations for the extra footprints, she got up and headed toward the yet-unexplored part of the tunnel.

Her little flashlight had a narrow beam and illuminated only a small section of her surroundings at a time, so she had to keep it in constant motion to see what each region she passed through looked like. But apart from varying numbers of stalactites, one section of the tunnel was pretty much like another.

Then her light showed her something new.

Ahead of her, the tunnel branched in four directions.

Which way to go?

Deciding that the easiest way to keep track of where she'd been was to start with the one on the right, she resumed walking.

After she'd gone about fifteen yards down the chosen passage it ended at another metal door. Though there was no lock on her side, the door refused to open, immediately raising the concern that if there were no way out on this side of the bat colony, she'd have to go through those devils again.

Reminding herself that worrying about things prematurely was wasted energy, she retraced her steps to the original tunnel's branching point and took the second fork.

Three minutes later, she found that this one too, ended

at a locked door. On her way back to the branching point, the thought of another dash through the bat colony was a little harder to dismiss.

Tunnel three ended like the other two. Figuring it was likely a waste of time, but needing to finish the job, she headed down the fourth tunnel, already thinking it might be better, when she left, to turn off her flashlight as she passed the bats. Maybe they wouldn't pee so much if they weren't upset.

Should she get a series of rabies shots when she got out? They weren't as painful as they used to be, so maybe that'd be the safe thing to do. But she'd have to find someplace that had the vaccine. Surely Linville Methodist had some . . .

It gradually became apparent that this passage was longer than the other three. By now she'd lost all sense of direction, so she had no idea where she was in regard to the landmarks above ground. She walked for another couple of minutes before the final door appeared in the beam of her light.

Without any real hope that she'd finally found an escape route from the bats, she grasped the metal handle on the door and pulled.

And, by God, this one opened.

Passing through it, she found herself in a brick-lined stairwell.

But where was she?

She went up a short flight of metal steps to a small landing that led to a second set of stairs in a switchback. Reaching the much larger landing at the top of the latter, she saw two more metal doors, one straight ahead and one to her left.

Advantage Marti, for when she tried the door straight

ahead, it didn't even creak as it opened. From the landing she played her flashlight into the room beyond and saw stacks of old furniture and computer equipment. Apparently she'd surfaced in the storage building where she'd obtained the extra furniture for her office, or in another structure much like it.

Not interested in salvage shopping, she withdrew and turned to the remaining door, where she leaned on the long metal bar that served as a latching mechanism. The fresh air that rushed in as that door opened cleansed her lungs and lifted her spirits. Stepping outside she found herself facing a secluded section of the parking lot lined on two sides with woods and on a third by the front part of the storage building. From where she stood she couldn't see the main hospital or any of the other satellite structures.

Finding all she had seen extremely interesting, she set out across the parking lot to her car, which she reached about three minutes later. Even though it was a rental, she didn't want to climb in with her shoes and clothes so filthy.

Only one thing to do . . .

She went around to the trunk and opened it. After a quick glance around to make sure no one was watching, she took off her shoes. She did the same with her blouse, wrapped her shoes in it, and tossed the package in the trunk. She then hurried to the front seat and climbed in, knowing that if she got a flat tire on the short drive home, she was just going to keep going.

Nightfall was still about forty minutes away, so the driver of the eighteen-wheeler who passed Marti on the highway got a good enough look at her in her bra that he leaned heavily on the truck's air horn in a show of approval. Fortunately, though Clay was home when she passed, he was in the house, so she didn't have to explain her unusual driving attire to him.

When she reached her cottage, she went right inside and climbed into the shower, already wondering if Sheriff Banks would be in his office this late.

CHAPTER 21

AS HER HAND reached for the cottage telephone, Marti reflected on how she'd been on the Gibson staff only a week and already had to throw out two changes of clothing. And she hadn't brought much to begin with. Then she remembered the bolt cutters she'd left in the hospital basement.

Nuts.

At some point, she'd have to retrieve them and get them back to their owners. But right now she had something more important to do.

She dialed information. "McNairy County Sheriff's Office, please."

They put the call through, and it was promptly answered by a gruff male voice.

"This is Dr. Segerson. I was there a few hours ago talking with Sheriff Banks. Is he still in?"

"Gone for the day. Can I be of help?"

"Could you relay this call to him or give me a number where he can be reached?"

"We're not allowed to do that. You have business with this office tonight, you're gonna have to go through me."

"I'd rather call back when he's there."

Marti hung up, irritated at what had just happened. Damn it, this was important. She needed to speak with Banks; no one else would do.

She tried information for the sheriff's home phone number, but it was unlisted.

Now what . . . Drive over to the office and try to convince the people there to give her the number? That didn't seem like a productive way to go. She could wait until he was back at work in the morning, but she was too keyed up to let that much time pass.

Playing a long shot she left the cottage and climbed into her car.

CLAY ANSWERED THE door in his history professor uniform.

"You look like you're going out," Marti said.

"Retirement party for two of our faculty. The dean will be taking names and checking them twice for anyone in absentia. Did you figure out how Odessa could have done it?"

"I've got a few ideas, but I need to talk to Banks again. He's gone for the day and his office won't tell me his home number."

"C'mon in. I may be able to help."

He stepped back and Marti went inside.

"Back here," Clay said, heading for the hallway.

Marti followed him to the den, where he sat down at a

dark antique desk with bears and other wildlife crudely carved into the sides. He pulled a box of Rolodex cards over in front of him and began flipping through them. While she waited, Marti dropped into one of Clay's tree-limb chairs beside a lamp table of the same construction.

Having found the number he was looking for, Clay reached for the phone and punched in a number. While it rang, he looked at Marti. "This is a guy who serves on the volunteer fire department over in McNairy. I think he knows Banks"—His eyes shifted to the desktop—"Eddie. . . . Clay Hulett. . . . How you doing? . . . Yeah, I know what you mean."

They exchanged some fireman small talk, then Clay got down to business. "Do you happen to have the home number of the sheriff over there? . . . Yeah, that's him . . ."

Clay nodded to Marti and scrabbled in the desk drawer for a pen. He peeled a blank card from the Rolodex and scribbled down a number.

"Okay, thanks, Eddie. No, I won't tell him who gave it to me."

Clay got up and gestured for Marti to take his place.

As they swapped seats, he said, "Bet you didn't think it was going to be that easy."

"I don't believe I'd bet against you on anything."

Marti's call to Banks was answered by a woman.

"Sheriff Banks, please."

"May I tell him whose calling?"

"Dr. Segerson."

"And what is this about?"

"It's a long story."

"Condense it for me."

Marti assumed this was Banks's wife. Rather than

feeling upset with her for being so protective of her husband's time off, Marti respected her for it. That didn't mean Marti was going to spend a lot of time explaining things to a third party. "If you'll just tell him who's calling, I'm sure he'll want to speak with me."

There was no response, but the line remained open, so Mrs. Banks was either thinking about what Marti had just said or was carrying her message to Banks.

There was a scraping noise in the background followed by a thump, then the sheriff came on the line. "Dr. Segerson, what can I do for you?"

"I guess you knew that the night of the murder over there, Odessa was in seclusion."

"Yes."

"Doesn't it strike you as a little odd . . . the one night when something happens he might have been responsible for, his normal routine is altered?"

"It certainly got my attention."

"And no one checked on him the entire night, did you know that?"

"Doctor, with all due respect, this is all old news to me."

"I just came from the hospital basement. The main door to the seclusion cellblock doesn't lock automatically when you close it. You have to turn the key. The same is true for all the cell doors. Suppose whoever put Odessa down there forgot to lock the doors or thought they locked automatically. After they left, he could have just walked out. Such a mistake would probably have been discovered the next morning, but why would the person responsible admit it? Especially if there was a chance the mistake had led to the murder of someone."

"Odessa was taken to seclusion by two orderlies on

the night shift," Banks said. "He was removed the next day, by two who work days. So you see, there'd be no reason for the ones discovering the mistake to lie about it."

"Unless they were good friends with the other two and knew how much trouble they'd be in."

"There's no evidence of that kind of friendship. Believe me, I checked the point thoroughly. And the two on the day shift swear both doors were locked when they went down to pick him up. I've had a lot of experience with liars and there's no doubt in my mind they were telling the truth. In addition to that problem, we have to explain why Odessa returned to the hospital after the murder. Do you have an explanation for that?"

"Maybe he figured it would give him a good alibi."

"So how did he lock himself in when he got back?"

"I don't know. But I found a way he could have gotten out of the hospital basement without being seen. There's a tunnel from the basement to a storage building with an exterior door opening onto a section of the parking lot isolated from any of the other buildings. Were you aware of that?"

"I saw the entrance in the hospital basement, but it was padlocked. How could he have gotten in there?"

"I admit there are a few things yet to explain . . ."

"Doctor, you make it sound as if we're dealing with a couple of minor points. The things we can't explain are huge. I can't take a theory with that many holes in it to our DA. He'd think I've lost my mind. You seem very invested in proving Odessa's our man. May I ask why?"

Unwilling to tell him the true reason for her interest, Marti slipped the question. "If he did it, he needs to be punished. We owe it to the victim and to her family."

"Can't argue with that, but you've got to do better than what I've just heard."

"I'll work on it."

She hung up and looked at Clay, who said, "Work on what?"

"He had an objection for everything I told him."

"Valid or reaching?"

She leaned back in her chair and folded her arms over her chest. "It was all reasonable. But that's only because we haven't been smart enough to fill in the blanks in what happened."

"Don't take offense at this, but—"

"What?"

"Maybe he *didn't* do it."

Marti rocked forward in her chair and hit the desk with both fists. "He *did*."

"Would you be as convinced if you'd never heard of him before?"

Marti's hands slid from the desk into her lap. Disappointed and defeated, she wilted, her collapse pushing the air out of her in a rush. "Honestly . . . I'm not sure."

Clay looked at her across the desk for a few seconds, wishing he could think of something to say that would cheer her up. But this thing was so complicated and charged with significance he didn't know where to begin, so he copped out. "Maybe if you sleep on it you'll wake up in the morning with a solution to one or two of the things that are puzzling you."

As lame as she found his suggestion, it warmed Marti to have someone she could talk to openly about the situation. "I don't seem to have any other choice."

She got up and slowly walked toward the doorway, her head down, but her mind active, looking for a way through the logical escarpment that stood between her and proof Odessa was responsible for the Blake murder.

Clay followed her into the living room, then moved up so he was beside her. He raised his right hand toward her shoulder, intending to give her a supportive hug. Then, unsure of whether he should follow through, he hesitated.

At exactly that moment, a couple of words from Clay's suggestion came bouncing back from wherever they'd gone in Marti's head, one of them slightly modified: *solution . . . puzzle . . .*

Mouth gaping in amazement, she looked at Clay. "I have to go back to the hospital."

"Why?"

"I've got an idea."

"What is it?"

"Too complicated to explain. I'll talk to you later."

"I should be home around ten. Let me know."

WHEN MARTI ENTERED Two East B, she immediately spotted Harry Evensky sitting at a table by himself, working on the latest newspaper with a pair of blunt scissors. She looked around the dayroom to see if Odessa was watching, but he wasn't there. Evensky looked up as she approached.

She leaned down and spoke in a voice she hoped only he could hear. "I need to talk to you."

"Sure. Go ahead."

"Not here . . . in the interview room."

Evensky scooped the *R*'s he'd cut from the paper into an envelope, then, envelope and scissors in hand, he got up and headed for the dorm wing.

In the interview room, Marti shut the door and turned

to the old man. "Your riddle: What's tall and fair . . . you think it's here but it's really there?"

Evensky's eyebrows lifted and his head craned forward on his neck in anticipation of what she was about to say.

"Is the answer Vernon Odessa?"

The old man's face lit up. "Now, was that so hard?"

CHAPTER 22

"YOU SAW ODESSA outside the hospital one night when you were out, didn't you?" Marti asked the old man.

"I thought you understood that."

"When was it?"

"The night the woman in Blake was killed. I read about her the next day in the paper. I think he did it."

"Why on earth didn't you tell someone?"

"Eventually, when it became clear that the murder wasn't gonna be solved unless I spoke up, I tried, but nobody was willin' to think about what I was sayin'."

"Where did you see him?"

"He came out a side door of the big building where they store stuff and got into a tan rec vehicle."

The tunnel, Marti thought. *Those* were *Odessa's footprints on the floor.* "What happened after he got in the vehicle?"

"It drove away."

"Who was at the wheel?"

"I couldn't tell."

"Did you get the license number?"

Evensky shook his head. "Too dark, and it left too fast. Besides, I wasn't out there takin' notes."

"I may want to talk to you some more about this; but for now, go back to the dayroom and don't tell anyone what we discussed."

"What are *you* gonna do?"

"I don't know. I need time to think."

After Evensky left, Marti hit herself in the head with the palm of her hand. Odessa had help. *That's* how he got out. Someone went down to seclusion after he was locked in and released him. The same person must have unlocked the tunnel door and then gone upstairs and out of the building to the vehicle they left in.

But who would do such a thing?

She paced the room, trying to fit various people on the staff into the picture, but failed to make any progress, probably because she hadn't yet come up with any motive for such behavior.

Motive . . .

That approach stumped her too.

Motive . . . think . . .

She finally realized she was being too logical. She wasn't letting her mind run free.

Okay . . . open up . . . let the possibilities in . . . don't get in the way . . .

Somebody in the hospital had a grudge against the victim and talked Odessa into killing her for them . . .

Not bad, but even that was too logical. Odessa was a creature of emotion. He wasn't a contract killer. He'd certainly kill a stranger, but she had to fit his victim profile.

Try again.

Somebody in the hospital had a warped sense of adventure. They longed to kill someone themselves, but didn't have the nerve . . .

Boy, was that sick. Could someone that mentally ill hold down a job?

Been done before. Jeffery Dahmer worked at a chocolate factory.

C'mon, try again. Get creative . . .

Her mind went arid for about twenty seconds, then she hit the mother of all creativity.

Jesus, was that idea out there. She tried to discard it and find more fertile ground, but it wouldn't go away. Giving it a little more consideration, she thought back to her reading of Odessa's file when she first arrived. *Is to be given no neurotropic drugs . . .*

That fits.

And Odessa's explanation for behaving himself at Gibson but not at his previous hospital.

Another fit.

His transfer initiated shortly after . . .

Marti's palms began to sweat as one more fact locked into place.

She left the interview room and went to the nursing station, where she found the night nurse.

"Olivia, when was the decision made to use the old seclusion facility for Odessa?"

"It's a standing order from Dr. Quinn that if Odessa ever becomes violent, he's to be locked down there. The directive is posted on the glass by the medication work area."

"May I see it?"

"Of course."

They went into the nursing station, where Marti noted that the directive was dated just two months before the night Odessa had his behavioral lapse, almost as though . . . "I notice the order doesn't say anything about suspending the usual three-hour log check. When was that procedure initiated?"

"The night we had to forcibly control him. Dr. Quinn spoke to us personally about it. He wanted him to be down there in the dark, totally cut off from any human contact. He wouldn't even let anyone take food to him. It sounded kind of cruel to me, but as I said earlier, Dr. Quinn wanted Odessa to have no doubts about how seriously we viewed that kind of behavior."

"Do you remember what time Odessa was sent to seclusion?"

"I think it was around eight o'clock."

"And Quinn was in the hospital then?"

"He might have been here, or maybe someone called him."

"But you didn't."

"No."

"How long was it between the time Odessa was locked up and Quinn appeared on the ward to lay out the additional rules?"

Olivia thought about it a moment. "Around an hour."

"Okay, thanks. Is there an outside phone book in here?"

Olivia showed Marti the directory, then went off to her duties.

Marti suspected that Quinn would have an unlisted number, but to her surprise she was wrong. Using a pen from a cache in a leather cylinder near the phone, she jotted his address on a nearby notepad. She tore off the top sheet and carried it back into the dayroom, where she headed for the table where Harry Evensky was back at work cutting *R*'s out of the paper.

He looked up at her approach. "That nurse help you figure out what you're gonna do next?"

"You said you lived around here all your life. Do you know where Claiborne Road is?"

"Gimme that piece of paper and I'll draw you a map."

MARTI PULLED TO a stop at the big wrought-iron gates and studied Oren Quinn's house in the failing light. Despite her dislike of the man, she grudgingly had to admire his home, a fairy-tale mansion built in the shape of a widely spread *V* with the arms joining at a half-circle turret. The two wings of the house were clad in cobblestones with red-brick trim around the windows. The turret was mostly red brick with patches of cobblestones. It seemed like a place that would be home to a man with no dark secrets. But if she was right about Quinn, that would be far from the truth.

As she looked at the house, the two lanterns beside the marble flanking the entrance came on, startling her.

Was Quinn back early from his meeting?

She hoped not, because she needed the freedom his absence gave her.

She watched the house, waiting for more lights to come on, but the rest of the house remained dark. So the two fixtures by the door were probably just on a timer. She scanned the gates in front of her car looking for a security camera.

None there.

The entire estate was surrounded by a wrought-iron

fence at least seven feet tall. It wouldn't be a cinch to climb over, but it was doable. The estate, which appeared to consist of about four acres of grounds, was mostly lawn strategically interspersed with small groupings of evergreens. But where to go in?

The land bordering the property on the right was scrubby pasture that wouldn't provide any cover. But on the left and behind it, there was an orderly pine forest that was probably eventually going to be harvested for paper pulp.

The choice wasn't difficult.

MARTI HOISTED HERSELF over the pointed tips of the fence and dropped to the grass behind Quinn's house. Half expecting to suddenly hear a siren and be blinded by a spotlight, she quickly got her balance and sprinted for a large bronze statue of a wood nymph that faced the house over a bed of some kind of plant with lush red flowers.

From behind the statue, Marti scanned the back of the house, looking for any sign of life, but she saw no movement. The only light was one over a door that opened onto a columned walkway to the garage.

Taking a deep breath, Marti darted from behind the statue, took a direct route to the house, and flattened her back against the cobblestone wall.

Still no sirens or additional lights.

She ducked below a bank of oval windows and scuttled to the columned walkway, which was shielded from the road out front by the angled wing of the house. Protected from view by anyone passing the house by car, she moved confidently to the end of the walkway and tried the door to the garage. It was, of course, locked.

She played her flashlight through one of the mullioned glass panes and tried to see inside, but the angle was so poor she didn't learn anything.

If you didn't count trespassing, Marti hadn't so far done anything illegal. But that was about to change. Lacking the skill of Harry Evensky with his paper clips, she turned her flashlight around and drove the handle through one of the panes in the door.

The sound of breaking glass was much louder than she'd anticipated, but once again it didn't kick off any alarm . . . at least not one she could hear. Aware that a control panel at some security service or even at the sheriff's office might that very minute be signaling the breakage, she figured she might have only a few minutes before someone arrived to see what was going on.

She cleared away the sharp edges of the broken pane, reached inside, and opened the door.

She flicked on the light switch by the entrance, but still couldn't see anything because the main part of the garage was around a corner. When she was beyond that obstruction, her hopes were destroyed, for the garage, big enough for two cars and the other vehicle she hoped to find, was empty.

How can that be? Everything about the idea that had brought her there fit together . . . It was insane, of course, but at the same time it explained almost everything. So where was the proof?

Was she wrong about Quinn?

Had she concocted this wild hypothesis simply because she disliked him so much?

Whatever the explanation, she had accomplished nothing by coming here. And she needed now to get back to her car.

She was on the columned walkway heading away from the garage, when something that had been subconsciously troubling her made her stop and turn around.

The rear of the garage extended into the backyard at least ten feet beyond the walkway, but . . .

She returned to the door she'd damaged, went inside, and again turned on the garage lights—which also controlled a light in the admitting alcove.

The left end of the alcove was no more than two feet away.

She went back into the main part of the garage and sighted along the wall separating it from the alcove, alternately looking on one side then the other.

It was just as she'd thought. The back wall of the garage was in line with the same wall of the alcove, which meant . . .

This was all taking too long, but with her curiosity now aroused, she was willing to risk being caught to explore the idea now demanding her attention.

She went outside, left the walkway, and checked the back wall of the garage, where she saw no windows or doors. There were two windows on the far side of the garage, but both were placed well toward the front. So she was right . . .

There was a hidden room in the rear of the garage.

CHAPTER 23

MARTI RETURNED TO the garage and studied the back wall, which was lined with pegboard. Hanging on the boards were all the usual garden tools one would need to keep up the grounds, and all looked well used.

She walked down the wall looking for places where the joints between the pegboard occurred at the same place as those in the baseboard.

There . . .

She knelt and played her flashlight over the joined baseboards at a raking angle. They were so cleverly done that casual inspection would not have revealed it, but the overlap was not sealed with paint.

About three feet farther on, she found another spot like the first. And three feet beyond that, another.

So how was the hidden door opened?

Thinking that one of the hanging tools might actually be a switch of some kind, she went back to the left end of the wall and worked her way down, adjusting each tool

on its hanger. But even after she'd manipulated every implement on the boards, she still hadn't found the way in.

By now, she was so invested in what she was doing
she didn't even think about how much time was elapsing.

There was a workbench on the wall that separated the
main part of the garage from the entry alcove. Starting at
the right end of the bench, she ran her fingers lightly
along the underside of the top. When she reached the opposite end, she felt an obstruction: a metal housing
capped with a button.

She pressed the button and the garage was filled with
the sound of activated levers and pistons. The garage wall
parted in the center exactly at one of the suspect joints,
and a section on each side that ended at the other joints
she'd identified swung open.

Inside was a tan rec vehicle.

Marti entered the hidden room and went around to the
door of the big bus. Before trying the door to the vehicle's living area, she looked around at the bench that
ringed the room. From the circuit boards, soldering
equipment, and spools of wire littering the bench it was
obvious this was an electronics lab, exactly what she expected to find.

The door to the rec vehicle wasn't locked. She
climbed the metal steps and went inside, where she found
that the interior had been completely gutted and re-
worked. The result looked like a CIA listening post with
a big comfortable chair bolted to the floor in front of an
instrument panel containing stacked power supplies on
each side of two tiers of oscilloscope monitors. Below
the panel was a stainless-steel work surface, where Quinn
probably took notes.

There was a wall across the rear of the vehicle with a

door in it. Curious as to what lay beyond, Marti turned
the knob and pulled the door open. Inside was a small
space with a shower on one side and a small chest of
drawers under a mirror on the other. In the top two drawers she found some large bath towels; in the bottom, a
box of rubber gloves and another of surgical shoe covers.

Faced with clear evidence that the wild idea she'd followed to come here had hit the mark, Marti began to feel
ill.

How could a man with Quinn's standing in the scientific and medical community be capable of what he'd
done? She'd believed from the moment she'd met him
that he was rude and arrogant. But she had no idea someone who'd achieved what he had could be so depraved.
She'd never accepted genius and insanity as different
sides of the same coin, but this changed all that. She was
now a convert.

"I'M CONVINCED THE maximum depth we'll ever be
able to record from with noninvasive techniques is three
to four millimeters," John Casey said. "It's all a function
of electrode quality and I'd have to say we've got the best
in the world."

"What do you think about that, Oren?" Jackson
Hunter asked.

Oren Quinn detested braggarts and Casey was among
the worst.

Best in the world . . .

Quinn had electrodes fifteen times better than that, but
he'd told no one. He didn't know why he came to these
mixers; he didn't like them and he didn't like most of the
people there. He attended meetings like this only because

he felt that as the leader in the field he was obligated to keep everybody else on the right path.

"John, you're underestimating human ingenuity," Quinn said. "Four millimeters is not only achievable, it's surpassable."

"Where's your evidence?" Casey sneered.

"Ask the question tomorrow during the panel discussion, and I'll show you."

Quinn had brought some of his old four-millimeter data to show if his hand was forced. Unlike most scientists he didn't feel the need to run to a microphone every time he made a little discovery. To his mind, the true scientist was driven by the need to know, not a desire to strut. In his case, he published just enough of his work to maintain his credibility and allow him to show the misguided in the field the correct path. That was his chosen philanthropy. The books and the patents were done just for the money, so his research wouldn't be dependent on the cubic zirconia staffing NIH study sections.

All he really cared about was understanding the human brain. It mattered not if anyone else shared in his knowledge. It was enough that he knew. And he *must* know all. It was what he was born to do.

Quinn was spared further inane conversation with the two men by the sound of his cell phone. He excused himself and stepped aside to answer the call.

But this was no ordinary call, because it came from the automated dialer he'd installed in the hidden room where he kept his mobile EEG lab. The dialer was linked to a set of cameras that relayed photos to his phone of anyone who entered the room without inactivating the call mechanism.

And who was in those photos?

Marti Segerson.

Quinn rarely cursed. But seeing Marti caught in the camera's lens as she reached for the door of his mobile lab, he muttered, "Damn that woman." And he actually moaned when he saw her open the door to the shower room, his reaction attracting curious stares from the two men he'd been talking to.

He harbored no illusions about the seriousness of what he'd just seen. If Segerson was in his garage, she'd probably figured out everything. And no one would understand what had motivated him. That could mean his life was over.

But Oren Quinn was not a man who jumped to conclusions, nor was he a quitter. *Put yourself in her place,* he thought. *What would you do next?*

I'd gather as much evidence as I could so no one would doubt my story.

But was she that careful?

He didn't know, but he was certainly going to find out before he accepted the loss of all he'd worked for.

If I were her, and I hadn't been there already, I'd find a way to get into my research office, Quinn thought, wishing he'd been more careful about what he kept there.

Hoping it wasn't too late, he punched the number for Gibson's security office into his phone and waited for an answer.

TOMMY JOYNER'S GRANDFATHER had been a cop in Jackson, his father retired as a lieutenant from the Memphis force, and his older brother was a sergeant in Nashville, so it was natural that Tommy would seek employment in the same profession. But an abnormality in his retinas that had caused them to detach numerous times had so damaged his eyesight, he couldn't pass the physical for any real police force. As a result he'd had to settle for security work.

Tommy's daddy had told him it didn't matter what a man did in life as long as he did it to the best of his ability. So Tommy was as diligent and loyal an employee as Gibson had. But he still sometimes made bad decisions, such as leaving the security cell phone in the office with the TV on tonight when he went to the john, so he didn't hear Quinn's call.

QUINN LET THE phone ring ten times before giving up in anger. He shoved his phone back in his jacket pocket then scanned the crowd, looking for Carl Hatch, the symposium organizer. At six foot six, Hatch was easy to spot and Quinn found him in just a few seconds. Consumed with dread, Quinn threaded his way through the throng to Hatch's side.

"Carl, I'm sorry to do this to you, but I've got an emergency at home and I have to leave."

Hatch's face showed his disappointment at losing Quinn on tomorrow's panel. "I understand. You go and don't worry about us, we'll do fine. Hope everything works out."

So the hell do I, Quinn thought, practically running from the room.

CHAPTER 24

MARTI BELIEVED THAT her discovery of the mobile EEG lab was solid evidence Quinn and Odessa were both involved in the Blake murder. But her experience, in which even her eyewitness identification of Odessa as her sister's killer had not persuaded the Los Angeles DA to prosecute him, made her want more proof, especially since she still didn't understand why Odessa came back to the hospital after the murder.

So where should she look now?

The office in Quinn's research lab seemed the most likely place. If the door to the lab had contained a glass panel, she'd have just gone back to the hospital and broken it as she had the garage door. But the lab door was solid oak. There was no way she could force her way in through it. Fortunately, she had an answer for that.

· · ·

MARTI KNOCKED GENTLY on the sleeping room in the dorm wing of Two East B.

"Who's there?" a voice inside said.

"Dr. Segerson."

The door swung open and Harry Evensky looked out at her with a pleased expression. "Did you figure out what to do next?"

"Is anyone else in there?"

"No. The guy who won't talk is in the john. . . . Don't ask what he's doin', you don't want to know. My other roommate, Chick, is under dorm lockdown."

"That's what I heard."

"I don't know what happened, he just lost it at dinner . . . knocked over a cart and started screamin' at the cooks. And the food ain't that bad. You gonna talk to him?"

"Tomorrow. Right now, we've got more important things to do. May I come in?"

"Sure."

The old man stepped back and Marti went inside, then turned and said, "Better shut the door."

Evensky did as she asked.

Marti reached in her pocket, got the two paper clips she'd picked up in her office before coming to the ward, and held them out to the old man. "How'd you like to put these to use for a good cause?"

"You got a lock you want picked?"

"Dr. Quinn's research lab on the fourth floor."

"Dr. Qui—Why do you want in there?"

Marti had thought about what she'd tell Evensky if he asked that question, and she'd decided to be truthful with him . . . to a point. "I think he let Odessa out of solitary the night you saw him."

"Why would he do that?"

"I'm not sure. That's why I want to get in his office and look around."

"Seems to me I could get in big trouble for this."

"If everything works out as I hope, Quinn will soon be in a position where he won't be able to do anything to you."

"Suppose it don't work out?"

"I'll try to take all the blame, but some certainly might spill onto you."

"You know what?"

"What?"

"I don't really care."

Marti got Evensky out of the ward by telling Olivia Barr she was taking him to her office for the second half of a timed memory test they'd begun earlier that day.

Marti hadn't wanted to take her flashlight onto the ward so she'd left it in her office. They picked it up when they crossed over to the west wing through the administrative area. Two minutes later, as they were about to turn the corner on the floor where Quinn had his lab, Marti stopped moving and spoke to the old man. "You wait here and I'll make sure no one's there."

Halfway to Quinn's door, Marti looked behind her.

There was Evensky standing right out in the open. She motioned for him to get back.

Reaching the lab, she tried the door, then knocked.

No answer.

She knocked again and waited a reasonable amount of time before taking a few steps toward where the old man waited. "It's okay, come on . . ."

He didn't reappear.

Thinking the old man might have run out on her, she hurried back to where she'd left him, and there he was.

"I said, 'Come on.'"

"Sorry, sometimes my hearin' ain't too good."

They walked back to the lab together and Marti said, "Okay, show me how it's done."

Evensky looked at her with a furrowed brow. "I didn't know I was gonna have to pick the lock on *this* old gal."

"You can't do it?"

"Not with paper clips. I need somethin' more substantial . . . like a couple pieces of a coat hanger about six inches long."

There were some coat hangers in Marti's office, but she had no idea how she was going to cut one into pieces. Then she remembered the bolt cutter she'd left in the basement.

"I'll need a few minutes to get what you want. In the meantime, come back to the stairs with me and wait out of sight on the vacant floor above this one."

WHATEVER TOMMY JOYNER had eaten that had caused him such intestinal discomfort wasn't about to loosen its grip, and Tommy was beginning to think if he lost any more fluid down the toilet, he'd soon start to shrivel up. In the security office, where the phone had been quiet for nearly three minutes, it began to ring again.

TONGUE PROTRUDING SLIGHTLY from the corner of his mouth as he worked, Harry Evensky knelt in front of the door to Quinn's lab clicking two pieces of coat hanger around inside the old lock. Marti glanced again down the hall toward the steps, worried that at any moment some-one might come around the corner and see them. Look-ing back at the old man and the sweat pearling on his forehead, she began to doubt he'd be able to do the job. But suddenly there was a click from inside the lock mechanism. Evensky stood up and opened the door with a flourish.

"Had you worried, didn't I?"

"Not for a minute," Marti said.

The only windows in the lab were on the right, facing some lawn and the woods bordering the creek Evensky had followed the night he'd appeared in Marti's bed-room. Having no idea what the night security man's rou-tine was, it seemed possible he might that very minute be taking a tour of the grounds and would notice if they turned on the lab's lights. So she left them off. Worried that the guard might even see her flashlight, she went to the windows and made sure all the blinds were closed.

She then led Evensky to Quinn's office door. "Time for you to go back to work, Harry."

The old man looked up at her. "You called me 'Harry' . . . like we were friends. That was nice. Can I call you by your first name?"

"Only when we're alone."

"Perfect. It'll be like another secret we have together. It's Marti, right?"

"Yes."

"I like it."

"Now get us in this office."

"Sure thing, Marti."

And he did, using his paper clips so effectively it took only a few seconds, explaining his speed on this lock with two words, "Cheap goods."

Because Quinn's office had no windows, Marti felt comfortable in turning on the lights. To keep an eye on the lab door to the hallway, she left the office door open.

She then went to Quinn's desk and tried the drawers, only to find them locked as well.

"Harry, can you open these?"

Harry looked at her as if to say, "Is there any doubt in your mind?"

"Sorry, will you *please* open this desk."

And he did, with almost no effort. While Marti started through the drawers' contents Harry tried to open a big walnut armoire against the left wall. But this, too, needed his lock-picking skills.

Marti found nothing of interest in the first drawer she examined, nor the second. She was just pulling out the third when Harry said, "Hey, look at this."

Joining him at the armoire, where both its doors were now standing open, he showed her a DVD case. "This has your name on it."

She took the case and looked at the label on the spine. Marti Segerson . . . He wasn't joking.

There was a DVD player and a TV on a stand to the right of the desk. Marti carried the DVD to the stand, turned everything on and slipped the disc into the player. Picking up the DVD remote control from beside the TV, she hit PLAY.

DOWN IN THE security office Tommy Joyner felt as if he could finally pull up his pants and rejoin the rest of the world. As he opened the bathroom door, the ring of the phone sent him scrambling to reach it.

"Security."

"This is Oren Quinn. Where the hell have you been?"

"I was . . ."

"Never mind. I have reason to believe someone will try to break into my research office tonight. She may be up there right now."

"Don't you worry, Dr. Quinn. I'm on my way."

CHAPTER 25

THE DVD MARTI had put in Quinn's player ran for a few seconds with no picture, then an image abruptly appeared. And it made Marti gasp, for it was a film of her last boyfriend showing him from the lower ribs up, on his back, in bed, breathing hard. At the bottom of the frame two feminine hands could be seen splayed across his chest. Clearly this was a sex film with the camera being held by someone just behind the woman straddling him.

"Jesus, would you look at that," Harry murmured.

Marti was so shocked, she had no reply. How could Quinn have obtained such a film? Had this guy been a porno actor before he went to medical school? But he looked the same as when she'd last seen him. Surely he wasn't doing porno films and a surgical residency at the same time. And why was her name on the thing?

Then the camera turned to a new angle. As it rotated, she saw the wall behind the bed, then a chair with clothes thrown over it, the edge of a dresser, the dresser mirror . . .

Oh my God . . .

In the reflection from the mirror, Marti saw that the woman on top of her boyfriend was *her.* And there *was* no cameraman.

While her mind tried in vain to comprehend what she was watching, the scene abruptly ended and for a few seconds there was just darkness on the screen. Then, the sensation of movement . . . someone falling . . . struggling . . . a door opening . . . but more darkness beyond. More movement . . . turning . . . advancing . . .

Suddenly there was light and she saw on the screen . . . Harry Evensky . . .

In her bedroom.

"That's *me*," Harry said. "I didn't know you had a camera in your house that night."

"I didn't," Marti murmured.

The screen went dark.

Stunned, Marti stood in front of the TV, too numb to move . . . too confused to think.

The disc continued playing, but there were no more images on it.

Noting that she wasn't reacting, Harry took the control from her and pressed fast forward.

After a few seconds he turned it off. "Doesn't seem to be any more on there." He turned to Marti. "I'm sorry for seein' you . . . in your birthday suit, but what *was* that?"

Marti was so deep in thought she didn't reply. She was thinking about the first day she and Quinn had met at the scientific meeting in D.C. and his wild idea about theoretically being able to make memory movies. Except he wasn't talking about something that someday might be . . . he'd already perfected it . . . and had used it on her.

She *had* been drugged the day of the mind-reading test. And while she was unconscious he had raped her mind.

The enormity of this conclusion made her want to reject it. Memory movies . . . it wasn't possible . . . couldn't be done. But as difficult as it was to accept such a crazy explanation, she couldn't discard it, because it was the only thing that would account for what she'd just seen.

With her resistance to the concept of memory movies shattered, her mind began to fit that reality into other things she'd learned since arriving at Gibson. The experiment Nadine had shown her where long-term memories of mice once again became as fragile as short-term memories when those memories were tapped into . . .

Tapped into . . .

By the animal remembering or . . . electrical stimulation . . . Nadine didn't say that but . . .

That's why she had no memory of Harry coming to her room—the act of stimulating and recording a memory must erase it.

Must erase it . . .

She turned to the armoire where Harry had found the disc, and she saw others, a long row of them, arranged alphabetically by the names on the spines. She began scanning the names in reverse alphabetical order.

There . . .

Vernon Odessa.

Hands shaking in anticipation of what she was about to see, Marti took Odessa's disc from the shelf and slid it out of its case. She carried it to the player, removed her disc, and put Odessa's in.

Harry handed her the controls. Did she really want to do this?

No . . . and yes.

Her finger pressed PLAY and the machine began running.

Darkness . . . darkness . . . then the dim image of her sister struggling in bed. Mercifully, there was no sound so she couldn't hear Lee's voice as she tried to buck Odessa off her and remove his hand from her throat. Then a blur appeared in the upper right of the screen . . . Odessa's hammer coming down.

Unable to take any more, Marti shut it off.

Extremely shaken at seeing Lee's murder through Odessa's eyes, Marti was still capable of constructive thought.

This was why Odessa had passed the brain fingerprint test . . . Quinn had Odessa's memory of Lee on tape and because of that, Odessa no longer possessed it. And Molly Norman . . . she must have known Quinn let Odessa out of seclusion the night of the Blake murder. To keep her quiet, Quinn had erased *all* her memories, giving her total amnesia.

Suddenly hearing the sound of a key in the lab door, Marti darted for the light switch and flicked it off. Just as she eased the office door shut, and Harry closed the armoire, she saw a security guard come into the lab.

"Could you tell who it is?" Harry whispered.

"Security," Marti whispered back.

"Did he see you?"

"Don't think so."

"What do we do now?"

Marti had been so focused on Quinn's desk and the films she hadn't really paid much attention to the layout of the office. But from her earlier visit the day Quinn coerced her into taking the mind-reading test, she thought there was a side door in the right wall behind the TV stand.

She played her flashlight in that direction and saw what she was looking for. "We get out of here . . . over there."

Harry reached the door first and found it locked. "Boy, this guy doesn't leave anything open," he whispered.

IN THE LAB, Tommy Joyner had turned on the lights and was checking to make sure no one was crouching behind any of the equipment or cabinetry. Satisfied that the lab was secure, he headed for Quinn's office.

HARRY MADE SHORT work of picking his third lock of the night, and he and Marti slipped into the adjacent room just as Joyner opened the office door. Once again Marti didn't believe they were seen. But they still might be trapped. If they were caught, the guard would likely call Quinn and tell him what was going on. That would be disastrous, for then he'd know she was on to him, and she wasn't convinced she had enough evidence yet to persuade anyone else to accept what would sound like an unbelievable story.

She played her flashlight around the room and saw a lot of electronic equipment and a big dental chair in the center of the room. This could be where Quinn made his memory movies. But was there a way out? Moving her flashlight to the right, she found a door that must lead back into the lab.

Too risky.

They'd have to cross the entire lab to get to the hall. She raked her light to the left, down a wall of cabinets and banks of stacked power supplies . . . and found another door.

With Marti holding the light for Harry, he picked that lock too, and once again they escaped just as Joyner came in from the opposite side.

They were now in the room where Marti had been drugged the day of the mind-reading test and she could see now how easy it had been for Quinn and Nadine to move her from there into the chair next door to roam through her brain.

The door that led to the last room in the series was unlocked, so this time they evaded detection by a safer margin. But even as they moved on, Marti knew they were about to run out of real estate. And she was right, for this time there was just a blank wall where all the other means of escape had been.

And what was worse . . .

She played her light onto the wall where every other room had a door to the lab.

Cabinets . . . nothing but cabinets.

Angry at not being smarter, she whipped her light around and raked the back wall with it. Because her view was obscured by some white coats on a hook, she almost didn't see the doorknob. When she did, her hopes rose.

Harry saw it too and beat her to the spot. So he was the first to discover he needed to work his magic again. He wasn't quite as fast this time, and he was still working when they heard Joyner mistakenly key the unlocked door from the next room.

Joyner came in just as Harry opened the back door. But the security guard's line of sight to the rear of the room was blocked by the door he'd just opened, allowing Marti and Harry to get out unseen. Nor did he hear them, because Marti had the foresight to ease the door shut behind them.

Marti and Harry found themselves in the back hallway, which led to the stairwell each ward used to reach the cafeteria, which meant they could now either go down the rear stairs or circle around past the entrance to Quinn's lab and escape the front way.

It wasn't an easy choice. If they chose the back route and the security guard came out the way they just had, he'd hear them on the creaky old stairs and might give chase. On the other hand, if they picked the alternate route and he left the lab the way he came in, they'd run right into him.

"Over here," Marti said, pulling Harry toward the mesh door that guarded the back stairs.

IN THE ROOM they'd just left, Joyner walked to the rear door and tried the knob to see if this one was unlocked too. Finding it secured, he used his key one more time.

AT THE LAST second, the alternate route suddenly seemed a better choice to Marti. She grabbed Harry and veered to the right. "No, this way."

The corridor leading to the front stairs was only a few steps away and they were around the corner and out of sight by the time Joyner leaned his head into the hall for a quick look.

Tommy's retinal problem didn't affect his ears. Thinking he heard the sound of soft footfalls from somewhere close by, he came into the hallway and started walking toward the intersecting corridor, where Marti and Harry were still in plain sight.

Just as Tommy was about to turn the corner, his phone rang.

"This is Quinn. What have you found?"

Tommy was so intimidated by Quinn he froze where he stood like a bird dog on point. "Everything is fine, sir. No problems here."

"I want you to spend the rest of your shift in my lab with my office door open so you can see if anyone's in there," Quinn said. "Do not enter my office again unless you do so to apprehend a trespasser. Have I made myself clear?"

"Absolutely, sir. You can count on me."

"That better be true."

DOWN THE HALL, Marti and Harry turned the corner and were no longer visible from the rear corridor.

QUINN WAS IN a short line for the Northwest ticket counter at the Atlanta airport. As he folded his cell phone and put it back in his pocket, the person at the head of the line stepped up to the agent, leaving him two back.

With all that was at stake it was hard waiting his turn, especially since the flight he wanted to catch was leaving in just ten minutes.

Standing there, each second that passed was another knife in his chances of getting on the plane. Then, after an eternity, he was next . . .

But the old woman ahead of him engaged the agent in some interminable conversation, making him want to rush the counter and throw her aside. Quinn's money and influence alone would have made him impatient at being held up by a commoner. But his long career, in which he had never met a mind equal to his, had shown him he was also a superior intellect. So why should *anyone* be helped before him?

Having reached the end of his tolerance, he picked up his bag and charged toward the counter. But before he had to insist on being served, the old woman turned and headed for the concourse.

"One seat on flight eighty-two thirty-three, first class," he said, slapping his credit card on the counter.

The agent's eyes dropped to his keyboard and his fingers began flying over it. "They're about to leave. But I'll call and let them know you're coming. You'll have to hurry. You're lucky the gate is close and the airport isn't very busy tonight."

A few seconds later, as Quinn hurried toward the security check point, clutching his boarding pass, he certainly didn't feel lucky.

VERNON ODESSA RAN his finger lightly along the blade of the case knife he'd been sharpening for hours.

Good. It should do the job nicely.

He thought about the first two people who'd be tasting its bite. He wasn't happy about the very first one, but the second would be a pleasure. The problem was he didn't know when that would be. Soon, he thought, but like most of his life, it was a decision that was out of his hands. And it would come, he was sure, without warning. So he had to be prepared.

He went to his bed and pulled the sheet off the mattress at one end. Hospital policy didn't allow locks on the sleeping room doors so it was possible one of the orderlies or nurses might just barge in at any moment. Working fast, with his back to the door, he used the knife to cut two long, narrow strips from the fabric. He then tucked the damaged sheet back in place. Sitting on the side of the bed opposite the door, he pulled up one leg of his pants and tied the strips snugly around his calf about two inches apart. He then carefully slid the knife behind the strips, tugged his pant leg down, and tried walking.

Not bad . . . not bad at all.

CHAPTER 26

MARTI TOOK HARRY Evensky back to the ward, then she went to her car and drove home, confused about her next move. Her discovery in Quinn's office of the film proving he'd been in her brain and had erased her memory of Harry's visit the night he escaped was only circumstantial evidence he was also responsible for Molly Norman's amnesia.

Circumstantial but convincing . . . at least to her.

The film of her own memories was probably sufficient evidence to charge Quinn with *something* . . . assault, maybe, but that was so minor compared to what she believed he'd done. And even if she did want to proceed with some kind of lesser charge against him, she hadn't been smart enough to take the disc with her when the security guard had interrupted.

As she turned onto the dirt road leading to her cottage, she saw that she was losing her focus. Quinn was not her primary concern. He was important only as a conduit to

Odessa. But wait . . . If Quinn had a film of Lee's murder, maybe he also had one of the Blake killing . . . and it might have even been on the disc she'd been looking at.

Idiot.

She hit the brakes.

That's the one she should have taken.

She sat for a moment with her headlights lighting up the road ahead, considering turning around and going back to the hospital. But she quickly realized it was too soon. That guard might still be in the lab, or close by. Better to wait a few hours and let the situation cool down. Other than her own impatience there was no hurry. Quinn wouldn't even be back until day after tomorrow. Just stay calm.

QUINN GOT OFF the plane in Memphis and hurried to his car in the long-term parking lot close to the terminal, his mind still occupied with trying to think of a way to get rid of the mobile lab when he got back to Linville. He'd cleaned the shower up as best he could after Odessa had used it, but he'd never gotten around to checking the result with Luminol, the chemical any forensic team worth a damn would use to look for blood. But this issue aside, the mere presence of all the equipment in the vehicle would give him away. So he needed it out of his garage and hidden where no one would ever find it. But how could such a trick be accomplished? As he pondered the problem he tried to put the possibility out of his mind that when he got home, he might discover it was already too late.

• • •

IT HAD NOW been two hours since Marti and Harry had been chased from room to room in Quinn's lab. As she passed Clay's cottage on her way back to the hospital she saw from the presence of his truck that he was home from the retirement party he'd attended.

She stopped and looked at Clay's front door, thinking it would sure be a lot more comforting to have Clay with her than Harry Evensky. But she needed Harry. And three seemed like too big a troupe to be sneaking through the hospital's corridors. So, reluctantly, she stepped on the gas.

During the short drive to the hospital, she worked on an explanation for why she would be taking Harry out of the ward again tonight and at such a late hour. By the time she reached the hospital parking lot, she'd decided to just say the memory test he'd been taking required another session.

She'd closed the blinds in Quinn's lab when she and Harry broke in, but it seemed likely that if the overhead lights were now on, she'd be able to see them from the lawn along the building's west wing. And if the lights were on, the security guy was probably still there.

She parked her car at the westernmost part of the lot, got out, and stepped up onto the curb, where she set off on a diagonal course across the newly cut grass.

The lights from the wards on the first three floors were obvious from the outset. The fourth floor, where Quinn's lab was located, looked dark. But she needed a better angle to make sure.

Ten seconds later, because she was looking at the hospital instead of where she was going, she stumbled over a knee-high evergreen tree. Thankful it wasn't a big oak, she untangled herself from the little tree and resumed walking, this time keeping her eyes on the ground.

When she reached what she believed to be as good a vantage point as she could get, she turned her attention back to the hospital. And now there was no doubt . . . a thin rim of light could be seen around each of the windows in Quinn's lab. She couldn't go back up there now. As difficult as it would be, she'd just have to return home and wait a while longer.

QUINN SLOWLY DROVE past his home, appraising it with a suspicious eye. Everything looked just the way he'd left it . . . no crime scene tape strung around the garage . . . no official vehicles in the drive, the only lights on, those that should be. But was it a trap? Were cops hiding on the property, ready to grab him when he appeared?

He drove down to the pine forest and turned around on a wide part of the shoulder. On the way back, he stopped at the eastern end of his land and stared at the house.

Go in or run?

It was as difficult a decision as he ever had to make.

Finally, deciding he had to know one way or the other, he nudged the gas and slowly approached his driveway. When he reached it, he almost drove past, but at the last moment, he turned in.

As tense a situation as this was, his hands weren't sweating, his blood pressure was normal, and his heart was beating at its usual rate. For while it was true he couldn't control what was about to happen, he *could* control his reaction to the situation, and he wasn't going to tremble over it like a child.

He made it to the garage with no surprises. A little

more optimistic now about the next few minutes, he got out of his car and signaled the garage door to open. The fact that it did so without disgorging a contingent of cops was gratifying.

He went into the garage, turned on the lights with his remote, and closed the door behind him. Now believing he already knew the answer to the question that had haunted him all the way back to Memphis, he nevertheless walked to the bench with the hidden button and opened the room where he kept his mobile lab.

And once again, there were no surprises.

Now it was time to create one for Marti Segerson.

ONCE AGAIN MARTI almost stopped at Clay's cottage when she passed it on her way home from the hospital. As much as she wanted to see him and tell him what she'd found, she was afraid such a talk would naturally lead into a discussion about what she was going to do next. And she didn't want to hear any arguments about why she shouldn't try once again to get that disc from Quinn's office. Better to wait and tell Clay what she'd done after it was finished. So once more, she resisted the temptation to see him.

As she walked into her cottage a few minutes later, the phone rang.

"Dr. Segerson . . ."

"Doctor, this is Sheriff Aiken here in Hardeman County . . . I know it's late, but I'd like to talk to you tonight about one of your patients named Vernon Odessa. Would it be okay if I came over? It's extremely important."

Marti's curiosity was intensely aroused. What could

the Hardeman County sheriff want to talk to about? "All right. Do you know how to get here?"

"I believe I do. I'm on the other side of the county right now finishin' up with somethin' we'll be discussin', so it'll take me about an hour to get there."

"I'll see you then."

"One other thing . . . this is a very sensitive matter, so we would need to discuss it in private."

"I understand."

With any other patient and on any other night, Marti would probably have told Aiken to come to the hospital in the morning to talk. But he'd mentioned the one name she'd drop everything to learn more about. And his visit would help pass the time until she could make another run on Quinn's office.

QUINN HUNG UP the pay phone at the Circle K convenience store on the west edge of town and shoved the paper towel he'd used to distort his voice into his pocket. With his first call from the phone, in which he'd pretended to have reached a wrong number, he'd learned that Clay Hulett was indeed in the way, just as he'd feared. With the second call, he'd bought himself a little time to work, but an hour wasn't very long, so he'd have to move fast.

CHAPTER 27

STILL STANDING IN front of the Circle K, Quinn took out his cell phone and called the hospital. Without waiting for the call menu to finish reciting all the options when the connection was made, he punched in the number for the nursing station on Two East B.

"This is Quinn. I want Vernon Odessa sent down to seclusion in the basement immediately for lack of cooperation with a member of the medical staff. I will not have the patients obstructing our routines. Have I made myself clear? This is to be done immediately. He's to be put in cell number three. I'll call back in a few minutes to verify that my orders have been carried out."

Quinn went to his car and got in. He was under no illusion that this was all going to end the way he wanted. There was just too much out of his control. He didn't even know how Segerson had figured out what had actually taken place the night of the Blake murder. And she must have done so, or she wouldn't have been in his hid-

den room. But on the positive side, the lack of police activity around his home tonight suggested she hadn't yet
gone to the authorities with what she knew.

Even if everything did work out tonight, it would be
the end of Odessa's usefulness, which was truly a
shame. And Segerson . . . she was a bright, resourceful
woman with the potential to be a fine psychiatrist. Her
death would be an even greater loss. If she had only
stayed in California, none of this would have happened.

IT WAS PAST the time for lights out on Two East B, but
Harry Evensky was sitting on the edge of his bed reading
a "Spider Man" comic book in the beam of a penlight.
Even though it was a pretty simple story, he found it hard
to concentrate because he was still tingling from his
caper with Marti earlier in the evening. He liked the word
caper and had long wanted to be part of one. But to this
day, he'd only been involved in two . . . the one tonight
and the visit to Marti's home while she slept. And both of
them had made him want more.

He looked at the empty bed normally occupied by
Chick, who was still on ward lockdown for his outburst
in the cafeteria. *That* was a caper . . . not as good as his
two, but it *was* one. Old Chick had manufactured a caper
right under everyone's nose.

He reflected for a moment on how Chick's caper was
so out of character; then Harry's other roommate, Frank
Hoyt, or was it Holt, he wasn't sure because Frank didn't
talk, began to snore. Harry got up, walked over to Frank's
bed, and shook him by the arm. His sleep disturbed,

Frank rolled onto his side, where, except for an occasional lip smacking, he was usually quiet.

As Harry was walking back to his bed, he was galvanized by the sound of clanking chains from the hallway. Pretty sure he knew what that meant, he went to the door and looked out.

Sure enough, two of the night orderlies were taking Odessa out the back door in chains, and they were almost certainly headed for the basement.

Convinced another woman would be killed that night, Harry was infused with purpose. . . . He had to tell Marti what was happening. He tossed the penlight onto his bed, then bolted from his room and charged down the hall to the dimly lit dayroom, where he headed for the nursing station.

Seeing him approaching, Olivia Barr came out to meet him.

"I have to use the phone."

"Why?"

"I need to tell Dr. Segerson somethin' important."

"I'm sure it can wait until tomorrow."

"It can't. She'll want to hear what I have to tell her, believe that."

The remaining orderly, a stocky guy with long hair and a mustache, came up behind Harry and took him by the arm. "C'mon, Mr. Evensky. Go back to bed. You can talk to Dr. Segerson in the morning."

Harry pulled his arm free. "Tomorrow will be too late, you idiot." He turned and tried to push past Olivia, but the orderly rushed in and got him in a bear hug from behind. Harry kicked and flailed to get free, but he was no match for the younger, heavier man. "Damn your hide, let me go. Somebody's gonna die tonight."

Mistaking Harry's last comment for a threat, Olivia said, "Just hold him right there."

She went into the nursing station, got a small bottle from the refrigerator, and quickly plunged the needle of a syringe through the rubber top. Even though Harry put up a good fight, the needle was soon in his arm, dispensing the Haldol and Ativan cocktail that would calm him down.

"Now let him cool off in the lockdown," Olivia said, putting the plastic cover back on the syringe needle.

"Chickadee is in there already," the orderly reminded her.

"Take him down to the first floor, then."

By now Libby Sullivan, the redheaded junior nurse on the night shift, had joined the group.

"Libby will get the doors as you go," Olivia said. "I'll let them know you're coming."

"You all are aidin' and abettin' a felony," Harry shouted as the orderly hauled him toward the door. "I know what I'm talkin' about. Will someone listen to me? There'll be blood on your hands if you don't."

Olivia went into the nursing station and punched in the extension for One East. "Carrie, this is Olivia on two. Hope you don't have anyone in lockdown because I'm sending you one of ours for a time-out. . . . You don't? Good. . . . We rarely have two go off on the same night, but that's what we're dealing with. He's been given a bolus of H and A so he shouldn't be any trouble. Thanks. Any time we can reciprocate . . ."

As she hung up, Olivia realized it wasn't *two* of her patients that had warranted punishment tonight. Counting Vernon Odessa, it was *three*. Months without any problems like this, then all these on the same night. If she

didn't know better, she'd think the three events were
somehow related.

VERNON ODESSA'S OPPORTUNITY had come sooner
than expected. Now it was up to him to make the most of
it. But was he able to take the first hurdle? And could it
be done in the dark? Not yet ready to proceed, he sat on
the floor of his dank cell, closed his eyes, and tried to prepare himself.

IN THE FIRST floor lockdown, Harry Evensky stood at
the heavy Plexiglas panel that allowed him to be viewed
from the hall, screaming . . . pleading to be taken to a
phone, his fist slamming against the door. But the orderly
who'd just locked him in was already thinking about
something else.

QUINN PARKED HIS car well off the shoulder, being
careful to choose a spot that wasn't so soft he might get
stuck. He was also worried about imprints his tires might
leave that could be used to link him to this place. Because
of the latter, he'd drive to Jackson tomorrow first thing
and have them all replaced, and he'd pay cash so there
was no record of the transaction. He wasn't happy that
he'd had to use his own car, but in the time available
there just wasn't any other option.

He checked the road in both directions.

No one coming.

Already wearing surgical booties over his shoes so he
wouldn't leave any identifiable footprints, he grabbed the

flashlight and the plastic bag on the seat beside him and got out of the car. Before setting off down the dusty farm road into the cotton field beside the car, he stopped at the license plate and wrapped the plastic bag around it so the numbers were obscured.

There was a three-quarter moon in the sky providing enough illumination that Quinn didn't have to use his flashlight as he traveled along the hedgerow. But it also made it more likely he could be seen by anyone passing on the road where he'd parked. To minimize that possibility he tried to stay in the hedgerow's shadows.

About seventy yards from where he'd started walking he came to an intersecting hedgerow that ran to his left. This one didn't have a road beside it but the cotton field it bordered was no impediment to his progress. And he was now shielded from the road.

Worried that this was taking too much time, he picked up the pace and hurried along the second hedgerow for about eighty yards. Then, through a break in the trees he saw he was almost directly across from the barn he'd chosen before making his calls from the Circle K.

Quinn picked his way through the trees and bushes and ducked through the metal fencing surrounding the pasture on the other side. There was now nothing shielding him from the road, but the barn obstructed the view of anyone in the farmhouse, so he didn't feel too uncomfortable using his flashlight to avoid the piles of horse dung that littered his route.

He soon arrived at the big open side door of the barn and went inside. Playing his light over the interior, he quickly found the ladder to the hayloft. But before going up, he needed to find some rope.

He wandered down the row of stalls, looking in all the

places where he imagined a coil of rope might hang, but found none. Then he encountered a horse in one of the stalls. He'd never been that close to a horse before, and he was surprised at how large its eyes were and how expressive. He considered freeing it, but a big portion of the fenced area just outside the barn could be seen from the house. And if someone there saw the horse roaming around loose, they might come down to lock him up and ruin everything.

It was a hard decision, but the welfare of humans had to come before animals. It was even in the Bible . . . or at least he thought so. Of course, since the human in this case was Quinn, it didn't really matter whether it was there or not.

But that was all a moot issue until he found some rope.

You would think if there was a horse, there would be some rope nearby. But there wasn't. What kind of farmers were these people anyway?

After another futile two minutes looking for rope, the time crunch began to get serious. Damn it, he should have brought it with him. Now that he couldn't find any in the barn it was easy to forget he'd come without it because he couldn't think where to get some at that hour anywhere else either.

He'd chosen this barn because he'd driven past it every day on the way to the hospital and knew the layout was perfect . . . had even seen them storing hay in the loft.

But without rope how could he . . .

Then he got an idea.

He hadn't climbed a ladder in twenty years. And he discovered as he ascended to the hayloft that he wasn't as agile as he imagined. And by the time he stepped onto the flooring up there, his knees ached.

There was a chance his idea wasn't going to pay off. . . . If they used some kind of cable instead of . . .

But his flashlight quickly showed him that the pulley used to haul hay bales up to the loft was strung with a nice cotton rope.

With his pocketknife, he cut a sufficient length of rope off the pulley and took it back to the ladder, where he wedged one end of the rope between two floorboards and let the other drop to the ground below. Even if the baled hay hadn't been so heavy, working in the dark with only a small flashlight that just couldn't be set anywhere so its beam did much good made it hell trying to get a bale on top of the rope to keep it from coming loose.

But eventually he managed to do it.

Sweating from the exertion, he gathered up an armful of loose hay and piled it on top of the rope on the lip of the loft flooring.

Finished up there, he grabbed the flashlight and backed down the ladder. Reaching solid ground, he went over to the dangling rope and cut it at chest level. After making sure there was no hay on the ground anywhere near the rope, he took out a book of matches and set the tip of the rope on fire.

He watched it for several seconds until the fibers were well lit and the flames were climbing steadily toward the loft. Satisfied that he'd have time to get back to his car or at least be nearly there before the fuse he'd made would set the place on fire, he headed for the big door through which he'd come.

•   •   •

IN THE BASEMENT of Gibson State Hospital, as Vernon Odessa made the first cut with his sharpened case knife, he had to bite his tongue to keep from screaming. He knew no one would hear if he did, but it was a matter of pride that he keep silent.

CHAPTER 28

BREATHING HARD AND sweating like a longshoreman, Quinn unlocked his car with his remote but hung back in the shadows of the hedgerow until he was certain there was no traffic coming. Then he dashed for his car, pausing at the rear just long enough to pull the plastic bag from his license plate. Since he traveled this road regularly, once he was under way, it wouldn't matter if anyone saw his car in the area.

Moving as fast as he could, he went to the driver's door, yanked it open, and piled in sidesaddle so his feet were still outside. He stripped off his surgical shoe covers and stuffed them into the bag he'd used to hide his license plate. His rubber gloves went into the bag next.

As he pulled away from the shoulder, he glanced in the direction of the barn and saw smoke curling around the loft door. He checked his watch. From his call to Segerson to now had taken twenty-three minutes, so he'd have to really hustle to meet the hour deadline he'd set himself.

CLAY HULETT LOOKED at the phone and thought again about calling Marti. He was dying to know what the idea was she'd mentioned before heading back to the hospital after he'd helped her get in touch with the McNairy County sheriff. But it seemed to Clay that if she wanted to talk, the ball was in her court. She *must* have seen his truck when she drove past, heading home a little while ago. So she knew he was there.

Maybe she felt she was imposing too much on him with her problems. And wouldn't that be an unfortunate situation . . . for her to believe such a thing when it wasn't true. Having reasoned himself into taking the initiative, Clay picked up the phone. He entered the first digit of Marti's number and was reaching for the second when he heard the wail of the fire siren. Heeding the call, he slammed the receiver back in its cradle and charged out the door and into his truck as fast as any volunteer in the department.

QUINN MANEUVERED THE mobile EEG lab through the hospital parking lot toward the hidden alcove beside the furniture storage building, not at all happy now to be driving the thing that could help put him in prison. But it could also help keep him safe, which made the situation one of weighing the debits against the credits. And right now, he couldn't see any other way to do things.

•   •   •

IT HAD ONLY been around forty minutes since Sheriff
Aiken had called Marti, but every few minutes she still
looked out the window that gave her a view of the road
to her cottage. She couldn't see Clay's house from the
window, but she'd heard the fire siren and assumed he
was out answering the call. So between wondering what
Aiken wanted to discuss and thinking about her investigation of Quinn and Odessa, she worried about Clay's
safety.

QUINN UNLOCKED THE door to the east wing of the
hospital, darted through it, and headed for the stairs to the
basement. He was carrying a fresh plastic bag containing
a flashlight, a pair of rubber gloves, and some clean surgical shoe covers so Odessa wouldn't get any bat shit on
his shoes when he went through the tunnel. The weakest
part of his plan was that even if Segerson hadn't spoken
to the authorities about whatever she'd learned, she could
have told a friend, like Clay Hulett, the guy he'd seen her
with at the restaurant. But that was just something he'd
have to live with. He'd do what he could, then try to
weather what followed. Maybe he'd succeed, maybe not.

At the foot of the stairs, after unlocking the big door
to the seclusion facility, he flicked on the feeble lights in
the main room and picked up the cell key from the trestle table. He'd given all the ward personnel standing orders that no one was to be placed in any of these cells
without his permission. And it looked like they were following orders because all the cell doors except the one
for number three were standing ajar.

To be absolutely sure no one would overhear his conversation with Odessa, he went to each of the unoccupied

cells and made sure they were empty. Only then did he go to cell number three, where he reached in his pocket and got out the black control box he'd picked up in his office just before coming down there. No way he'd confront Odessa without that.

"It's Quinn, and I *am* prepared. Step away from the door."

Holding the control in his left hand, thumb poised over the button, he keyed the cell lock and pulled the door open.

He expected to see Odessa standing a few feet from the door, eager to get out. Instead, his prize patient was sitting on the floor against the left wall, his legs sticking out of deep shadow that obscured the rest of him.

Senses alerted, Quinn stepped inside. "What's wrong?"

"Nothing," Odessa replied. "Are we going out tonight?"

Quinn had realized from the start that Odessa would be the first suspect the cops would consider when the Blake victim was discovered. Though he believed county sheriffs to be rubes with little investigative ability, he nevertheless wanted to cover his tracks as much as possible.

To make sure Odessa wouldn't give himself away in any trick questioning or other interrogation techniques, Quinn had connected Odessa to the memory movie equipment in the mobile lab right after Odessa had showered following the murder. He'd then taken the memory before it had a chance to move from short-term to long-term storage, where he might never find it.

Because Odessa's short-term memory had been erased before they had returned to Gibson and he had made his way back to his cell through the tunnel while Quinn took the hospital route, Odessa remembered all that part of the trip. But he had no memory of the murder itself. He had deduced what had happened and his role in it when he saw the story of the killing on TV the next day, an event Quinn had anticipated and had accepted as the cost of doing business.

The longer-range version of the black control box Quinn had installed in the mobile lab had ensured Odessa's return to the lab after the murder, but it wasn't needed to get him to go on the hunt. The film of the intended victim Quinn had shown him in the seclusion staging room before they departed and Odessa's predatory personality had made him more than willing to do that without coercion. In Quinn's world such evil was a valuable commodity. So it was with great sadness he had decided that when Odessa returned from dealing with Segerson, he would have to be made like Molly Norman.

Knowing what had happened the last time he was sent to the basement, it was natural that when Quinn sent him there again tonight, he believed he'd be going out again.

"Yes, but this time you'll be on your own."

"How is that going to work?" Odessa replied, still sitting in darkness.

"I discovered your psychiatrist, Segerson, snooping in the mobile lab. I don't know how she learned of its existence but it suggests she's figured out everything . . . or at least enough to be a danger to us."

"And you'd like for me to take care of her."

"Is that a problem?"

"No. I've actually been thinking about her a lot lately. This other problem aside, she's a smart-ass who needs to be taught a lesson. And there's something else about her . . . I can't put my finger on it, but it makes me feel that I'm supposed to hurt her . . . like it's unfinished business."

"This is exactly that . . . business, not pleasure, although I expect the difference may be difficult for you to appreciate. In any event, this one must be done only with a knife . . . no hammer. I don't want your signature on it."

"You said I'm going to be on my own. Where is she?"

"At home, waiting for a fictitious police officer to arrive."

"You did that?"

"I needed to be sure she'd stay put."

"And you think *I'm* the psychopath?"

"What do you mean by that?"

"You may be rich as hell and have the world fooled into thinking you're this genius who writes books and invents shit, but you're just as fucked up in the head as I am."

"I don't think so."

"At least I don't try to fool myself about who I am."

As much as Quinn appreciated Odessa's uniquely wired brain, to be spoken to like that by such an inferior creature got under Quinn's skin. "I hardly think someone like you is qualified to judge me."

Odessa laughed, a guttural snort that sounded to Quinn as if the effort caused him pain.

"Doc, you just proved my point."

Quinn felt like pressing the button under his thumb and holding it down until Odessa screamed for mercy, but there was too much at stake for such an indulgence. Instead, he swallowed his anger and stayed focused. "We don't have time to debate the status of my mental health.

I arranged for Segerson to remain at home for one hour. And that time is rapidly running out."

"Where does she live and how am I going to get there?"

"She's renting a place on the property just east of the hospital grounds, about two hundred yards from our containment fence line. A few days ago, a rotten tree about eighty yards south of the rear wing of this building fell on our fence and flattened it. It hasn't been repaired yet, so you can go on foot and cross over at that point.

"There's a dirt road on the other property almost directly opposite the rear of this building. She lives at the end of that road. But she'll probably be watching out a window for the cop who isn't coming, so don't approach her house by the road. Go through the woods between the road and the highway."

"Any other houses over there?"

"One . . . near the point where the road curves toward the highway. She's much farther in. You don't have to worry about the occupant of the closer house. He'll be gone for at least another hour. When I leave, you go out through the tunnel, and I'll meet you where I left you off last time."

Even though Odessa had returned to his cell through the tunnel the night of the Blake trip, his memory of going the other way had been erased. So Quinn went over the route with him.

"That means when you reach the point where the tunnel branches into four choices, you bear left. You can't get out any other way. At the top of the stairs you'll encounter when you leave the tunnel, go out the door to your left. I'll meet you there and give you the weapon I want you to use."

Quinn threw the plastic bag he'd brought onto the bed. "There's a flashlight in there, some rubber gloves, and shoe covers. Put on the glóves and the shoe covers before you enter the tunnel. Take the covers off after you've cleared the bat droppings and put them in the bag. And bring the bag out with you. Do not leave it behind."

Quinn disliked the tunnel, but knew that later in the evening, after *all* of Odessa's memories were gone and he had become like a newborn child, he would be incapable of finding his own way back through the tunnel to his cell. Quinn would then have to escort him . . . just one more annoyance Quinn would have to tolerate until this situation was resolved. And somehow he'd have to come up with a plausible rationale for why another person at Gibson had suffered a complete loss of memory.

But he couldn't think about that at the moment; maybe later, while Odessa was taking care of Segerson. Right now he had to explain something else to Odessa that had been erased along with the Blake murder. He held out the control box so Odessa could see his thumb poised over the button. "The mobile lab is on the grounds, so I not only have the ability to track your movements for a considerable distance, I have long-range control of you. I'll give you reasonable leeway, but if you stray out of the set limits, I believe you know what will happen. Now come on, we've wasted enough time talking."

"I couldn't agree more," Odessa said, as he got to his feet.

For a second or two after he stood, he remained in the shadows where Quinn could barely discern his outline against the brick wall behind him. Then he came into the light.

When he saw Odessa clearly for the first time, Quinn

gasped, for there was blood on Odessa's neck, and both his hands were covered with it. There was something shiny in his right hand . . . a knife . . . As Quinn's mind reeled with what he was seeing, he thought for the briefest moment that Odessa had killed someone, then as Odessa raised his left hand, turned it palm up, and opened his fingers, revealing what he held there, Quinn knew that all the blood was Odessa's. Because in his palm was the electrode Quinn had implanted in his neck months ago so he could be controlled.

The thought was almost beyond comprehension . . . *Odessa had cut the electrode out of his own body.*

Among the thoughts flooding Quinn's mind was the awareness that he was now in more trouble than he had ever been.

"Now say good-bye, old man," Odessa hissed, suddenly charging across the cell.

Odessa's first knife thrust went into Quinn's belly with such force an inch of the handle disappeared inside him. The power of the blow was so great Quinn's abdominal wall was driven an abnormal distance inward, allowing the tip of the knife to nick his aorta.

Quinn went down on his back with Odessa on top of him. Even if Odessa had known his first thrust had inflicted a mortal wound, it wouldn't have mattered, for he was finally free to be himself. And as he stabbed Quinn again and again, first in the abdomen, then in the chest, driving the knife through Quinn's ribs, crushing them with the force of his blows, Odessa realized he had underestimated the pleasures that could be had with the knife.

And when he finally stood over Quinn's devastated body, Odessa was already thinking of Marti Segerson and how the knife could be used as a phallus . . . penetrating into her deepest reaches where he could become her total master. The thought had come into his mind as something that could be done at his leisure, after she was dead, but then he realized it would be far more fun to do it while she could still appreciate it.

CHAPTER 29

THE THREE-QUARTER MOON was bright enough to navigate by when Odessa was in the open, but made the going tough when he entered the dense woods flanking the road leading to Marti's cottage.

When he had emerged from the storage building after coming through the tunnel at the hospital, he'd replaced his sharpened case knife with a big hunting knife Quinn had waiting for him in the mobile lab. And he found he liked the feel of it in his hand almost as much as a claw hammer. He also had the flashlight Quinn had given him, but it was stuffed in one pocket because he feared that using it might betray him. So he moved forward along the fringe of the woods as a shadowy specter, there one minute, gone the next.

The exertion he was putting forth should have made the fresh wound in his neck throb with pain, but the excitement of killing Quinn and the anticipation of showing Marti what the fox could do dominated all other sensation. Even so, he was aware this would be the final chapter in his life, for he would never allow anyone to lock him up again. And knowing that, he decided to make the most of it. Segerson and Quinn would just be the beginning of the end.

MARTI CHECKED HER watch and looked out the window one more time. It was now eight minutes beyond the hour Sheriff Aiken had said it would take for him to get there.

Eight minutes . . .

Not long enough to worry that he was going to keep her pinned at home to where she couldn't make another run on Quinn's office. Besides, it was probably still too soon to even be thinking about that.

As she turned from the small window overlooking the road, she pivoted to her left, so a split second before the big window with the lake view exploded inward, she saw the dark shape hurtling toward it.

Amid a shower of glass and wood, Odessa hit the floor and stumbled forward, but remained on his feet. Through her confusion and shock, Marti recognized who it was. At nearly the same instant she saw the big knife in his hand. She lunged for her cell phone on the small table by the door. In her confusion, she forgot that Clay was not home, and she punched the preset for his number.

AT THE BARN fire, which was now raging, Clay's face felt like his skin was cooking, but he held on to the throbbing hose and directed its powerful flow at the barn roof, where the intensity of the flames seemed to be turning all the water to steam. He felt his phone vibrate in his pocket, but it was beneath his fireman's protective gear where he couldn't reach it. And even if it had been accessible, he couldn't have taken the time to answer.

ODESSA CHARGED ACROSS the room to Marti and with a vicious swipe of his arm, backhanded the phone from her grip, sending it hurtling into the far wall. Turning to face him, Marti now saw blood streaking his skin under his left jaw line. Believing he must be wounded there, she instinctively brought both her fists around in an arc and slammed them into each side of his neck.

Marti's fist missed the epicenter of the fresh wound where Odessa had cut out Quinn's electrode, but she hit close enough to send him to his knees in pain. She should have finished him then, but her first response had bought her a moment to think and that had reminded her to be afraid of the knife.

So she wasted the edge she'd gained and ran for the back door, which, even with the deadbolt she had to open, she managed to get through and out into the night before Odessa could recover.

To Marti's right was the field in which the flowers and weeds were no more than waist high. If she took the path through it to the creek, Odessa was sure to see her in the moonlight. So her only choice was the woods to her left. She'd traveled the path that led into those woods from the backyard a couple of times since she'd moved in, so she wasn't heading into unknown territory. But as she ran for their protection, she realized she'd be able to see very little once she was inside.

It was about ten yards to the woods, which was a

shade too far, for just as she hit the path, Odessa came out
the back door and saw her. He pulled the flashlight from
his pocket and gave chase. He was a bit slow because,
since Marti had hit him, each step was like another fist
pounding at his wound. But there was no way he was
going to let that stop him.

Hearing him on the porch, Marti believed he'd probably seen her. She couldn't run as fast as she was able because the path was only vaguely apparent before her as a
negative image, an absence of trees rather than a tangible
presence. But she found she could follow it with surprising accuracy, so that even with the hindrance of the dark,
she managed to maintain the lead she'd had going in.

The path followed a circuitous route through the trees,
giving her an occasional glimpse of the beam from
Odessa's flashlight, but largely preventing them from
seeing each other. Marti knew she couldn't just count on
physically outlasting Odessa in a footrace. A root that
might catch her shoe, a turn missed, and he could be on
her. She needed a plan.

At exactly that moment, she ran smack into a tree, and
everything went black.

CHAPTER 30

MARTI REGAINED HER senses just as she hit the ground. Her first perception was of a sharp pain in her forehead where the bark from the big persimmon she'd run into had scraped her skin. If she'd been wearing her glasses, her injuries might have been worse. For a moment she was disoriented, unaware of where she was. But then, the sound of a twig cracking as Odessa stepped on it, mere yards away, brought everything back.

It was too late to get up and run. So she rolled to the side of the path, hoping she wouldn't be blocked by some sapling growing inches away. Her first 180-degree turn put her face into a wet, leafy plant that smelled as though a dog had just urinated on it. Still unimpeded, she kept rolling . . . onto her back . . . then again onto her face . . . onto her back . . .

And that's as far as she got, because she was finally stopped by the sapling she'd been worried about. She couldn't be more than a few feet off the path and she had no idea whether she'd be visible when Odessa got there. So all she could do was wait and hope.

She could hear Odessa breathing hard as he rounded the last curve visually separating them. Then she could see the beam of his flashlight, which to her horror he was raking into the woods on each side of the path as he came toward her.

As Odessa turned his light to her side of the path, she lost sight of a portion of the beam. It was then she realized she was lying under the trunk of a large wind-toppled tree. Maybe he *wouldn't* see her and would just go on past.

ODESSA DIDN'T GET much exercise in the hospital, certainly none that prepared him for this, and he was winded. He'd heard the quail from time to time as he pursued her, but he hadn't actually seen her. Now, he realized, he didn't hear her any more either. So he stopped running to catch his breath and listen more carefully.

MARTI COULD SEE Odessa's legs up to his knees. She was physically in good shape, so she wasn't advertising her presence by labored breathing, but if he decided to lean down and look under the tree just to check it out, there would be nothing she could do. She thought about a preemptive strike . . . try to knock him down . . . and . . .

What?

What would she do then that she couldn't have done with more favorable odds back in the cottage? Still, wouldn't it be better to do *something* before he discovered her and had all the advantage?

ODESSA STOOD, UNMOVING . . . listening . . .

Damn it. Other than his own breathing, there wasn't another sound in the woods. Had she gotten *that* far ahead of him? She didn't have a flashlight, so it didn't seem likely she could have moved fast enough to be out of earshot. And if she'd left the path, she'd have made a lot of noise. No . . . she was nearby and she was hiding.

"I know you're here," he said aloud. "Trying to hide from me, which means you must be afraid. And you know what . . . that's the right reaction, it really is, because when I find you, you'll wish you'd never come to Gibson, that you'd never heard of me. But I'll always have fond memories of you, of the last time I saw you."

As Odessa spoke, he worked the woods with his light.

"Of course you won't look very much like you do now."

Just to the left of the path ahead, the beam of his flashlight picked out a rotten ten-foot-tall stump of a tree that looked as though it might be hollow on the side facing away from the path, an excellent place for a frightened quail to hide.

Playing the light down the path so the rotten stump was illuminated only in the periphery of its beam, he moved forward, his breathing now heavier as he anticipated an end to the chase.

UNDER THE TREE where Marti was hiding, the needle on her stress gauge dropped only a fraction of a point.

Sure, he'd moved away from her tree, but that didn't mean he was leaving.

ODESSA SILENTLY EDGED past the rotted stump and stopped. He took three quick steps to the stump then brought his knife hand around in a looping arc toward the side facing away from him, which if the quail was there, would surely impale her.

But his knife merely punctured a decaying inch-thick wall of Shumard oak before punching through into the stump's rotten central cavity.

No quail.

So where was she?

He directed his light down the path and saw another likely hiding place . . . a massive century-old poplar blown partially over so that many of its huge roots had lifted up out of the ground, forming a dozen places Segerson might have crawled into. Eagerly, he moved forward to see if that's where she was.

WITH ODESSA NOW about fifteen yards away and hidden from view by the persimmon Marti had run into, she rolled from under the tree hiding her, got to her feet, and headed back toward her cottage, where she could claim her car keys and get the hell out of there.

She reached the cottage a few minutes later and entered through the back door, which was standing wide open. Inside, she went directly to the small table by the door, where she always unloaded her keys when she got home.

They weren't there.

Where the hell were they?

Fighting to control the panic that threatened to consume her, she searched the floor thinking they might have fallen from the table when she was scuffling with Odessa. Not finding them near the table, she widened her search until she had scoured every inch of the living room's well-worn pine floorboards and its two small area rugs.

No keys.

Maybe she hadn't left them on the table.

She went off on a mission, looking in every conceivable place she might have put them. But it was activity destined to produce only frustration. Finally, she had to admit she wouldn't be leaving by car.

The phone . . . 911 . . . At least she could call for help.

She went to the cottage phone and yanked the receiver off the hook. Her fingers had two of the three numbers entered before she realized there had been no dial tone before she hit the first button. She pulled on the cord and found it severed cleanly from the part still in the jack, obviously cut by Odessa before he followed her into the woods.

Her cell phone . . .

He'd knocked it from her hand and it had flown . . .

She turned and scanned the floor for it.

There . . .

She hurried over and picked it up only to find it smashed and no longer functional.

She now seemed to have only one choice: get to the highway on foot and flag down a car. Because of a strip of impassable swamp that flanked the highway for miles, she couldn't go through the woods, but would have to use the dirt road leading out.

Before leaving she went into the kitchen and yanked

open the drawer where she kept the steak knives. Compared to the monster Odessa was carrying, a steak knife wasn't much protection, but it was all she had.

It would be a lot easier running along the dirt drive to the highway than it had been careening through the woods, but Marti still felt that a flashlight would be useful. The one she'd used in the tunnel at the hospital was locked in her car, but Clay had provided tenants of the cottage with a rechargeable model in the outlet by the back door. She hadn't had a chance to grab it earlier when she'd been running for her life, but a little less pressured now, she pulled it from the outlet and took it along as she went back outside.

On the porch she paused and looked at the path into the woods, afraid that Odessa might have given up and returned to the cottage to see if she was there. But all was dark and quiet.

The side yard opposite the woods was an open patch of grass easily navigated by moonlight, so as she leaped from the porch and set out around the cottage on a dead run, she kept the flashlight off.

Reaching the dirt road, she thought about veering up into the woods to keep from being so obvious, but chose instead to stay on the road, where she could run full tilt without worrying about hidden roots and uneven terrain.

It felt good to run unimpeded, and with every step that left Odessa farther behind, she felt freer and safer. She had no idea how he had gotten out, but this would prove to any doubters he could, and if he did it tonight, he could have done it when the girl was killed in Blake. So once she got to a phone and Odessa was in custody, she'd show the cops Quinn's mobile lab, then take them to his office and get those discs. And that would be the end of both of them.

After she'd run about twenty yards she came to the small rise blocking Clay's house from view. She lost a little steam going up the hill, but was encouraged by the knowledge that on the other side, from the bottom of the hill, the terrain was flat all the way to the highway. So as she topped the rise, she felt her confidence surge to an even higher level.

But then she saw something that made her jolt to a stop.

Someone was walking toward her.

Clay . . . back from the fire.

She started running toward him, but then saw a flash of something in the moonlight . . .

A knife . . .

CHAPTER 31

ODESSA MUST HAVE taken the leg of the path in the woods she'd never followed and he'd come out ahead of her. They faced each other for a brief moment in the moonlight like a pair of cowboys in a western show-down. Marti had the steak knife from the kitchen, but now it seemed even punier than when she'd picked it up.

She looked to her left . . . toward the trail through the field to the creek. There were several places along the route where she could hide, and at the creek there were even more, where the bank had eroded away from the roots of some huge trees. But could she get a big enough lead on him so he wouldn't see where she went?

She looked back at him . . .

From what she'd seen in her short time at Gibson, it didn't seem like he got much exercise. He was probably already winded from his trek through the woods. Believing that in a footrace she could beat him like a rug, she bolted for the trail.

• • •

ODESSA GROANED WHEN he saw her start to run, for his side ached and he could barely get his breath. Now he was going to have to chase that bitch in the open. Then, he remembered . . . Grinning, he ignored Marti and set off as fast as he could for the cottage.

•

AS MARTI'S LEGS settled into a powerful pumping rhythm, she thought about the old childhood warning against running with a knife. Good advice if you weren't being chased by a psychopath. She hurtled along the trail at full speed for about eighty yards before she turned to see how close Odessa was.

What she saw made her brain howl.

The headlights of a car, just fishtailing onto the trail . . . *That's* where her car keys were . . . Odessa had taken them. And he was coming now with the gas pedal to the floorboard.

She had reached the triple fork in the trail. The closest place to hide was the old barn to the left. She veered that way and began to chew up real estate at a pace she hadn't thought possible.

For a few seconds, she was out of the car's headlights. What would she do when she reached the barn? Then she remembered something she'd seen there on one of her walks. With that she would at least have a chance.

She had nearly reached the barn when Odessa came sliding from the main trail onto the one she'd taken, igniting the trail with the car's headlights. She'd once met an Olympic-caliber sprinter who had told her you never look back because it causes you to lose time. Even knowing that, she couldn't help but take a quick glance to judge how long it would be before he reached her.

He was still about forty yards away, but he was really pushing it. She was about to veer off the trail and get to the barn, when she had another idea. If this one worked he'd never be a problem to anyone again. But it was a real long shot.

Deciding to go for a final solution, Marti ignored the barn and kept running.

In a few seconds she could hear the car's engine behind her, closing fast, its lights burning into her, but also showing her the way ahead, allowing her to make her decision at just the right time.

BEHIND THE WHEEL of the car, Odessa was a happy man. In just a few seconds he'd have her . . . and the fun could begin . . . although this was actually fun too.

He was now just a few feet away.

Suddenly the quail veered to the left, off the trail and into some heavy weeds. Odessa hit the brakes, but before the car could even begin to stop, it hurtled off a railroad tie that marked the end of the trail. Just in front of the tie was a hole in the ground where the many warning signs Clay had posted over the years had inevitably been carried off by the local kids.

The car flew through the air and rejoined the earth with a dull whump, the sudden stop throwing Odessa forward, driving his chest against the steering wheel. By the time he'd recovered from the shock of what had happened, and the pain in his chest had receded to where he could think about something else, the car had sunk up to

the wheel tops in the bog quicksand Marti had lured him
into.

AS MARTI LEFT the trail, she stumbled on a half-buried
brick and sprawled onto her face, flattening the weeds in
front of her. Realizing as she got to her feet that she'd lost
her knife, she flicked on the flashlight still in her hand
and went on a rampage looking for it.

NOT YET UNDERSTANDING where he was, Odessa
threw the car door open, grabbed his knife and flashlight
from the seat beside him, and leaped out. When he hit, his
feet disappeared up to his ankles in quicksand.

MARTI HAD NOW flattened the weeds in a big circle,
but still had not found her knife. She was dimly aware
that Odessa had opened the car door, but had heard nothing for the last few seconds to indicate he was coming
after her.

She stood for a moment now and listened hard to see
if she was missing something. But no . . . the silence continued.

A part of her told her to forget the knife and run like
hell to put as much distance between her and Odessa as
she could. But she'd waited so long for revenge, the
thought that she finally had him snared kept her from
leaving. If her plan had succeeded, and it appeared that it
had, he was about to die. And that was something she just
had to watch.

Practically holding her breath, she left the weeds,

walked out onto the trail, and played her flashlight into the bog, where she could see the dim shape of the car and . . .

Yes . . .

Odessa too, struggling to lift his feet from the muck holding him captive.

She played her flashlight into his face to see his expression as he tried to lift his feet free of the restraining quicksand only to discover that the attempt made him sink deeper into it.

"I'm afraid you're trapped," Marti said, her heart beating high in her chest like church bells celebrating the end of a long and draining war.

Beside Odessa, the car had sunk up to the floorboards, and quicksand was edging through the open door.

Odessa held up his knife hand to shield his eyes from Marti's flashlight and he retaliated with his own light.

"You planned this?"

"No," she said sarcastically. "It was all just a big accident."

"So *you've* decided to be my judge and jury."

"The real ones do a lousy job."

"What do you mean?"

"We met once before, eighteen years ago at a beach in California, outside the house where you murdered my sister."

"I don't remember that."

"It's one of the memories Quinn took from you."

"Tell me about it."

"Go to hell."

"I'm sure I will."

"The sooner the better."

He was now buried in quicksand up to his knees. In the car, it had just about covered the seats.

"Oh, now I see," Odessa said, disappointing Marti by the lack of fear in his voice. "You took the job at Gibson just to get to me."

"You've been on my mind every day for nearly two decades," Marti said, through clenched teeth.

"So what was the plan? Were you going to kill me?"

"I thought about it."

"So you didn't have the nerve?"

"I'm not like you. I'm human."

"So what's this . . . aren't you killing me now?"

"You did this to yourself."

"That's a distortion of the truth and you know it. If you're so honorable, help me now."

Marti let out a guttural laugh. "You've got to be kidding."

"I promise not to hurt you."

"You must think I'm stupid."

"Okay, I would hurt you. Like I did your sister. I'll bet she pled for her life when I did it. I like it when they whimper and ask me to spare them. It's so naive and cute."

"Keep running your mouth. Pretty soon it'll be filled with the sludge you're standing in. Think what that'll be like . . . After your nose goes under, you'll hold your breath for as long as you can . . . until your chest is on fire for lack of oxygen, your brain will scream for air . . ."

"Did you love your sister? Is life empty now for you?"

"Finally, you'll take a breath and fill your lungs with sand and water and frog shit."

The quicksand had now reached Odessa's lower ribs. On the car it had risen to the controls for the windows.

"Have you thought about what her body must look like now?" Odessa crooned. "I understand the hair lasts the longest . . . and the fingernails. Did she have pretty hair? Did you look up to her?"

"Shut your damn mouth."

"Or what? What will you do to me?"

Unable to control herself, Marti pulled her arm back and hurled her flashlight at Odessa's head, but it missed.

Odessa had been holding his knife by the handle. Before Marti realized what was happening he had somehow turned it in his hand so he now had it by the blade. In a motion so quick, she barely saw it happen, he threw the knife.

And *he* didn't miss.

CHAPTER 32

ODESSA'S KNIFE STRUCK Marti in the thigh, blade first, penetrating all the way to the bone. In the instant before the pain began, she pulled the knife free and flung it into the bog.

"Whoa," Odessa shouted with glee, "Mark one up for the psychopath. And you thought you were safe. You'll never be free of me. I'll haunt your dreams till the day you die."

Struck by a sudden jolt of fire in her thigh, Marti bent over in agony.

"Does it hurt?" Odessa crooned. "Poor baby. Just keep telling yourself it's all in your mind. Pain is just an illusion of something real. You can't touch it, so why let it bother you?"

Weary of Odessa's voice, Marti turned and limped away, the pain in her thigh so bright each time she put her weight on that foot, it blossomed into something *very* real.

"And don't think you've accomplished anything." Odessa yelled after her. "When this is over your sister will still be dead and there's nothing you can do about that." The quicksand was now at the level of Odessa's sternum.

Back on the trail, though she could see it only poorly in the moonlight, there was now a bloodstain as big as her hand on the front of Marti's slacks. And even though she tried to favor that leg as she shuffled forward, each step seemed to widen the stain a little more.

Help was a long way off. Could she make it to Clay's house without going into shock? Without knowing how badly she was bleeding, there was no way to judge.

Damn it. Why had she thrown her flashlight at Odessa? Without it, she could barely see the margins of the stain soaking into her pants. She had to get a better look at the wound and maybe rig a tourniquet.

She was now opposite the old barn, where she could get off the trail and feel a bit more secure about what she needed to do. So she shuffled a dozen more steps, then, after checking her surroundings, loosened her belt and let her slacks down, turning toward the moon to take maximum advantage of its light.

She couldn't be absolutely certain, but the wound didn't seem to be pulsing blood in rhythm with her heart. If true, that was good, as it meant that if the blade *had* cut a major vessel, it was a vein, a low-pressure channel a clot could easily block. She put her hand gently onto the wound feeling for a rhythmic pressure head pushing against her palm.

She felt nothing, convincing her that the knife had not hit an artery. But she still needed to get off her feet and put some pressure on the wound until it clotted. Remembering a bench just inside the barn door, she shuffled in that direction.

The roof of the barn had a major hole in it. This admitted enough moonlight so Marti could easily find the parson's bench she was looking for. Gingerly, she eased herself onto the bench and stretched her wounded leg out in front of her, biting her lip at the pain that shot up into her groin. She pulled her slacks snugly against her thigh to help close the wound.

Except for an occasional skittering sound from what was probably a mouse scampering around the loose hay in the barn, the place was so quiet it reminded her that by now Odessa was fully entombed in the bog. So it was done. Her promise to Lee had been fulfilled.

She had often imagined how she would feel when this day came, and it was always with the expectation she would want to howl at the moon and beat her chest. But now that it was here, she was just tired.

So tired . . .

She lay her head back against one of the studs supporting the barn wall, closed her eyes for a few minutes, and withdrew into a land where there were no obligations and no decisions to make. It was pleasant there and she wanted to stay longer, but she was beckoned back to reality by the specter she had only glimpsed briefly in the last few days, but which now stood squarely in front of her.

Who was the real Marti Segerson?

What would her life be like without the direction and structure hatred had given it?

Was there any other person inside her?

The first thing she saw when she opened her eyes was the side of the horse stall directly across from her, and against the old boards, the dim outline of the object she'd thought about when Odessa was chasing her with the car.

Suppose she hadn't thought of the bog? What would have happened had she chosen the barn instead? There was a very real possibility she'd be dead and Odessa would be the one wondering what he was going to do next.

That suddenly made her want to be far away from there. She had probably been sitting long enough for her wound to clot but either way, she wasn't hanging around this place any longer.

HIS FACE STILL burning from the heat of the barn fire, Clay arrived home and just sat for a moment in his truck, reliving the excitement of the biggest fire they'd had in the county in a year. Finally, remembering the call he'd been too busy to take at the fire, he checked his phone to see who had tried to contact him. When he saw it was Marti, he started to ring her back, but then, realizing this was an opportunity to see her again, he started the truck and headed up the road to her cottage.

MARTI'S WOUNDED LEG had stiffened from being held so long in one position and she found it difficult to get up. But eventually, she managed it.

Moving carefully so she would put the least amount of weight possible on her bad leg, she shuffled the few steps to the door and stepped outside. As she did, something hit her in the face with enough power to drive her staggering backward into the barn, where her heel caught in the dirt. Trying to keep from falling, she stutter-stepped backward, each footfall on her bad leg a rimshot of pain that echoed off the throbbing fire in her nose, where blood was now oozing from both nostrils. Failing to find her balance, her back slammed against the side of the stall and she slid to the ground on her butt.

"I guess you didn't know the quicksand was only five feet deep near the edge of the bog," Odessa said, charging into the barn after her. "Honest mistake. I forgive you. But we now enter the penalty phase of our game . . . the part where you die of a crushed skull. Now it's time our challenger picks a weapon. Marti, I'll take bare fists for a hundred."

WHEN CLAY SAW that Marti's car wasn't in front of her house, he got out his cell phone and tried to call her on her cell.

"I'm sorry, but that number is not in service."

From where his truck was sitting, Clay couldn't see the smashed window on the side of the cottage, so although he was puzzled at why Marti's phone wasn't working, he turned the truck around and drove home.

ODESSA CAME AT Marti hard, blotting out what little light there was in the barn. She tried to lift her legs to fend him off, but the pain in her wounded thigh was so bad, she could only manage to raise the other leg, which he would surely just swat out of his way. As she shifted her hands on the ground to get more leverage to resist him, her right palm dropped onto something hard and round.

Realizing it was the handle of the rusty old pitchfork

she'd thought about before she got the bog idea, she rolled to her right, got hold of the implement in both hands, and brought it around it front of her just as Odessa threw himself at her.

The force of the impact drove the handle of the pitchfork into Marti's stomach. Odessa though, took the worst of it, because two of the tines went into his neck, tearing both carotid arteries. Blood immediately began spurting from the impalement points, showering Marti with it.

Unable to hold him dangling on the end of the pitchfork, Marti shifted it to her right and let Odessa's body fall to the ground.

Just before he lost consciousness, Odessa gurgled his final words on this earth. "Your sister is still dead."

Then Marti, too, passed out.

CHAPTER 33

INCREDIBLY, ODESSA GOT to his feet, the pitchfork hanging in front of him, its tines still buried in his neck. He grabbed the handle of the tool, pulled it free, and turned the bloody tines toward Marti, who was still on the barn floor. It was now dawn and Marti could clearly see what was happening. Grinning, his teeth smeared with blood, Odessa drove the pitchfork into her, causing her entire body to convulse in agony.

Then, with the tines buried in her belly, he began to shake her from side to side like a shark with a piece of meat in its mouth.

"Wake up . . . Marti, wake up . . ."

Marti opened her eyes into a world of subdued light, and there was Clay Hulett bending over her.

"Where . . . what's going on?"

"You're in the hospital. But everything's okay. In a few days you'll be pretty much your old self . . . except for maybe the bruising around your nose . . . that could take a little longer."

"Odessa . . ."

"Dead. And so's Quinn; apparently Odessa killed him in the hospital basement before he came after you."

"How long have I been asleep?"

"About thirty hours."

"Thirty . . ."

"You were pretty banged up. I'm sure you needed the rest. I think they gave you a mild sedative."

Though she'd just re-entered consciousness, Marti was aware that thirty hours meant . . .

She looked at the side of the bed where Clay was standing, then turning to her right, saw the collection bag on the opposite rail. Shifting her pelvis a little she now felt the catheter between her thighs. Ordinarily, she would have accepted being tethered to a urine collection bag as just one of those things life sometimes requires of you and would have had no feelings about it one way or the other. But for some reason, having her plumbing visible to Clay embarrassed her.

"How long have you been here?" she asked.

"Pretty much the whole time."

"Only on that side of the bed?"

Puzzled, Clay said, "Yes."

Figuring then that he hadn't seen the bag, Marti relaxed. "Your vigil would explain why you need a shave."

"I understand in LA that's a hot look."

"Never cared for it, but considering how you got it, I may have to change my mind."

The door opened and a thin, dark-haired guy in a white coat whisked into the room. "Well, look who's back with us." He turned up the lights and came to the bed. I'm Dr. Gilbear . . . I know it says *Gilbert* on my coat, but trust me, the *T* is silent. Now let's have a look at you."

He examined her eyes with his penlight and checked her pulse.

"How are you feeling?"

"Like I don't belong here any longer."

"That's a good sign. Can you stand up?"

"Am I wearing one of those gowns where my butt is going to show?"

"Good point." He looked at Clay. "Could you give us a moment?"

"Sure." Clay got up and went into the hall.

"I'm also tethered to a Foley," Marti said when Clay was gone. "Could we get rid of that?"

"Of course."

Gilbert picked up the house phone and called the nursing station. "Would you send someone to two twelve stat. Dr. Segerson needs her Foley removed."

"I don't know all the details of how you got your injuries," Gilbert said while they waited for the nurse, "but it sounds like you had a harrowing experience."

"I wouldn't like to do it again . . . or even talk about it," Marti replied, giving him a broad hint that she didn't want to be drawn into a discussion about what had happened.

The awkward silence that followed was ended by the arrival of a nurse with the syringe needed to draw the air out of the small balloon that held the catheter in Marti's bladder.

With Gilbert discreetly looking out the window while the nurse worked, the job was quickly done and all traces of the thing removed.

Back now on purely medical turf, Gilbert once again became his old self. "Now let's see how you do on your feet," he said brightly, coming over to stand between the bed and the door to the hall.

Marti threw her sheet back, slid her legs over the side of the bed where Gilbert was waiting, and got up, holding her gown closed at the rear even though there was no one behind her to see anything.

"Any dizziness?" Gilbert asked.

"No."

"Let's see you move around."

Her first step sent a mild shock wave up into her groin from her bad leg.

Noticing her reaction, Gilbert said, "That'll be a little tender for a few days."

After she'd taken a couple of steps, Gilbert said, "Okay, you can lie down again."

"I don't want to do that. I want to leave."

"I'd like to see you eat something first. If you can handle food with no problem and then can walk down to the nursing station and back with no bleeding and are steady on your feet, we'll get you out of here. Deal?"

"I suppose," Marti replied, reluctantly getting back in bed.

"I'll have a tray sent in."

Gilbert swept out of the room and Clay returned.

"What's the verdict?" he asked.

"I'll probably be released in an hour or so. Who found me?"

"I did. I'm sorry I didn't get there sooner. I know you tried to call me, but I was working a barn fire and couldn't answer the phone. When I got home I came up to talk to you but your car was gone. As I was leaving, I noticed fresh tire marks leading into the trail through the field. I drove down to the bog and when I saw your car in it with the door open . . ." He shook his head. "I thought you were buried in there too.

"But then I saw wet muck on the railroad tie and that made me think you got out. I started looking around and found you in the barn . . . you and Odessa's body. I can't stop thinking about how you were down there fighting for your life and I was sitting in front of your house like an idiot, doing nothing to help."

"You had no way of knowing what was happening."

"I could have seen those tire marks a little sooner."

"There's nothing to be gained from that kind of thinking. Believe me, I know from long experience."

There was a knock at the door.

"It's okay, come in," Marti said.

It was Sheriff Banks, looking well groomed as ever in his crisply pressed uniform.

"Morning," Banks said, coming to the bedside. "How are you feeling?"

"Not bad, considering . . ."

"You ought to be proud of yourself. You prevailed over a pretty nasty situation."

"I don't feel proud."

"Sorry, maybe that was the wrong sentiment. I just dropped by to give you this." He handed Marti the big envelope in his hand.

"What is it?"

"Oren Quinn kept a journal. When your county sheriff started his investigation of what happened the other night, he found several volumes of it in Quinn's office. Among other things, the volume Quinn started when he arrived at Gibson includes an explanation of how Odessa got out of seclusion the night he committed the Blake murder, so the sheriff made a copy of that entire volume for me. You won't be surprised by what you read in that part of it, but there are some other sections you'll find interesting. I didn't copy all of it for you, just the highlights. But it's enough to give you a good picture of what's been going on."

"Why are you giving it to me?"

"All the guilty are dead, so it can't do any harm. And considering your recent and past personal involvement in the situation, I thought you deserved to see it."

"What do you mean, my past involvement?"

"Eighteen years ago . . . at the beach."

"You know about that?"

"I did a little checking around. Have you given the county sheriff here a statement yet about what happened the other night?"

"Apparently I've been asleep since then."

"I'm sure he'll be wanting one. I wouldn't mention that you've seen those pages. Because then he'll ask me if I gave them to you, and I'll have to say no."

"That surprises me."

"How so?"

"You don't seem like the type to lie."

Banks emitted a baritone chuckle that seemed to rise from the deepest part of him. Then he turned and left, still chuckling as he went out the door.

Marti opened the envelope and took out the stapled pages inside. The first entry was dated nearly two years ago. She began reading aloud.

" 'O has arrived. Now to make sure I can control him. Surgical suite in my lab nearly ready. When the time comes, will give him something to make it appear he has appendicitis. Will say that with such a potentially dangerous patient am reluctant to send him out for surgery, especially since my facilities can easily handle such a simple procedure, and that I know a fine surgeon who would be willing to do it on site. Will bring in someone who looks the part, but will make the implant myself. O can recover in our infirmary, where a temporary staff who won't care that he has a neck wound in addition to an appendectomy incision is already in place.'"

Marti looked up from the pages and turned to Clay, who had wandered over and dropped into one of the vinyl-covered visitor's armchairs. "When I first saw Odessa after I got to Gibson, I noticed a scar on his neck. This implant must have been the cause. Quinn's comment about controlling Odessa with it sounds like it was some kind of stimulator that could activate spinal cord pain pathways."

"The night I found both of you in the barn, he had a big gash in the back of his neck in addition to that pitchfork in him," Clay said. "I thought he got the neck wound while you were fighting, but I wonder if he cut that implant out of himself. That would explain why he was able to get to Quinn."

"It makes sense . . . not that *any* of this really does."

"What else does Quinn say?"

Marti scanned the next entry silently then mumbled, "Of course . . ."

Seeing that she was continuing to read to herself, Clay said, "Explanation, please."

"Sorry, I forgot you were here."

"Oh, now *that* hurts."

"You know what I mean . . . I just got so involved in this . . . Anyway, Quinn had some equipment that could roam through a person's brain stimulating memory circuits and making movies of the memory."

"That doesn't sound possible."

"I agree, but he could do it. I've seen the proof. But whenever he made a memory movie, it erased the memory from the mind of the owner. To get subjects, he tricked people into participating in a supposed mind-reading experiment in which he drugged the subject and put them in the memory movie apparatus. He had an assistant named Nadine, who helped him."

"Sounds like both of them could have been arrested on assault charges just for that."

"And they did it to me. That's why I called you asking about the man who escaped from Gibson and came to my house. I had no memory of it because Quinn stole it. Shortly after I confronted Nadine about what she did to me when I supposedly fell asleep after drinking a Coke she gave me, she committed suicide. There should have been a medical examiner autopsy of her body, but Quinn got her cremated without one. When I went over to the crematorium, the guy who runs the equipment showed me a melted black object he found in the oven after she'd been cremated. I didn't know then what it was, but I do now . . ."

"The same thing Quinn implanted in Odessa . . ."

"The proof is right here." She looked down and began reading.

" 'Nadine Simpson is now mentally stable. But with her background, she would make a first-rate assistant. So I have decided to keep her at Gibson. To ensure her discretion about our memory movie enterprise I will also give her an implant. It may appear odd to some of the staff that two patients in the hospital became ill with appendicitis at about the same time, but it's not something people will spend much time thinking about.'"

"He didn't give a rat's you-know-what about anybody, did he?" Clay said.

"Just himself . . . that's about it."

Clay wiggled his index finger at Marti. "Go on . . . let's hear some more."

Marti turned to a fresh page. "This is dated"—she did a quick calculation—"nine months ago.

"'Implants working fine. O very cooperative. Have discovered that unlike other psychopaths, his amygdala and prefrontal cortex function normally when he's shown material with an emotional content. Very exciting but also puzzling. Must know more.'"

She looked at Clay. "The next entry is a week later.

"'Am becoming increasingly convinced there is only one way to truly understand how Odessa's brain functions. But the price is too dear.'

"A few days later he says, 'God help me, I have decided to proceed. Even as I write this, the vehicle I purchased two days ago is being gutted to receive the necessary equipment. It should take about six weeks to get everything ready. Am not yet emotionally ready to pick a subject. In any event, whatever happens, there will only be the one. I can't be responsible for more than that.'"

"What does he mean, 'pick a subject'?" Clay asked.

"I think he's about to tell us."

"Okay, keep going."

"Here's the next entry: 'Have found a suitable subject in Blake, Tennessee. She's slim and has long blond hair, like all the rest of O's victims.'"

"Blake . . ." Clay said, sitting forward in his chair.

"Jesus, he's talking about choosing the girl Odessa killed."

"I know."

"Why's he doing it?"

Marti didn't need to have anyone explain that and at first she was surprised Clay hadn't figured it out from what she'd already read. But then he didn't know everything she did, and to an outsider, the story was surely so bizarre it wouldn't be readily apparent.

"He's decided that the only way he can understand how Odessa's brain functions is to make wireless EEG recordings from his brain while he's murdering someone."

Clay's mouth dropped open and for a moment he just stared at Marti in astonished horror.

"And they put this guy in charge over there? I thought his brain-rape hobby was perverted, but this—"

"I'm not sure Quinn himself knew what he was capable of before he got involved with Odessa."

"Doesn't seem to me they were all that different from each other. Does Quinn describe what happened in Blake?"

Marti turned back to the journal pages and continued reading.

"'Subject lives alone in a small apartment down a wooded path behind a single-family home. Street in front of primary dwelling is deserted in the morning hours. Situation is ideal. Next trip will bring video camera. Do not know subject's name and don't wish to know.'

"Next section—" Marti said.

Before she could begin reading, a nurse came in carrying the breakfast tray the doctor had ordered.

"Sorry to interrupt," the nurse said, "but Dr. Gilbert wants you to eat something before you're discharged."

She put the tray on the bed, pinning Marti between its legs, then stood back and beamed at her accomplishment. "Doesn't that look good?"

Marti glanced down and saw that the two eggs and single piece of bacon on the institutional plate had been arranged like a smiling face. Earlier, when the doc had mentioned breakfast, it hadn't seemed like such a bad idea, but now, after Quinn's details of the Blake victim had personified her in Marti's mind, eating was out of the question. But she played along. "Can't wait to dig in."

When the nurse was out of earshot, Marti said to Clay. "Do you want this? I can't handle it."

"Me neither."

"If somebody doesn't eat it, Gilbear with a *T* might balk at letting me leave."

"Sure you couldn't force it down? He wouldn't have suggested eating if it wasn't in your best interests."

"Can't and won't."

"I shouldn't help you fool your doctor, but I guess, being one yourself, I'll just consider your stubbornness a second opinion."

Clay came to the bed, picked up the plate and the fork, and carried them into the bathroom, where he scraped the food into the toilet and flushed it. Returning to her bedside, he put the plate and fork back on the tray and set the whole thing aside. "Okay, read."

As Clay retreated to his chair, Marti found her place in the journal pages and read the next entry.

"'Showed O film of the girl in Blake—response all I had hoped for. After film, let him into the tunnel and went around to meet him at the exit. Hopes high for a success-

ful experiment, but in Blake, disaster . . . equipment mal-
functioned. A life wasted for nothing. Can't do this again.
Price too high.' "

" 'Price too high,' " Clay echoed. "What a caring guy."

"The equipment he mentioned here and earlier was a
mobile EEG lab he'd had constructed so he could record
from Odessa's brain while he killed the girl," Marti said.
"I found the lab in a hidden room in Odessa's garage the
night Odessa came after me. Quinn must have found out
I was onto them and sent Odessa to kill me."

"That barn fire the night you were hurt was arson. I'll
bet Quinn set it to get me out of the way."

"Seems plausible."

"I need some help here . . . Suppose Quinn's equipment had worked that night in Blake and he *had* learned
something important. He'd never be able to publish the
results. So what's the point?"

"I don't think he cared about publishing. He just had
to know. To him, the knowledge was all that mattered."

"I don't understand that kind of mind."

"He wasn't wired like the rest of us."

"No, I'd say not. I wonder if Nadine knew Quinn was
responsible for what happened in Blake?"

"That may be what drove her off the roof. If she was
mentally stable as Quinn said, she was probably racked
with guilt over the mind-rape experiments, if not the
Blake murder. And she was trapped . . . forced to help
Quinn and too afraid of the pain he could inflict on her to
turn him in."

Clay shook his head. "Where does such evil come
from?" He gestured to the journal pages in her hand.
"What else is in there?"

Marti took a moment to locate the next new section, then began reading again.

"'More trouble. That idiot, O, took a souvenir from the Blake subject's home . . . a small wallet-size picture of her. Molly Norman, one of the nurses on his ward, found it in his room. Realizing who it was from the girl's picture she saw on TV and knowing that O was a suspect in the killing, she brought the picture to me. Had to put her in the memory movie apparatus and burn away everything she knows. A dreadful business. At least I can count on Nadine's silence. Pain is a powerful ally.'"

"Poor Molly," Clay said. "If she'd just gone to the sheriff with what she found instead of to Quinn."

"Oh, my God," Marti said, reading ahead. "I was wondering why Quinn kept the mobile lab around. Two months ago he decided to try his experiment with Odessa again. He already had the next subject picked out."

"It's a damn good thing you came here when you did. Whoever that girl is, she owes you her life."

"I don't know about that. Odessa was probably planning to kill Quinn at the next opportunity whether I was around or not."

"Maybe so, but after Quinn was dead, Odessa still would have been free to go find the girl if he knew where she was. And if he didn't know, he would have found someone else."

"I suppose that's true."

Marti had read nearly everything in the packet Banks had given her. She turned now to the last page . . . and . . . "He mentions me: 'Marti Segerson . . . curse the luck. Today, while exploring her brain, stumbled into a recent memory that should never have been in long-term storage. To have this happen when I make every effort to avoid the short-term areas is infuriating. If I'd just known about Harry Evensky breaking into her bedroom I could have anticipated that the emotional content of the experience would have moved its memory into long-term storage quicker than normal. There's virtually no way she will fail to notice this memory lapse. Can only hope she won't figure out when it happened. If she does, it'll be bad for both of us.'"

"He was right to be worried," Clay said. "That mistake was what led you to Molly and from her to Blake."

There was a knock at the door and the nurse who'd brought the breakfast tray came in without waiting for a response.

"How are we coming with that food?" Seeing the empty plate, her already pleasant demeanor brightened even more. "Well, you made short work of most of it."

"Went down just as nifty as you please," Marti said, giving Clay a sly glance.

"No interest in the juice or toast?"

"Had enough."

"All right then . . . If you're ready, I'll get you another gown you can slip on over the one you're wearing so you're fully covered, then we'll take that little walk Dr. Gilbert asked for."

"I'm more than ready." She looked at Clay. "I don't have any clean clothes to leave here in. Would you go to my house and get me some?"

"Sure. What do you want?"

She described the outfit she had in mind and reminded him not to forget her underwear. Her mention of the latter made Clay blush, a reaction Marti found charming.

"It'll take me a while," Clay said.

"I've got a couple of phone calls to make, so that'll help pass the time."

"You weren't wearing your glasses when I found you in the barn. Were they lost while Odessa was chasing you?"

"I'm pretty sure they're at the cottage."

"I'll bring them too."

Believing this wasn't the time to explain that her eyesight was twenty/twenty, Marti just said, "Thanks."

When Clay was gone, Marti proved to the nurse it wouldn't be malpractice to let her leave the hospital. She then used the phone book in her room to look up the number of the first place in town she needed to contact to discuss a matter involving Harry Evensky. Her initial call went so well she didn't have to make any others.

She was now looking at the beginning of her new life, whatever that was going to be. And frankly, the steps leading up to it appeared even steeper than she had ever imagined.

CHAPTER 34

CLAY PULLED INTO a space in the Gibson State parking lot and cut off the engine of his pickup, which now had his camper top on it to protect Marti's suitcases.

"I won't be long," Marti said.

"Take whatever time you need," Clay said.

She was there to officially resign and say good-bye to the few people she'd grown close to. When she was finished with that, Clay would drive her to Memphis and she'd get on a plane back to LA, where she could start seriously thinking about who she wanted to be when she grew up.

Clay had not seemed like himself since he'd picked her up at the Best Western, where because of the damaged window at the cottage, she'd taken a room until her final business in Linville could be concluded. Missing his easy manner, Marti tried to coax it back one more time. "I appreciate you not holding me to my lease," she said.

"Considering the condition of the place and what happened to you there, it wouldn't be right."

"And taking me to the airport . . . that's very sweet of you."

"It's the least I could do."

"I *will* call you when I'm settled, I promise."

"I believe you. But I still don't understand why you're leaving."

"Staying was never part of my plans."

"Life can't always *be* planned. Sometimes it just happens."

Marti was having a hard time defending her return to California because it wasn't so much a decision as an instinct to be where she'd grown up, an injured animal seeking familiar surroundings to recover. Depleted of things to say about the situation, she left the truck and headed for the hospital's front entrance.

Inside, she went first up to Two East to see Harry Evensky. Her hopes that she could get in and out without running into Ada Metz were not to be, for Metz was standing just inside the ward entrance.

They stared at each other without speaking for a moment, then Metz, her eyes still lingering on the bruises Marti hadn't been able to hide even with heavy makeup, said, "You look terrible."

"Thanks for noticing."

"I didn't mean . . . Look, I know I've been hard on you since you came here, but I want to tell you I appreciate what you did. They're saying some terrible things about Dr. Quinn, and I don't know if they're true or not. All I know is he always treated me fairly, and I liked him. It sounds like there's not much doubt Odessa killed him before he came after you. The way I was brought up was that if you're the friend of my friend, then you get the benefit of the doubt from me. Odessa killed Quinn . . . you killed Odessa . . . that means I give you no more crap. Deal?"

Metz extended the hamhock she used for a hand.

The woman's premise that the killing of Odessa somehow made Marti and Quinn friends was so skewed Marti didn't know what to do. Finally, just to get past the woman, she shook her hand.

Just then Marti saw Harry Evensky come into the dayroom. "There's the man I came to see."

With a benevolent nod of the head, Metz stepped aside, leaving the way clear. Seeing Marti, Evensky met her halfway.

"I *knew* he was coming after you that night," Evensky said. "I tried to get to a phone to tell you, but they put me in a room where I couldn't get at the lock."

"Interview room," Marti said, taking him by the arm and steering him in that direction.

When they were behind a closed door, Harry said, "The news said you got him with a pitchfork. Man, I'd give anything to have seen that."

"Wish *I* hadn't."

"Yeah, I expect it was touch and go there for a while. Who was the guy who found you?"

"A friend. Harry, I'm not here to talk about me."

"Why *did* you come?"

"I want you to level with me. You don't ever think seriously about killing yourself, do you?"

"Yes, I do."

"And you don't really believe old letter *R*'s are going to be valuable someday either."

"You're wrong about that, too. And your disbelief is

why they will. Takes a man with foresight to go against the tide."

Marti walked over, took Harry by the shoulders, and looked into his eyes. "Harry, tell me the truth."

Under Marti's unrelenting scrutiny, Harry withered. "All right . . . of course, I don't believe that crap about the letters. And I'd never kill myself either. I just say I will because . . . well, I have to do these things to justify bein' able to stay here."

"And why would you want to be here instead of free?"

"It's safe here."

"What are you afraid of?"

Harry gently pulled free of her grasp, crossed his arms in front of him, and looked at the floor.

"What are you afraid of?"

Harry looked up. "Years ago when I had my own lock-smith business, I made a mess of things—went bankrupt, my wife left me . . . I couldn't make it on my own. I got confused, so I was sent here. Then, when I got to feelin' some better, I found I didn't want to leave."

"Harry, lots of people lose businesses and wives, too. It hurts, but they keep going."

"Why?"

"Because if you don't, you might as well be dead."

"I'm not dead in here."

"Yes, you are. Isn't there some small part of you that wants to try again in the world, to see if maybe what happened was just bad luck? Don't you ever long for friends who can carry on a decent conversation? Don't you get tired of the food here? Have you never awakened on a fall day and wished you could take a leisurely ride and look at the leaves? Don't you ever want to go fishing? Do you never miss the feeling of being needed, of being pro-

ductive, of standing back and looking with pride at a
tough job you've completed?"

"I don't fish."

"What about the other things?"

"Sure, I feel all that from time to time."

"So what do you say we do something about it."

"What do you mean?"

"I've found you a part-time job that includes some
locksmithing duties at Barker's Hardware. Most of the
time you'd probably just be making keys and helping out
as a clerk, but they offer lock installation and you'd be
the one doing that."

"I dunno . . ."

"It's only three hours a day."

"Could I still live here?"

"I'll see what can be arranged. If I can make that happen, will you take the job?"

"And we'd still be able to talk?"

"That's a problem. Harry, I'm going back to California."

"Why?"

"I came here only to see that Odessa was prosecuted
for murdering my sister. Now that he's dead, there's no
need for me to stay."

"What will you do in California?"

"I'm not sure."

"How are you getting to the airport?"

"My friend is driving me."

"The guy who found you the night Odessa attacked
you?"

"Yes."

"Do you like him?"

"He's a very nice man."

"Would you say he's good lookin'?"

"Yes."

"Have you got a boyfriend in California?"

"Harry, this conversation is getting a little too personal."

"You mean for a mental patient talkin' to his doctor?"

"No, Harry, I don't have a boyfriend."

"I see."

"What does that mean?"

"When is the most progress made with the fewest steps?"

"Another riddle?"

"Think about it."

"You never gave me an answer about the part-time job."

"Then we both have things to think about."

There was a knock at the door and Ada Metz leaned in. "Trina Estes is out in the hall with someone who wants to meet you."

"How did they know I was here?"

"I told them. I thought you'd want to see this person."

Marti turned to Harry. "I'm not prepared to leave here without you agreeing to try that job. So when I'm through in the hall, I'm coming back to finish our conversation."

"I'll be here."

When Marti went into the hallway she found Trina Estes standing beside an attractive older woman wearing a white knit shell under a wide-lapel bouclé jacket and skirt accented with a peach scarf. On the floor beside the woman was a suitcase. Marti assumed this was probably a new psychologist Quinn hired before he was killed. As nice as she looked, Marti thought her pearl necklace and earrings were maybe a little too dressy for a mental hospital. Why this woman would want to meet her was a mystery.

"Hi, Trina." Marti offered her hand to the other woman. "Hello, I'm Marti Segerson."

The woman smiled warmly and took Marti's hand. "Yes, I know. I'm Sarah Holman."

Sarah . . . The name sounded familiar, but for a moment Marti couldn't remember why. Then it came to her. Sarah Holman was the woman whose medication she'd changed to treat her severe depression. But this couldn't be the same person.

"I wanted to introduce myself to you and let you see the real me," Sarah said. "Because what you saw before you rescued me from the hell I was living in was someone else." She let go of Marti's hand and hugged her. "Thank you so much for giving me my life back."

When Sarah released Marti, Trina said, "Hospital regs say you were supposed to sign her discharge papers, but you were kind of not available so I authorized it myself, because she was so eager to leave. Hope you're not upset."

"Not at all. Sarah, I can't tell you how pleased I am for you. You go out there and have a happy life."

"I'm dying to talk to you about everything that's happened," Trina said. "But I need to deliver Sarah to her family who's waiting in the lobby."

"Of course, you go ahead."

As Marti watched Sarah walking down the hall, totally transformed from what she'd been, Marti felt as though a space heater had come on inside her, suffusing her body with the most relaxing, wonderful heat she'd ever felt. And in that moment, she knew the solution to Harry's new riddle.

She turned and let herself back into the ward, where Harry was sitting in front of the TV. She hurried over and sat beside him.

"I know the answer," she said.

"Okay, the most progress is made with the fewest steps when . . ."

"What you're looking for is right in front of you."

"Does that mean—"

"I'm staying."

"Then I'm takin' that job."

"Blackmailer."

"We loons do what we can."

She nudged Harry gently with her elbow, then got up and headed for the exit.

Outside, Marti went up to the driver's side of Clay's truck and motioned for him to roll his window down. When he did, she said, "I hear the rental cottage at Blue Sky Farm needs a tenant. Do you think the landlord would rent it to me after the repairs are made?"

Clay's stony expression melted. "If I put in a good word for you I think that's a distinct possibility."

"And you know what?" Marti said, taking off her glasses. "I don't really need these."

AUTHOR'S NOTE

Although there's some truth in what I wrote about memory movies, we're a long way from developing anything like that. On the other hand, brain fingerprinting is an actual technique that has already been ruled as admissable evidence in the courts of at least one state.